# THE
# LAST DAYS
# OF PUBLISHING

# The
# Last Days
# of Publishing

A NOVEL

## Tom Engelhardt

University of Massachusetts Press
*Amherst & Boston*

LC 2002155563
ISBN 1-55849-402-2
Designed by Jack Harrison
Set in Monotype Dante by Graphic Composition, Inc.
Printed and bound by The Maple-Vail Book Manufacturing Group

Library of Congress Cataloging-in-Publication Data
Engelhardt, Tom, 1944–
The last days of publishing : a novel / Tom Engelhardt.
    p. cm.
ISBN 1-55849-402-2 (Cloth : alk. paper)
1. Publishers and publishing—Fiction. 2. New York (N.Y.)—Fiction.
I. Title.

PS3605.N45 L37 2003
813'.6—dc21
                                    2002155563

British Library Cataloguing in Publication data are available.

# CONTENTS

# part i

# Chapter 1
## THE LAST DAYS OF PUBLISHING

When you visit Pompeii, as perhaps you have, as up to a million people do each year, and walk stony expanses that were once bustling streets in a Roman West Palm Beach, you are, of course, a tourist at the end of a world. You'll inspect rehabilitated villas like the House of the Faun, sealed under twenty-three feet of pumice and ash that red-hot August day nineteen centuries ago. Perhaps you'll venture to the outskirts of what was once a town of twenty-five thousand, with baths, stadiums, gladiatorial barracks, and a port for galleys carrying Phoenician wine and Egyptian jade. There you'll enter the Villa of the Mysteries, where Dionysian murals still stain walls the ocher of dried blood, the artistic blood of a lost age. As you stroll the town, you'll note excavations that were once rooms or gardens or temples but now look like the graves they became. At the Antiquarium, a name reflective of the deep dive you're taking into the stony pools of time, you'll see

[ 3 ]

plaster of paris casts of people buried in their lives that morning in 79 A.D. which, as Pliny the Younger wrote Tacitus, turned into the darkest of fiery nights.

Pliny's decision to refuse an offer of a boat ride to Pompeii from his uncle Pliny the Elder undoubtedly saved his life. ("I replied that I preferred to go on with my studies.") The Younger was surely the first tourist at the end of his world, and in the letter he composed long after, his tone is fittingly observational, at times even antic. There's something thrilling in such a stance, as in his cool description of his asthmatic uncle's beachside death from sulphur fumes. ("His body was found intact and uninjured, still fully clothed and looking more like sleep than death.")

Tourists often experience a chill on viewing those Pompeian figurines with the frozen peace of so many George Segal sculptures. We all yearn to be reminded that worlds can end without us. Take a look at the Grain Lady, named for her proximity to a thresher, or the Lovers, who died clutched in each other's arms, but who, for all we know, were the Haters, or the Strangers, or the Pimp and His Whore.

In Pompeii, you may also catch hints of our own world's end, for you can penetrate the rubble of history just so far before reaching all that could possibly end now. But never forget that you're in an archaeological theme park, viewing historical pornography— something I find no less moving than the nicknames we give those who were consumed by the unimaginable, or the gift shops that sell obliteration as entertainment.

My favorite among the town's many Pygmalions-in-reverse is the Scribe. He was found in a sitting position in the House of the Scholar and near at hand was a stylus, the assumed instrument of his trade. I like to imagine that while others fled, he was consumed by his work. No scrolls were found near him as at the Villa of the Papyri in nearby Herculaneum where the writings of a previously unknown stoic philosopher were recovered virtually intact, so we can't guess how he spent his last minutes. We can't even know whether he was the Poet, the Letter Writer, the Accountant, or simply a man who found himself near a stylus in the final moments of his life. He was probably one of countless Pompeians who helped the rich carry out the niche activities that wealth invariably allows. In fourteenth-century Hangzhou, the French scholar Jacques Gernet informs us, an aristocratic Southern Sung household would have employed a man solely to train pet crickets, just as in West Palm Beach today a family may employ a personal shopper.

If you visit the National Archaeological Museum in Naples with its trove of Pompeian mosaics, you can, as I did, buy a T-shirt with the image of the Scribe on it. Some find it ghoulish, but the thought of world's end spawning a vigorous trade in images of the long dead pleases me.

Sometimes, to amuse myself, I think of the Scribe as the Editor. On the day his world ended, the Romans still wrote on papyrus imported from Egypt, and reading was normally done aloud in the presence of others, not to the self alone. Much would happen after his town was buried. That Christian invention the book would not arrive for centuries, and long after his world ended others would open for Boccaccio and Dante, Pirandello and di Lampedusa, Primo and Carlo Levi, all now obliterated from this earth. Only later would the sonnet, the novel, the memoir, the comic, and the hypertext be spun out by pen, typewriter, and computer. Only later would nationalism, fascism, communism, Auschwitz, and the bomb make their appearances. And yet he's not completely of another time, for Mount Vesuvius still steams.

For an extra gratuity, your Italian guide will drive you to the foot of the mountain and take you on a trail up wooded and vined slopes to its "lips"—the mouth, that is, of one of the only volcanoes in Europe that might still belch hot gas, glowing ash, and pumice onto human populations in a deadly *nuée ardente*. As you approach those lips an almost lifeless terrain confronts you, the result of a mini-eruption that greeted Allied troops advancing up the boot of Italy in 1944. In medieval times, the records tell us, vineyards grew on the mountain's midslopes, producing a wine of some regional renown until, in 1631, several thousand people once again died in a local apocalypse.

Perched on those lips, looking into the crater, you might remember that Spartacus, the slave who raised an army and defied Rome, hid there around 54 B.C. Then, tangles of vines, bushes, and flowers lent it an almost unimaginable lushness. So it goes. In 1980, a flow of lava burned our own Mount St. Helens's slopes free of life, yet scientists were astonished by the blinding speed of its return, just as Hiroshima and Nagasaki today are bustling urban megascapes.

Worlds beyond measure may succeed our moment, and for each of them except the last there will be tourists. Every death is the end of the world for someone. And someday, of course, the world will end. In the meantime, smaller worlds end all the time. The urge to conjure up such endings has been unceasing, even if how we choose to imagine them says more about what has yet to end in us.

Facing the future of the book, my ex-wife, Connie Burian, thought an age, a world, was ending. She told me so. She was, you might say, my Pliny the Younger. And since she assumed the world ending wasn't hers, her comments rang as strangely to my ears as his might have to his uncle's, had he miraculously appeared on that sulphurous beach so long ago.

I returned to work early on the Monday morning she was to take up her new post. April 24, 2000, to be exact. Byzantium Press was deserted. I strolled down our hallway, looking into offices where computers throbbed and message lights blinked. A phone rang four times before being automatically answered. At eight, the air-conditioning came on, a hissing intake of breath that filled the air with subtle murmuring.

I felt like one of those cinematic survivors of atomically emptied cities as I stepped into the office that was no longer Margo Deare's, that had once been John Percy III's, and came face-to-face with my only best-selling author, Walter Groth. I stepped back in surprise, then laughed—a startlingly hollow sound when you're alone in the world—for "Walter" was a cardboard cutout. On a yellow Post-it where his jacket pocket might have been, someone had scrawled, "Margo, tell us what you think!" The shelves still held Margo's books, arranged by spine color, but our former managing director's desk had been swept bare and its drawers, when I sat in her chair, were empty.

I stared out at Times Square. Even in the light of morning, the sides of buildings boiled with imagery. Somewhere below, traffic moved and people headed for work, but from the twelfth floor the world was soundless and uninhabited. Kicking at the desk, I spun myself until the office turned to a ghostly blur. Before Percy III sat here, this had been air.

Byzantium's old building, that gargoyled edifice on Spring Street, is now stuffed with Italian designer boutiques. From his father, John Percy II—"Second," as he was called until his death in 1963—Percy III inherited a shabby, fifth-floor corner office with creased walls and a large walnut desk. Second had been William Dean Howells's last publisher. Howells, so the story went, commandeered his office to oversee the production of his final book and died there of gout. Growing up with "Old Percy," that domineering Protestant patriarch of police gazette fame, Second had been unfazed by Howells's presence. Before he went to war in 1917 and came back blinded in one eye ("a reasonable fate for a publisher," Percy III once told me), the building had housed a telephone exchange and, in the previous century, a shirtwaist factory. An Indian burial ground was rumored to lie under the building.

Sometime in 1980—I had been an editor for seven years—I received a proposal for a book about publishing from a promising young academic. The first chain bookstores were just spreading into the malls and the first wavelet of publishing takeovers just rising to sight. It was the year before Byzantium would be swallowed up by the Desmond & Dickinson Publishing Group. But when I

[ 7 ]

took the proposal to Percy, normally an editor's publisher and a thoroughly diffident man, he laughed and waved it aside. "Koppes," he said—he called all his editors by their last names—"there is no reason to write about publishing." There was something impressively modest in his feeling that ours was not a business worth writing about. For him, all that mattered was being subsumed in the final product.

As I twirled at Percy's desk, I could almost see the old Byzantium volumes from the days before Desmond & Dickinson itself was swallowed up by Bruno Hindemann's Multimedia Entertainment. They had once briefly lined these walls, too, some specially bound in Moroccan leather with touches of gold leaf on their spines. They had lent this space an unearned gravitas. A question came to mind and I made myself ask it. "What," I said into the mechanically vibrating air, "are you doing here?" Our voices were never meant to speak into space emptied of humanity. Still, I had said it and, as if beckoned, an answer rose. I was, I decided, waiting for a world to end.

It wasn't my habit to feel my way along inside myself as I might in a manuscript. But I had spent two weeks alone. I had gone nowhere, done nothing. I had barely used the phone, hadn't turned on the computer or the TV or read a book or looked at a manuscript. The only people who rang my bell were Jehovah's Witnesses, and they were indecently polite about my desire not to talk to them.

On the page, I could edge up to myself in the confusion of others. Without a manuscript, I was remarkably clueless, but—and this was a discovery—not lacking in curiosity. In those few minutes alone, twelve floors up, there turned out to be revelation of a modest sort. I sensed—I hardly have the words to describe it—that I had reached the end of an editing path. It was something like bumping into a wall you hadn't known was there. And when I touched it, to my surprise, it was a little like touching the heart of a manuscript.

So there it was. The most natural act of my life, the only skill that left the sixties with me, the way I fell in love with Connie Burian, through which I felt usable and well used, with which I grasped the world and was grasped by it, by which I offered value without need of return, from that I was, it seemed, barred. I wasn't tired of editing. It wasn't something you could be tired of. I still felt ready to be used by anyone whose words mattered to me, just not by what had come to pass for an editor's life. The oddest thing was, banging around inside one last time I couldn't find regret, only a small spark of what might have been anticipation, not unlike the way it felt just before you turned the first page of a manuscript, just before the journey began.

Back in my office, I poked at the mess that had flooded my desk and scrolled down the 276 e-mails backed up in my computer, all the while thinking of the Scribe carrying out the small tasks that must have been his life. Tossing papers in my outbox, writing notes, piling books on the floor, looking over p-and-l statements, I imagined my body already coated in ash.

The resiliency of the human spirit is overpraised in my opinion, but there I was, resilient as hell, when my assistant, Joy, arrived at nine, and there Margo Deare wasn't. I found not a word from her, but—no longer anyone's managing director—perhaps she was being resilient as hell somewhere else. Joy was ecstatic. Connie Burian had e-mailed her, making friendly sounds, and all she wanted to do was smother me in appreciation for a favor she had no way of knowing I'd never done.

"Joy, I didn't say a word to her the other night."

"But you were the one who made me go!" Her body was so wired she was practically dancing.

"I invited you to a restaurant to protect myself from Connie and then stuck you with her assistant. Was he a disaster?"

She burst out laughing. "With guys, that's a strong word. Okay, it was sort of a jerky evening"—her joyous eyes did a loop-de-loop for my amusement—"but I don't hold anything against you."

I missed her already.

"You're an impaired species, but he wasn't stupid. Not for a guy. And she's bringing him here, I think. He didn't quite say it but . . ." She considered the possibilities. "I might see him again. I might." Her upside-down half-grin admitted to an unstaunchable pride. "He did ask me."

When she looked at me through those glorious eyes, she didn't see the Scribe. She wasn't curious about where I'd been or why, or what if anything had happened. Children aren't. Still, Connie had e-mailed her. That was something worth considering. Maybe I had done it. Maybe Joy was Connie's e-mail to me.

She wanted to thank me again. She wanted to give me a kiss. She didn't know what she wanted, except to share the great good fortune then blossoming in her fantasies.

"All you got was an e-mail."

"But I got it! What are you going to do without me? Tell her today that she needs me. Please!"

She made me laugh. "We just have to wait."

"Wait? I want to take my life by the throat and drag it where it's got to go! Couldn't you see her? You have an edge on anybody in this building."

"You mean divorce?"

"I mean, she trusts you."

I held up my hand. "She said she'd come by and she will. Just be calm about it."

"Look at me! Do you think calm? Can you imagine me working with her? I mean, how cool would that be?"

For all I knew it would indeed be cool, especially if you were still a relatively unlayered being in an unlayered world.

And so we waited. I, at least, had faith. By whatever route, Connie was on her way.

I first caught sight of her that Wednesday. I was revolving out of the lobby in search of a sandwich just as she was heading in, one door away. The following Monday, when the elevator opened on the sixth floor, I saw her standing alone in the opposite elevator. Her face sparked to life just as the doors shut.

But that was all. For the rest of that week and part of the next, the pace of editorial life slowed. There were no meetings, for Margo Deare wasn't there to organize them. It was remarkably peaceful, deceptively like my earliest years at Byzantium when we moved at a pace more suited to the long, slow run of the book.

And here was the funny thing: The slower I went, the faster went the paperback of Walter Groth's third book. He wasn't in the country for publicity, but it no longer mattered. *The Masculine Journey* had floated free of the clutter of entertainment life. We had a quarter million copies in print, and however often we went back to press, we couldn't keep up.

If nothing else, that insured Connie's arrival. On the Wednesday of that third week, she burst in without warning, arm in arm with Kate Hughes. Kate held one of the many vice presidencies that had proliferated at Desmond & Dickinson. She was also managing director and senior editor of Dickinson Publishing. Those titles, read back to front, summarized her career in the building. She was, at a guess, in her early forties, with cropped, bright-red hair, and a squared yet delicately angular face, all subtle planes jutting at you. The odd way she held her body, tilting toward you from the waist, gave her the look of a dancer. She seemed, even at rest, to be on her tiptoes, leaning your way at a gravity-defying angle. Strange to say, seated, the effect was no different.

You're seldom aware of the spatial prohibitions that surround you until someone violates them. Kate Hughes did that. Though her lower body remained at a tolerable distance, her face was always too close for comfort. She made me self-conscious. In a restaurant booth, she had the unnerving habit of slipping in beside you, even when no one else was expected. Her eyes, only inches from yours, shone with curiosity, which was why I always tried to meet her in my office, barricaded behind my desk.

Not that we were in regular communication, for she was an important person in the publishing scheme of things. But she did profess curiosity about me, or maybe she was just preparing herself for a moment like this, because our conversations were always filled with questions about Byzantium.

I haven't mentioned the one thing no one mentioned in her presence. She was Bruno Hindemann's baby. When he was in town, she was regularly at his distinctly overaged, thrice-married, still-married side. What she was doing there was the subject of endless speculation, for the fortunes of others fill empty time so agreeably. Everyone knows power has its perks, but what sort of perk Kate Hughes was—and so what sort of man Hindemann was—no one quite knew. At least she wore her borrowed power lightly. She didn't bully or invoke his name, and though her rise at D&D had not been slow, people who might have said worse claimed she was exceedingly competent.

She and Connie came in, faces flushed as if they had been on a mad dash in a cold breeze. They were laughing like schoolgirls. Connie collapsed on my little couch, Kate into a chair by my desk, panting and giggling.

"Ricky," Connie gasped, "I wanted you to meet your boss." That sent them into gales of laughter. "She's the new head of Byzantium," Connie managed, and they both stared at me expectantly.

I said nothing.

"Look how calm he is!"

"He's the Tao!" gasped Kate. She pronounced it as in Taos.

That broke them up. Kate half-staggered to her feet, pulled her chair around the desk, and seated herself within inches of my face. "Come on, Connie!" she said. "Sober up, girl. I don't know what's got into us."

I had the urge to retreat but that would have meant falling out of my chair. "*She's* running Byzantium?" I asked.

Connie was trying to suppress the next wave of laughter.

Kate leaned closer, her face radiating intensity. "Don't I qualify?"

"It probably wasn't the most judicious way to pass on the news," Connie said helpfully.

I took a breath. "Maybe I'm missing something, but Kate Hughes running an imprint? It's like the five-legged cow in the what's-wrong-with-this-landscape painting."

"You mean, Kate Hughes, protégée or maybe mistress of Bruno Hindemann?" said Kate evenly.

"No one thinks that," Connie said.

"Of course they do. Silence speaks with one voice. It's not just in fortune cookies. I live with it every day."

"Then he must, too."

Kate waved her hand. "Bruno doesn't make his way in the world. It makes way for him."

Connie slumped against the couch. "At the end of an era, who wouldn't want to be in the doge's palace?"

"That's where you think I am? That's who you think Bruno is?"

"Yes, Kate, you're inside the palace grounds, while people outside are getting trampled to death. I only hope I'm in there with you."

Connie, too, had Italian scenarios on the brain.

"You truly think we're at the edge of something new?" Kate asked quietly.

"Either that or a precipice. Take your pick."

"It's multimedia this, and e-book that. Everybody in the business talks the talk, but do any of us have the faintest idea how to walk the walk?"

Connie laughed. "I better."

"And this future, are you sure it's good for publishing?"

Connie laughed again. This time I caught the nervousness. "Rick doesn't think so. It makes him anxious. Then again, you don't look to an ex-husband for reassurance. This is the biggest gamble I've ever taken. Like transferring from ship to ship on the high seas in a storm."

Kate laughed, a warm and throaty sound, full of empathy. "You have a way with alarming images." She turned to me. "Was she always prone to this? And are you really anxious, Rick?"

I was staring deep into the hazel speckling of her irises. There wasn't space for a reaction.

"We need to do something to allay your fears."

"It's part of his charm," Connie said dryly.

"I don't see you in any danger."

"Given Walter Groth, you mean." He was, of course, my patron, my Bruno.

Kate cocked her head slightly and looked me over from such a close range that she could only have been examining the bumps and blotches age lends a face. "I'm surprised you think he's all you have to offer."

Walter, of course, wasn't mine to offer, but I just said, "If Margaret Boisoneau were my leading author, the three of us wouldn't be talking."

"Who?" Kate looked at Connie.

Connie shrugged.

"Well, she *isn't* your lead author and I think you underestimate how your editorial reach might expand, given the right environment."

I had heard those exact words not so many weeks before, and Margo Deare, who had spoken them, was now tossing somewhere on the high seas.

"A helpful hint, Kate: When he falls silent, his brain's spinning. I never could figure out what about. Say something, Rick. Tell Kate you're happy she's arrived."

I looked deep into her eyes. A web of tiny blood vessels forced themselves on my attention. It was eerie, actually. I wanted to jump out of my skin.

Kate sighed. "I've always yearned to run something small and classy. I've said so to Bruno many times. He always says, 'Small ist zee ant zat you smoosh mit your shoe. You do not vant to be zee ant.'"

Connie laughed.

"Really, that's what he sounds like. Like a Nazi in one of those old movies. I tell him, 'Bruno, not in English, not in public, it makes you sound like a thug.' But he doesn't care, and his German's quite gorgeous, in a manly, assertive way. He'll say, 'My darlink, I am a thug,' and laugh that beefy laugh of his. I can't make him stop and it's a public relations catastrophe. But Connie, you're the first colleague I've ever said that to." She turned to me. "I hardly know the woman and still I feel . . ." She paused. "It must be why you married her."

"I think it's why he divorced me, but I'm a notoriously good first date."

There was a sweetness in the room, the lightness of bonding, and I felt it unbearably.

Connie looked over. "By the way, Kate won't just be in charge of Byzantium. There are scads of imprints littered around this company. I'm going to pile them outside her door like Legos and let her grow them into a mini-empire. For your sake, Rick, we'll call the whole damn thing Byzantium and then we'll see how they sort themselves out."

"How they fall out, you mean."

"You see?" she said to Kate. "He gives everything the worst possible spin." They looked at each other and smiled. "Speaking of spin, Kate and I—it was really Kate's idea—have arranged for you to meet David Marsden."

I suppose I looked appalled.

"It's for your own good, a kind of inoculation for the future. An *inoculation*."

"You're our project," Kate added. "And David's part of the plan. Anyway, he's a fantastic guy, a visionary."

"When you look in the publishing mirror a couple of months from now, you won't recognize yourself."

And they giggled in unison.

I think I flushed. It was so improbable. The man who ran Multimedia from L.A., who was known in every business-page profile as Bruno Hindemann's adopted son, who had launched com.com as a joke and convinced Hindemann to buy StarServe when it was nothing but an electronic fanzine. But you know the story.

"And we think you'll interest him," Connie said. "Next Thursday, eleven A.M. And Kate, you'll take him up?"

Up forty-five floors, she meant.

"I wouldn't let him fly solo."

I made a dumb show of writing it down.

"Kate, check out your new office. Note how much nearer the street you are." Connie turned to me. "I'm in the same office three floors down. If things don't work out, we can see who hits Broadway first." She glanced at her watch. "Marty Beck's on his way up to introduce you to sales. I have a small favor to ask of my ex-husband and I prefer to do it in private."

"No problem." Kate dragged her chair to the other side of the desk and returned to shake my hand. She had a firm, honest grip. "I'm taking a few days off, a firebreak between jobs, but I'm looking forward to spending time together."

I only smiled.

When she was gone, Connie kicked off her shoes, stuck out a foot, and shoved the door closed.

Neither of us spoke. It was a comfortable moment, filled with a sense of ancient times, and so completely unreliable.

Finally she said, "I wish you could be just a little more polite. Kate would have appreciated it."

"I can see that."

She laughed. "That's the way! Give me an Eliza response."

I raised an eyebrow.

"The computer program that mimicked a therapist: 'So why do you feel underappreciated?' 'Do you want to tell me more?' You've learned a trick or two since my day, Ricky."

"You seem pretty chummy with Kate."

"I like her, but honestly . . ." She paused to consider honesty a moment.

"You're not obliged to be honest with me."

"But I can be. It's like spousal privilege. I know you won't rat me out."

It was true, of course. Whatever I did, I wouldn't rat her out.

"After all these years, it's amusing fessing up to marrying you. Don't you feel that?"

I said nothing. I knew things she couldn't know. I had been inside myself where no one had been for a long, long time.

"That's okay, I don't want you to rat yourself out either."

"You said you had a favor to ask."

"Oh, yes indeedy," she swung her legs off the couch and sat up. "I have something for you." She said it so sweetly. "I meant to mention it the other night." She reached under the couch, picked up a manila envelope, and handed it across the desk.

"What is it?"

"It's . . ." She hesitated. A beautiful pause hung shivering in the air. "A fiction. Stories, really."

"Are you sure it's me you want? I've rarely edited fiction."

"You and only you."

"Who's the writer?"

"Me."

"*You?*"

That made her laugh. "I've always written."

"Why didn't you tell me?"

"You'll understand when you read it."

I started to unclasp the envelope, but she was on her feet. "Not now."

I looked at her with curiosity. That she had been my wife made my life more fascinating than it had any right to be.

"You know," she said, dropping onto the couch, "stutterers don't stutter on the page. Writing was my private passion. Very, very private and very . . ." She faltered. "When I was a child, I kept a secret diary. My parents found it and read it. That was a terrible experience. The only time, you might say, I've ever been published."

She laughed. "I've kept my writing to myself ever since, but recently, maybe because . . ." An expression I couldn't begin to interpret swept across her face. She waved a hand as if clearing it away. "Well, it doesn't matter. It really doesn't matter."

A thought crossed my mind. "It's not—" I stopped dead. It was as close to a stutter as I was likely to come and it felt eerie, like a crash dummy splatting into an air bag. I looked to her for help.

She smiled. Triumphantly, I would say. "I hate to disappoint you, but you're not in it."

To my surprise, I felt something other than relief.

"I'm the only author likely to say such a thing—and mean it— but take your time. I'd love you to like it, but I want you to be honest, and right now I can't afford honesty."

"Then why not give it to me a month from now?"

She smiled. "I wanted it gone. Now, let's talk about something else."

"Okay, I have a favor to ask. Joy tells me you e-mailed. Are you thinking about hiring her?"

"In the bright light of day, should I?"

"She's a gem. Give her something worth doing and you won't regret it."

"I'm amazed," she said. "It seems a little . . ."—she paused— "emphatic for you."

It was my turn to smile. "Maybe you're facing a new me."

That amused her. "Miracles happen, just not in my lifetime."

"Promise me one thing?"

"Anything. Within reason of course."

"Whatever happens, you'll take care of Joy."

She threw her head back and laughed. "I swear, I promise. If you love her—"

"I do love her."

"Then I will, too. We'll have a love fest. But don't make it sound so dire. Nothing will happen, except what always happens. We'll publish books. Authors will tour, reviewers review, stores return, and then we'll complain about it all. Which reminds me, you remember my assistant, Todd? I'm planning to bring him to Byzantium. He's just pretentious enough, and these kids deserve the same chance we got."

She glanced at her watch. "I've got to check on Kate. Honestly, if I didn't like her, I wouldn't act differently. I need allies fast. And if she falls in love with me, she won't be the first."

"I know."

"Maybe she and I—"

"And Bruno," I said and we both laughed.

". . . and Bruno will have a more successful marriage than we did. Or maybe I'll really go out the window."

She stood up and slipped on her shoes.

I came out from behind my desk. "I always barricade myself when Kate visits."

"Her spacing's uncomfortable, poor thing."

We laughed again. Easily and together.

"What's the story with Bruno and her?"

She shrugged. "Your guess is almost as good as mine."

It felt like the note-sharing of people who have spent a lifetime together. She took a step toward me. Her eyes, those vertiginous eyes, met mine, and the next thing I knew we had our arms around each other. I felt her body against me for the first time in more than twenty years. She rested her head briefly on my shoulder. I heard her whisper, "Sometimes I miss having a good editor around." It seemed like a moment of grace. And then I did something Walter Groth would have loved. I stepped inside myself.

"Don't let this go to your head," she said, releasing me.

"Nor you." And we laughed together one last time.

"Really, ex-husband or not, I won't go easy on you."

"Nor I on you. It's not my nature as an editor."

She smiled and stepped into the hallway.

A few moments later I followed, colliding with Joy, who protested, "I was only coming in to . . ."

"Everything's okay," I said. "I'm not sure you needed me at all."

"It would be nice to think that."

Her face was alive with pleasure. I suppressed an urge to warn her. She would be in no mood for jeremiads about a publishing world of which she believed me unbearably ignorant.

If you've ever gone after bluefish on a party boat, you know the usual routine: You drop your line to the bottom, then herky-jerk it up, over and over, until the first blue hits. But there are times when you lean against the rail, play the line out little by little, and watch it drift toward the horizon. That week at the office, I played the line out, waiting for it to intersect with I wasn't sure what.

The only manuscript I might have read I stored in my still empty apartment in response to Connie's wishes. When necessary I dealt with requests impossible to ignore. For the first time in a quarter century I didn't edit a line of text. Once, I followed the automated suggestions on the American Museum of Natural History's phone system to Katrina Adambak's extension. But I didn't leave a message.

I spent my time idling. And no one could tell. No one except Joy actually knew what I did and, long after you stop editing, the work you did continues to stand in for you. For years to come, catalogs would feature descriptions of my books and the books would appear with acknowledgments offering thanks to my particular brand of "encouragement and dedication," or my "fine eye."

About ten that Thursday, a voice from world's end, maternal and with just a hint of a European accent, materialized on my phone asking for "Mister Rick Koppes." When I identified myself, I was informed that Mister David Marsden's office was confirming a meeting with Mister David Marsden for *exactly* eleven o'clock. I should be on time since Mister David Marsden put "a high value on punctuality."

Three-quarters of an hour later, Kate knocked politely on my open door. This was her fourth day in the office and, though we had been in a couple of meetings together, I had seen little of her, and nothing of Connie Burian.

"Ready?" she asked perkily.

"As I'll ever be."

She sat on the couch and checked her watch. "We shouldn't leave yet. It never does to look too eager."

"How's it going?"

"*The Masculine Journey*'s through the roof."

"I meant for you."

"Oh, beginnings . . . you know . . ."

"Kate, how does the honor of meeting David Marsden fall to me?"

"That's a fair question," she said and fell silent.

"Fair but inappropriate?"

She closed the door. "I don't usually like closed doors."

"I don't usually close doors."

"I've been looking over the account books and they stink."

Her surprise surprised me. Once, those were the only books publishers kept in their heads. All of Byzantium's business dealings had been efficiently filed in the brain of John Percy III, as in his father's before him. Of course, the business had been so modest then. Now publishers were inundated with information and had offices of people crunching it every which way, yet Percy could still have told you the results out of his head. Byzantium's bottom line would remain around four percent—and that would be in a good year. But all I said was, "And that actually surprises you?"

"Surprises me? Yes. Leaves me feeling sandbagged? Distinctly. I've spent years at Dickinson, but I never thought a place like Byzantium . . ." She stopped in midsentence. "With Walter Groth on the books! And the other imprints look worse. Any suggestions?"

"Make Walter Groth an institution?" I laughed.

But she didn't crack a smile. "It's crossed my mind. And I'm not alone."

"Kate, I don't think you should count on me."

"Why? Are you planning to do anything?"

"I can honestly say I have no plans, but my view of things . . ."

"You'll have to tell me about it one day. I've already read a curious memo on the subject from the previous managing director."

"Which I don't suppose I'll be able to see."

"Not even if you're very, very good. Anyway, it's time to go."

It was as if I had been eavesdropping on a conversation at the edge of the world.

Kate and I stepped from the elevator into the transnational heavens at exactly 10:59, according to one of a series of clocks embedded in the wall. The others showed the time in Bremen, London, Honolulu, and Tokyo. Kate directed me through glass doors set into an all-glass expanse etched with MULTIMEDIA and Bruno Hindemann's golden lion logo.

A receptionist greeted her deferentially and buzzed us through another glass door. Kate led me down a taupe hallway lined with Audubon prints into a vast conference room. Before me, the highrises of New York sloped to water's edge, while the river shimmered gloriously in the early summer sun. Billowing clouds swept at eye level over green cliffs splashed with honey-colored light. Forty-five stories below, the life of Man (as they said in my childhood) hummed on, ignorant of city, sky, sun, cliffs. I stood as if on the lips of some Vesuvius, a tourist surveying a world I had inhabited but never quite seen. I was reluctant to leave even when Kate took my arm.

We proceeded into a windowless waiting area. I don't know what I had expected—Chagall windows, chandeliers, plush curtains—but its walls were a motel tan and lacked decoration. Athwart two offices was a single desk behind which sat a prematurely gray-haired woman in a yellow blouse. A small coffee table and a pea-green couch were the only furniture.

"Lena," said Kate, "how's the day treating you?"

The woman smiled and, in the faintly accented English I had

heard on the phone, said, "I fear there has been a slight delay. It may take five minutes, but then again"—she offered us both an elegant grimace—"you know David."

Kate turned to me. "I'm so sorry. I promised Connie I'd shepherd you through this but"—she glanced at her watch—"I'm meeting the Pegasus staff in half an hour and I don't think I should . . ."

When she didn't finish, I assured her I would be fine.

"Then I'll leave you in Lena's capable hands," she said brightly, adding as she waved good-bye, "I'll check in later."

I sat down. Lena answered the phone and wrote herself a number of brief notes. Otherwise she did nothing except glance at me from time to time.

"It must be hard to sit in an office with no windows," I said.

"Not at all," she replied.

A little later I asked why the room was so undecorated. Mr. David Marsden, it turned out, was not often or for long on this coast. She was, by then, reading a *Vanity Fair* with Christina Ricci on the cover.

On the coffee table were D&D catalogs, Multimedia brochures, and a glossy stockholder's report with exquisite Eisen photos of the company's modernistic headquarters and of Bremen's Hindemann Square, where Bruno Hindemann's collection of monumental Oldenburg lipsticks had been installed to stunning effect.

When I asked if Mister David Marsden was often late, Lena replied, "This is his normal"—she pronounced it nor*mal*—from which I assumed that his was the punctuality of the powerful. "I assure you," she said the next time I inquired about his arrival, "when I know you'll know."

An hour passed. I concentrated on the blank wall as if it were the future, imagining this as the Zen exercise of an editor in transit. I was just sensing the stirrings of a most un-Zen-like appetite when the door sprang open. A spare, balding man of about my age, nattily outfitted in a light gray suit, red tie, and

[ 23 ]

blue silk handkerchief, strode in followed by a hulking, frizzy-haired fellow in a Phish T-shirt that said "Seminole Millennium."

I rose to my feet. "Rick Koppes," I said to the besuited man and stuck out my hand. He stepped back, startled. The other fellow began to laugh.

"You see, Arthur, It's always like this," and he put out his paw. "I'm Marsden." Then he added, "I should take greater effort to look like an entertainment oligarch." He draped an arm over my shoulder. "Make yourself at home in my home away from home," and he flung open an office door. "I'll only be a minute."

Which was how I found myself by a spacious desk staring out at the northern face of the imperial city dominated by the vast, green sweep of parkland that Olmstead and Vaux had blasted into being with more gunpowder than was used at Gettysburg. Fifteen minutes passed before I grew curious enough to read the letter from a Nokia executive that lay atop a very full inbox. It suggested ways the companies might jointly explore the "content possibilities" of an on-line future. I noted Walter Groth's three books piled at desk's edge. On picking up *The Masculine Journey*, I found it heavily underlined and annotated. For instance, Marsden—at least, I assumed it was he—had scrawled "Peter Pan Nation!" beside this familiar passage: "Fathers should, by nature, be cartographers. Among certain Amazonian tribes like the Iratube, as well as the Athapaskans of British Columbia, it is the father's task to present a 'dream map' to his son. Without that charting of the trails of consciousness, the path to adulthood would be unavailable to the next generation."

I hefted a paperweight, a gorgeous hunk of milky quartz suffused with sunlight from the world beyond. Incised in its polished base was "David Marsden, Entrepreneur of the Year, The Society of Internet Sponsors, 1998." I examined a golden Zippo lighter engraved on one side, "For D. M., with gratitude, B. H." When I spun the flint, a tongue of flame leaped skyward.

Then I noticed the triptych of photos in a jointed frame, the kind you might put in a traveling case. On the left was a youthful Marsden holding a guitar triumphantly aloft; at center, the Marsden I had just met, arm around a stunning young woman, a small boy in a red fireman's hat between them; on the right—I brought the photo close—against a rocky seascape, was Marsden, shoulder to shoulder with Rob DuVeen, decades older than I remembered him but distinctly himself.

"Anyone I know?"

I spun around. "That's Rob DuVeen!" I said breathlessly.

"Ah, Rob. I spoke at the funeral. Walter Groth says we pick our fathers where we can."

"I remember the passage."

"Yes, of course you do. The sarcasm is richly deserved. Rob took me under his capacious wing when I first landed in L.A. No one had a keener sense of the wiles of capitalism. What was your connection?"

"We lived together in a commune in the sixties."

"Ah, the famous commune in the sixties." He said it so mellowly, like decades-old scotch going down. The mockery would have been easy to miss. "Capitalism's a fatal mistress, or so they claim." He chuckled. "Whenever the business confounded me, I'd call Rob and he'd ask—it was his mantra—'What would the essential contradiction be for Uncle Karl?' He was teasing, but teaching, too. If you don't grasp the essential contradiction, which no situation lacks, you can't effectively exploit the world as it is. Of course the two of you had all the luck. By the time I came along, the only thing left was making money by making book." He laughed. "You're allowed to smile, even if you don't approve of my sort of cultural commissar."

I turned to the window. Not even a plane to mar the view, just the silence of buildings soaring to the heavens and that expanse of green like an overgrown scar on the body of the city.

"I missed the Vietnam war," he continued. "I was fourteen when the protests ended, a guitarist in a Berkeley garage band when Saigon fell. I was in film school, making short documentaries, pretentious crap, still dreaming about the sixties, wishing I hadn't missed it all, when I met Rob. He set me straight. 'The sixties are dog meat' was how he put it. 'Hey, man,' he said, only he said it, 'mon,' Rasta-style. 'Hey, mon, the sixties? There ain't no there there no more. You want to live?" He had that raspy voice and those slurry *r*'s. "Y'wann'r live? Try the eighties."

He had told this story more than once. There was probably more than one version to tell, but I could still hear some faint echo of Rob DuVeen, dead to me these thirty years. I felt, I don't know, a shiver maybe.

We stood side by side, staring out. "Ever been up this high?"

I couldn't tell if he was serious. I doubted it mattered. "To the top of the Empire State Building."

"I meant, ever been to the top of an imperial moment before?"

I didn't respond.

"You face your contradictions where you find them. I find them up here. I take pride in being a cultural imperialist. That's what Rob DuVeen taught me." He paused and looked my way. "With a little help from Walter Groth. I saw your piece about publishing in *The Threepenny Review*. It caught something of our world."

I was too stunned to reply.

"Just not the view from the forty-fifth floor."

I stood perfectly still. There was a path through this mix of stroking and bluntness in a language anybody from the sixties would almost have recognized. I simply didn't see it.

Then he put his arm around me. I remembered this passage from Walter Groth, too. I had wanted him to take out that whole silly section on "fathering gestures."

Marsden gave me a good squeeze. He exuded spontaneity and yet I doubted anything he did lacked forethought.

"Between us, we cover the high points of Rob's life. The movie producer I knew had a sniffer for the shit that passes as culture, and he was a seer. You know the last thing he said to me?"

He pressed both palms to the window and leaned his forehead against it. He reminded me of a little boy outside a toy store. I tried to imagine what toys he saw in the imperial city.

"My house sits on a cliff overlooking the Pacific and a storm was rolling in. Vast thunderheads, dark as death. A week later he would be a dead man. He said, 'Ya gott'r ride it out.' I asked, 'Ride what out?' He said, 'Every storm, ya gott'r ride 'em out.' I asked, 'Is there a meaning to this?' He said, 'I've ridden out a few storms in my life.' You could see the rain in patches, black, rippling sheets of it, like TV static, way out there over the water. It was a mean-looking son of a bitch. That's the Pacific for you, pure melodrama. And he says, 'Ya need t'buckle y'r seatbelt, sonny.' There were only fourteen years between us, but he dealt with me like I was a kid. Sometimes you know better than to speak. After a while, he says, 'Soon enough, books won't matter. A lot of publishers, they'll duck and cover, but if ya don't have y'r head up y'r butt, ya won't. Y'll ride it out. For a company like y'rs, nothin'll matter but copyrights. Get y'r mitts on those and y'll ride out any fuck-ing thing. Mon, there's going to be six, seven copyright oligarchs astride this fucking earth. They'll control every damn thing.' Now, that's a truth for the twenty-first century. Rob DuVeen saw it in the heart of that storm and it should frighten you. It frightens me."

I had entered his aura. The conviction you have forty-five floors up and five years ahead of the rest of humanity held me tight. It wasn't fuzzy like Walter Groth's "Coriolanus effect" and it wasn't a path, but it was as real as the paperweight.

"Think of the control possibilities on a global level. Seven spig-ots for content and seven CEOs to turn them on or off."

I looked at him then. He was leaning against the window, mo-tionless, while out there somewhere, beyond the sky, were the other six.

"You're thinking, he's one of them, he's a copyright oligarch."

"I guess I was," I replied in a whisper.

"Now, tell me about Walter Groth."

I felt something shift, and it wasn't just the subject. "What is it you want to know?"

"He's a phenomenon. He drives you to do things so sensible you can't believe you wouldn't have done them without him. *The Masculine Journey* sent me flying to Majorca for a week without my wife or son. The pitch you had him record for the sales reps last season, that knocked me out. He's a natural. There's no doubt his future's off the page. Do you realize that we own seven cable stations in major markets and—look, can you keep something between us?"

He hadn't moved an inch or so much as glanced my way, but there was something indescribably intimate in his voice.

"We're about to become a major content provider for Time Warner. A shot of content injected into the ass of a mega-entertainment enterprise, you can't begin to know what that means. Walter Groth could sell his style of wisdom to men across a full spectrum: print, audio, video, digital, product. We want to brand him awesomely. But we can't get there by ourselves. He won't return my calls or Connie's, and she's going to be coordinating this."

I should have been offended, but I found myself smiling.

"That amuses you," Marsden said without looking in my direction, "but it's an ignorant reaction. It means you don't grok the world we're entering. That television in your living room, a few years from now it'll be a broadband machine bringing you everything from shows to shopping, print to product, not to mention your date book, bankbook, and high school yearbook. It'll correlate your tastes, purchases, credit rating, and financial profile with what you watch. For the first time we'll be able to see you. So for the *Walter Groth Show,* advertisers won't have to pay for viewers only fifteen percent of whom might conceivably buy their products. We'll download Volvo ads onto Rick Koppes's screen, BMWs onto mine, and Chrysler minicompacts onto Joe Consumer's. We'll cohabit intimately with you alone. We'll be in bed with you."

"You're sure it'll happen this way?"

He motioned me to a chair and opened a desk drawer. "Fondle one of these babies from Nokia . . . " He brandished what looked like a chunky cell phone. "I mean, get a grip on this and the future's in your hands. A few years from now the grandchild of this machine will target you any time, anywhere on this planet."

His voice held such conviction that I could hear myself thinking, maybe, just maybe. And then the strangest idea came into my head: Maybe I can get him to write a book. It wasn't an editor's thought. It had something to do with gain and fame. It was the forty-fifth floor speaking. I was, I realized, still holding the lighter. I flicked it open and idly spun the flint. A flame leaped out, a shimmering of yellows and oranges, reds and blues, on the other side of which lay the future. Its flickering heart was no less mesmerizing than Marsden, that votary of a new faith—and it was gorgeous. In Rome, he would have been a priest of Augustus.

"Connie assures me you have some influence with Groth." He was leaning back in his chair. "She also says you might be the guy to put Byzantium in order."

"But Kate—" I began.

"Yes, Kate . . ." He paused. "Well, Kate may have more on her plate than she imagines. I'm treading carefully here. Connie says you're a minefield and I'll only know you're going off when I take the first misstep."

That made me smile.

"I generally don't misstep."

It was then—I don't know why—that I stepped out of the aura of his aura and the future vanished along with his book that would never be. I thought of Rob DuVeen, hair to his shoulders, hunkered down on a sagging couch in our sagging commune, speaking in an anxious whisper but with no less fervor of a future that was also not to be. "There was something that Rob and I always talked about . . . ," I began.

"And what was that?"

"Destruction."

He eyed me curiously. "You're saying Rob was what? A bomber?"

I laughed. "Not a bomber, no. But alone in the night with a little dope to stoke us, we had destruction on the brain. It was the great taboo. Maybe he would have called it the essential contradiction at the heart of our project. You didn't say it, not in public, not in daylight, not if you were half sane, because all we were accused of wanting was to tear things down and we were so desperate to build them up. But you can't be awake all the time and, in our dreams, when it did come down, it felt good. It felt familiar. After all, in the dreams we grew up with, everything was ash. I'll never forget—and this was in a dream forty-odd years ago—the burning sensation that seared my arm the first time I watched the mushroom cloud soar. And then there was the obvious. Our country was tearing a small land, a million miles away, limb from limb. Destruction was on the goddamn TV. Power, immense power, and all that desolation. And no matter what we did we couldn't make it stop. We were going crazy with despair. When it was over, despair and those dreams sent Rob DuVeen to Hollywood. It wasn't an accident that he made horror movies."

"Then it was what Schumpeter called creative destruction."

"You know what Rob would have said to that?"

He looked at me curiously.

"Fuck Schumpeter. We knew destruction wasn't creative. You just couldn't not want it. Just like you want it now."

"That's hardly fair."

"You like taking companies apart, don't you?"

"Well, that's not destructive."

I laughed. "Tell that to your employees."

"That's just life. That's the way it goes."

"You'd unravel the future if you could."

"The world's about to be a different place. That's inexorable. That's not me."

I reached over for the letter from Nokia. Then I raised the

lighter and watched as a tongue of flame leaped for a corner of the paper, licked it lightly, and started to burn. "I wanted to show you a contradiction," I said. A line of yellow flames, blue at their core, was already rushing from the paper's blackened edge down its white face, eating every word in its path. I laid those words being sucked into the void on his desk. "That's a contradiction." I picked up the next letter on the pile and lit it, too. "Here's another."

He was big, you know. And fit. And younger. He could have kicked the crap out of me. But maybe in those flames where a future seemed to dance, his vanished. He sat there, a look of confusion on his face, staring at the fire now nibbling at his blotter. It isn't often, I suppose, that you run into a contradiction so close at hand when you're forty-five floors up.

"I think," I said, "this is what Walter Groth actually meant by the spontaneous gesture."

"Hey!" he said. Then, "You fuck!" He rose to his feet as those two letters shriveled into black spheres and the first flames began to lick the edges of *The Masculine Journey*. He yelled, "Fire! Fire!" It was a wild cry, out of all proportion to the small contradiction that was flaming on his desk.

As I walked away, Lena passed me, a red fire extinguisher in her hands. I turned at the door. His desk was already covered in white foam and he was scrambling to rescue objects.

There was no need for someone to escort me out. I spun through the revolving door into the midday glare. The sun was nowhere in sight. Perhaps it belonged to the millennium just past. The ground shook from the staccato blast of a riveter and the deep bass pounding of a pile driver, the sounds of a city being taken apart. Crowds spilled past. In the distance, horns cried out angrily. I looked up. That sheer cliff of Mylar soared out of sight. I took a deep breath. The air had the distinct tang of New York, a mix of every mutant thing civilization has to offer. I began walking north along Broadway. I sensed a small opening ahead and in it a future only minutes away. I would follow my feet. It was no more complicated than that, for they seemed to be heading toward the American Museum of Natural History, where preserving the species was a matter of pride.

# part ii

# Chapter 2
## HISTORY

I bumped into Miriam Levy—quite literally—on the second afternoon of the convention that April day in 1997 as we both hurried toward the Jefferson Room of the Washington Sheraton. On impact, I felt a little burst of annoyance. Only then did I look down. She is, I would guess, barely five feet tall. Although we hadn't seen each other in more than a quarter of a century, I recognized her instantly.

Normally, you have to search for the past in faces blurred by life, as in photos too long exposed. With Miriam, it was the opposite. Time, like the wind in some dry land, had carried away whatever was extra in that face. The cheekbones stood out in a skeletal landscape. Her cheeks were sunk in shadow, as were her eyes. We were both veterans of the same historical moment, yet a glance told me she was a veteran of some harsher, more personal struggle as well. The odd thing was that she looked more alive than ever. I said her name without a hint of surprise.

She looked up, those contemplative eyes grown larger in their cavernous sockets. People sometimes speak of things written on a face. I could see her struggle and fail to read mine. Perhaps she recognized me but was unsure whom she recognized. That possibility touched me more than I can say. In her confusion I saw myself and I was a stranger. It wasn't the loss of hair, or the way my face had filled out, or the tweed jacket and paisley tie I wouldn't have been wearing those many years ago, but something else. I touched her shoulder gently, and said with more emotion than I might have chosen to display, "It's Rick, Rick Koppes."

Recognition dawned. At such moments, you know why images become clichés. It was indeed like light suffusing from a distant horizon. Pleasure slowly filled her face and then she laughed, an honest sound, and said, "Rick?" with astonishment, still staring at me. "Were you"—she used her chin to point toward the door—"going to this session?"

I nodded.

"Well, then,"—and she took my hand—"let's go in together."

I hadn't exactly been stirred by the thought of attending "Public History in an Age of Confusion," the convention's main session. But in a season when museum shows were suddenly front-page news, it had generated buzz around the book exhibits. My own relationship to scholarly gatherings had been changing. The new president of Desmond & Dickinson, recently hired away from a movie company, was being hailed for his "multimedia expertise," and the job of publishing history, once my meat and potatoes, had largely fallen to the university presses. Each year I left such conventions with fewer projects. This time, I hadn't come across one that had a chance of making it through our publication committee. I was at the Jefferson Room only because Bob West, whose book on McCarthyism I had once published, was on the panel.

As we wedged ourselves into adjacent seats in the second to last row, a young scholar, ponytail, corduroy jacket, jeans, and cowboy boots, squatted beside Miriam. She inclined her head, a perfectly calibrated gesture of attentiveness, and entered a conversation of which I could catch nothing. I felt a spark of jealousy, which shamed me. Here I was, long after the sixties died its untimely death, evidently neither wiser nor tougher. I noticed Bob West slumped at the end of a table on the distant stage. His glasses dangled from one hand, his head was down. He was rubbing his eyes.

As the other panelists took their places, Miriam's hand came to rest on mine. It had a weightlessness, as if her bones, like those of a bird, had been hollowed out for flight. I found it remarkable that such gravity and lightness could exist in one person.

A few moments later the panel was called to order by John Herman, Yale University's Distinguished Professor of American History, whom I had several times unsuccessfully importuned for blurbs on books, Bob's included. His shock of white hair seemed to justify the "distinguished." He dislodged a microphone from its stand and, freeing the cord, began to pace the stage delivering a series of one-liners—"those who ignore the past are bound to repent it"—and put-downs of politicians who feared "the historian's task of examining cherished national narratives." Here's one historian, I thought, who's spent too much time watching the Comedy Channel and Charlie Rose.

Miriam leaned so close her words brushed my cheek. "Would you believe," she whispered, "that this passes for politics in our lives?" And she laughed, soundlessly.

With her hand hovering above mine I drifted off, though had I known where I was going I would have stopped myself immediately, repression being a much-undervalued state of mind. In that unguarded moment I suddenly recalled the way Miriam and I had bumped into each other seven years earlier.

One day a colleague asked me to read a book proposal. A bit on the scholarly side, she said, but there was something to it. At the very least, history being my area, I could help her sort out a rejection letter. This was, as the reader may have guessed, Miriam's proposal for *Angels and Devils,* her book on the abolitionist Grimké sisters from South Carolina's plantation elite. The title was a play on the name—Devilina—that slaveholders had bestowed on younger sister Angelina, who would later marry the abolitionist Theodore Weld. Those to whom this much is familiar will recall that, on publication by the University of North Carolina Press, the book received a split front cover *New York Times* review and a National Book Critics Circle Award.

That, of course, was the future when I looked at the proposal and found the name of a woman I had last seen in a Toronto loft full of Canadian Trotskyites and American deserters so many years before. Lying to yourself is unavoidable, but lying about your younger self is another matter. So let me say, I had once been ridiculously in love with Miriam and, sitting beside her, found I still was—in love, at least, with the idea of her. Had I been able to conjure up the image of a hotel room, I would have gone to bed with the idea of her on the spot, but my imagination tends to fail me in such matters.

As movement comrades, Miriam and I had lived in a communal house, done draft counseling together, organized demonstrations, and produced leaflets against the Vietnam War. So when she asked me to drive those two deserters, yakking about Vietcong they'd offed, through Canadian customs, I agreed, despite my fears. The shorter one sat up front with me and made sputtering *duh-duh-duh* sounds while spraying passing suburbs with an invisible gun held in clenched fists. Miriam was in back with the taller, quieter one, taking puffs from the joints they were passing back and forth. ("Uncle Ho's gen-u-ine thing," the soldier beside me said.) In her quiet, steady way, she drew from each of them stories about a war locked in the car with us. I couldn't detect a trace of fear in her.

I was a knot of silent terror and, as always in her presence, jealousy. I hated that war but those soldiers frightened me. Though I had a class analysis of the world back then, I would never have admitted I was suffering from a case of class fear. Now, I feel a certain tenderness toward those two macho, wigged-out adolescents; at the time all I could think was: We would be arrested at the border, I was a coward, none of this was part of my unspoken agreement with Miriam—nor was the moment when she dipped her head through the window of our car, parked on Spadina Road in Toronto, kissed me on the cheek, and said, "See you in the States," only to turn up under a university letterhead two decades later in a life without me.

As an editor, I'm proud of my fairness. Yet Byzantium did not publish *Angels and Devils*. When I try to imagine why, I feel only puzzlement. It wasn't the first book I rejected that later garnered attention or sold its way off the shelves. Any editor has such tales to tell and little reason to feel ashamed of them. But this one shames me. In it I encounter an impulse I don't understand. Perhaps I didn't want her walking our halls, or couldn't face what had been lost in those years when she was swallowed up, or was embarrassed not to have gone looking for her. But perhaps not. Like a missing echo, no answer comes back.

Somewhere between Spadina Road and the Jefferson Room, I had no doubt, she had experienced a kind of immolation. Somehow, her face, from which much flesh had been burned away, set me thinking of the eight Americans who immolated themselves in that era of protest. Is that so strange? If nothing is remembered of them, why should those who were consumed much more slowly have been noticed?

As I emerged from my reverie, if that's what it was, a public historian from Wisconsin was imploring his university-based colleagues to experience life "on the ground" at a museum where "real publics are being faced every day." All around me, sensing adjournment, historians were stirring. Under the distant gaze of Bob West, I stirred, too. I stir now, remembering my sense of unease. Dread would not have been too strong a word. Given the blindingly bright lights on stage (a documentary of some sort was being shot), it might seem improbable that the gaze generating anxiety was his, and yet as the session ended and younger historians rushed to capture a moment of the Distinguished Professor's time, Bob hustled up the jammed aisle.

The sweat from those lights still glistened on his face. With an enthusiasm so at odds with his writing style, he exclaimed, "I was starting to think we might miss each other!"

I was fond of the Bob West I knew in print. He wrote with a restraint all the more impressive for the vein of emotion he tapped into. You could not, for instance, read the blacklisting chapters in his book on McCarthyism unmoved. Yet in life his weapon was the exclamation point and, though he seldom raised his voice, you had the distinct sense that he was shouting at you. If you met him first on the page, in person he seemed an impostor.

I introduced him to Miriam and he turned on her in full gush. "The Grimké woman! I'm a tremendous admirer!"

She looked at him with bemused curiosity. "I'm at a disadvantage," she said quietly. "I haven't read your work, though perhaps one day I will." She then graced him with a smile I recognized. I had last seen it twenty-seven years earlier on the other side of a national boundary.

If the future is beyond the scope of the historian, it's where editors spend a remarkable amount of time. You sign up a book but the manuscript doesn't appear for years; by the time it's published, to you it's ancient history. Think of a publisher's catalog announcing next season's offerings, signed up long ago by editors laid off by a management no longer in place for a house that, in all but name, may no longer exist. Its pages are like light from a distant star, telling you of a future that, to the editor, is long gone. It's a perspective that bleeds easily enough into life.

From the moment I noticed Bob staring, I sensed what would occur. I wasn't surprised, then, to find myself thigh-to-thigh with him at a too-small table polychromed with World War II news headlines ("Americans Cross Rhine," "1,000 Bomber Raid on Tokyo,"

"Aachen Taken") in the Sheraton's Zenger Lounge. I ordered a glass of Chardonnay, Miriam, a scotch on the rocks, and Bob, complaining cheerily of an ulcer, Evian water. For the first time, I found I could look directly at her. She returned my gaze with sympathy. It was as if Bob, just then praising my editing skills and inquiring about her work, were our child, the objective correlative of those missing years. This thought, for reasons I can't begin to guess, I found soothing.

"I've discovered a cache of letters between two sisters from Massachusetts," Miriam was saying to him. "One went south to work for the Freedmen's Bureau and stayed on to fight the return of white-rule regimes. The other remained in Dedham, became embittered that blacks, not women, had gotten the vote and took up racialist politics in the cause of women's rights. So you've got racial and gender backlash tearing up one family and, by extension, one country."

Bob half-whistled, a little sucking in of air. "That's topical as hell!"

"Well, the present came from somewhere, didn't it?"

"Sure, but where did *your* present come from? You obviously have a thing for sisters! How many sisters do you have to have a thing for?"

I nearly leaped from my chair. But Miriam only smiled, almost shyly, and after a moment's thought, replied, "Oddly enough, I'm an only child, but my mother had a twin sister who took a lot of responsibility for raising me." She paused. "I've always thought of her as a second mother. And I do, of course, have two daughters." Again she fell silent before adding, almost dreamily, "Maybe I do have a thing for sisters."

So she was the mother of two, formerly the child of two mothers. And I was the father of none, formerly . . . I sipped my drink. She and I had worked together for two years, a long energy high, and what did I know about her, except that she had gone to Mississippi for Freedom Summer?

"I should thank you," she was saying to Bob. "It's always hard to look in the mirror." And she began to elaborate on her project with quiet energy.

It was rare for me to hear someone describe a book as yet unwritten and not feel I was being asked, however indirectly, to publish it. But such was the case until Bob exclaimed, "Then we have something in common! My next project —Rick, this will interest you—is a reconsideration of the Carter interregnum."

"You realize," I muttered, "that each of your books skips the sixties in a different century?"

They looked at me oddly, then at the each other, and we burst out laughing.

I ordered a second glass of wine, and Miriam another scotch. Bob, glancing at his watch, refused an Evian. "Listen, give me a few minutes!" He beamed at Miriam. "I'll run back to my room, make a call or two, and we can adjourn for dinner!" He looked at her pleadingly, then at me. "Half an hour at the outside!" And in a whirl of motion he was gone.

I broke the ensuing silence, guilty consciences being what they are, by asking about the success of her book. She thought for a few moments—time enough for me to grow uneasy—and said, "You can't imagine how unsettling it was to be noticed." She paused, evidently to turn over her answer as she had my question. "So different from being noticed as a group. Do you remember the rush back from a demonstration to see if we were on TV?"

"I remember feeling a demonstration hadn't happened unless I saw it on TV."

That made her smile, which pleased me. I was tempted to mention our old commune-mate, Larry, as we were scheduled to lunch the following week. But recalling her visceral distaste for him I held back and, naturally, other topics arose.

At one point, she laughed lightly. I must have looked puzzled.

"I just remembered cops and robbers." She laughed softly a second time. "It's what we used to call you and Robby DuVeen when we all lived together. He stole from the icebox and you . . . you policed the house."

Yes, I remembered, though at the time, being a cop, no less a Koppes, didn't seem like a compliment. "I lost track of him years ago," I said, "but I catch his name in the papers from time to time. He's out in Hollywood making terrible films."

We chatted warmly then, though in a gingerly fashion, as if sliding around our common past. I wasn't surprised. I've noticed the odd constraint veterans of the antiwar movement feel whenever we might recount our equivalent of war stories.

At some moment, Miriam leaned toward me and said gently, "And you, Rick, are you . . . ?"

I waited as if breathing were beyond me.

"Are you . . . ?" And she looked to me, smiling, for help.

I smiled back encouragingly. It was all I could do.

"Are you happy?"

I don't know what I expected, but happy? Such an easy question really. Was I happy? No, I was not happy. But I felt certain that wasn't the question she meant to ask.

Perhaps I looked confused or perhaps my silence was enough, for she quickly added, "As an editor. Do you enjoy your work?"

Did I enjoy editing? It was a question without meaning, like asking whether I took pleasure in breathing. For fear of appearing a fool, I said, a bit foolishly, "I'm quite a good editor, actually."

"I'm sure you are."

I felt myself blushing, which confused me more than I can say. "That must sound like bragging."

She shook her head. "A person doesn't brag about such things. I'm quite a good historian. I believe that finally. I even take some mild pleasure from it."

We sat then in each other's presence for what seemed a long but not uncomfortable time.

Finally she said, "I hope you don't mind my curiosity, but are

you . . . ?" And here she stopped again. "When I look at you . . ."—
and indeed I realized I had been bathed in her serious, kind gaze these
many minutes—"I feel . . ." She suddenly said, "Are you married?"

"Formerly. In another life, to another editor. It was a curious
catastrophe."

"Are you alone, then?"

I stopped to consider that question. I was, of course, not alone.
I was with Sarah Dixon.

"I'm sorry." She looked stricken. "I didn't mean to embarrass
you. I just—"

"No, no," I said hurriedly, "you're not embarrassing me. It's a
perfectly reasonable question. It's . . ." And here I faltered. Ours
was a conversation incapable of completing a sentence.

"Honestly, forget I asked. It's truly not important."

"I'm with somebody. It's just that I . . . "

"No, really. I don't mean to pry."

"You're not. We . . . ," I began, but I couldn't say what was true:
that Sarah and I were waiting together for an aloneness sure to
come. How could I say that when we had yet to acknowledge it
to each other? To speak of it in the Zenger Lounge to this woman
I still loved who had two daughters and, undoubtedly, a husband
seemed like a betrayal. I felt stupid, then, and unhappy, as if I
had no access to words that would make things right. There was
surely a path through this moment, but I lacked an editor to show
me the way.

Suddenly, Miriam took us elsewhere, perhaps only to end the
awkwardness. "Do you have any idea how bizarre it is to run into
you?" Just the week before, she added, she had been thinking
about me again due to "an odd story" that had come her way, a
story no one in her present life could appreciate.

She searched for words, stopping several times before mentioning that she had been tempted to write it down. But serviceable as
her prose was, she said, she did not consider herself a real writer.
"A writer of *that* sort." Those were her words.

"I've seen your pieces from time to time," she added, "and I don't doubt you might make something of it."

This surprised me for my infrequent essays appear in magazines that, I often suspect, have more contributors than readers.

"If it appeals to you," she added, "maybe you'll write it up yourself." It seemed, however casually put, a request.

"Do you remember Jack Mills?"

I nodded.

"He was my lover back then."

This admission—or whatever it was, for it had nothing of the confessional about it—depressed me. Though we had all worked together, I had not liked him. A phrase from a San Francisco Mime Troupe play came into my head: "You can choose which side of history you're on, but not who's on it with you." That summed up my relationship to Jack, a movement leader with a brand of arrogance exceedingly familiar at the time. What appalled me, even so many years later, was that I had been ignorant of his involvement with Miriam.

"And you remember the photograph."

This wasn't a question. Even people not in Washington on that tear-gassy day in 1969 remembered it. I think it had been in *Time* magazine and you often saw it tacked to bulletin boards or magnetized onto refrigerator doors.

Unbelievably enough, more than three decades have passed since some unknown news photographer snapped it. So if you weren't born yet or don't remember it, imagine a ghostly white veil superimposed on the grainy shadow of a massive building; authority, you might say, losing its substance. In the shape-shifting foreground was Jack splayed on the sidewalk in an Army surplus jacket, face streaked with blood, arm thrown up protectively. Above him, helmetless, loomed a policeman, nightstick raised—you could feel the rage in the gesture—his bulky body riddled with whiteness. Behind him, a bandanna-shrouded face, a hand, body parts floated in that unnatural fog that concealed a rock or brick.

As an image, it lacked the terror of those years—the napalmed child running naked down the road, the mask of grief on that girl at Kent State—but it captured the mayhem, the Krazy Kat feeling of the time. A cartoon of terror, it lacked only a balloon with the words "l'il ainjil" inside. For some of us who ran through that fog, choking and gasping and crying, pumped on adrenaline or, like me, fueled by fear, it caught the surreal nature of the war at home. And if you were around when the fog drifted off . . .

"And you remember Jack afterward?" she said quietly.

"Of course." After he got out of jail, she meant, and I did remember, more or less. There were the ludicrous charges and the trial. He had, after all, been beaten nearly senseless. I remembered the officer in court in a wheelchair.

"We stopped seeing each other." She paused. "I stopped seeing him."

I said nothing. She was breathing quickly the way a small bird does if you hold it in your hand.

"It's always bothered me."

I had no idea what to say.

"And you remember that policeman?"

"Wasn't he paralyzed somehow?"

"He lost the use of an arm. Anyway, a few weeks ago Jack called me. He came across a copy of my book and used it to track me down."

"What's he doing?"

"He's a councilman in Monterey, California. He was calling to tell me his twenty-two-year-old son, an actor, had played one of the aliens in the movie *Independence Day,* which is strange enough when you think about it. But here's the bizarre thing: That police officer's daughter was part of the crew that digitalized the special effects, so that—you know the scene where the alien splats against the glass?" She looked at me. "You did see it, didn't you?"

I nodded, though I hadn't.

"That was, in essence, her. And, of course, the idiot hippies who

[ 46 ]

got vaporized in L.A., that was what was left of us. And there was that police officer's daughter taking a high-tech billy club to the image of Jack's son. They should have called that movie *The Alien Ate Us All.*"

There was something here I was still trying to grasp. "So did they get together?"

She looked at me oddly.

"Are they a couple now?"

"Of course. They burned the earth clean of us, then Alien and Eve started over." And for the last time that afternoon she smiled, a miraculous flicker on that serious face, strobing with some kind of pleasure. "I always suspected you of being a secret romantic."

And she reached across the table, once again placing her hand carefully on mine. I had the impression that her life was a current running into my hand. I was, as Dr. Mesmer might have said, galvanized. I was just imagining what I might say when Bob appeared.

"Done!" He sat down, waving a *Zagat.* "I picked it up at the newsstand in the lobby! Shall we choose a restaurant?" Miriam took a sip of her drink. She continued to look at me, or—so it felt anyway—into me, though I wasn't sure what was there for her to see.

I heard an electronic warbling. Her eyes faltered, then she bent her head, lifted her purse to the table, and extracted a black plastic square that unfolded into a phone.

"Excuse me," she said, "but I have to feed my turkey." And she placed it to her ear. "Yes?" she almost whispered. "Of course it's me . . . Are you sure? . . . All right . . . Twenty minutes at the out-side." She folded the phone back into the purse and zipped it shut. "That was my younger daughter. I'm afraid I have to go."

With that she stood up. I rose, too. Bob protested to no avail. She leaned over and shook his hand in a pleasant, businesslike way. She would take a rain check, she told him. Then she straightened up to the fullness of her tiny height and offered me that hand. Her face in the twilight of the Zenger Lounge seemed sunken and strangely lacking in expression. I thought of her smile, so like the light from a distant star, as I said good-bye and watched her leave, a woman whose only advance, however unmeant, I had rejected seven years earlier.

Bob West was waiting. We would go to dinner, just the two of us, at a restaurant of his choice, and I would hear about his new project and it would be my job to tell a man whose last book had sold less than four thousand copies in hardcover that, in publishing terms, he was history.

# Chapter 3

## TWO EDITORS EATING LUNCH

Larry and I rarely met for lunch. We scheduled meals on a monthly basis, but one of us usually backed out. To my surprise, on that day in November 1998, neither of us did. Larry had suggested Claus Carlsrad, an inexpensive German restaurant just off First Avenue and heavy on the *wurst* dishes. It was our regular spot. If we went anywhere, we went there.

To my mind, restaurants are like gas stations, meant to tank you up so you can get to your next stop, but Larry takes his food seriously. So Claus Carlsrad always seemed an odd choice. Its advantages were its tables, set far apart—he's a touch paranoid about others listening in—and the fact that no editors or authors seemed to know about it. Amid its nondescript clientele, we felt free to complain in peace.

But it had another advantage. It allowed us to indulge in two conflicting impulses from the sixties. One of us would always put the meal on his expense account, fulfilling an urge to rip off "corporate capitalism," as we called it back when we didn't imagine the half of it. Yet the amounts were so modest neither of us felt we were exploiting what we would once have termed our "class position." I mention this largely in the spirit of nostalgia, for neither impulse turned out to be relevant that day.

It was such a rare, summery November afternoon that I left the office early, jacket slung over arm, Alain Delon shades in place. On the long crosstown walk, I took in daytime Manhattan, normally experienced only through the Mylar-layered windows installed by Multimedia's energy-conscious managers. By the time I arrived at the restaurant, with the heat of the sun on my bald head, I was in a remarkably relaxed mood, until I realized Claus Carlsrad was no longer there. The whole block—a grocery store, a newsstand, a linens shop, and Peter's Place, a small bookstore I had always thought lacking in inspiration—was gone. Only skeletons remained; exposed beams, open doorways, wall-less walls covered by vast swatches of plastic sheeting. Blotting out the spot where Claus Carlsrad had been, a sign requested our patience while construction was completed on a new Barnes & Noble with a "twenty-thousand-square-foot multimedia center" and a Starbucks café.

I was laughing when Larry walked up. He took in the scene at a glance and said, "Perfect," in his laconic, poker-faced way.

His face retained the boyish look of another era. (Only the gray-flecked Zapata mustache wasn't a holdover from the sixties.) But his body was like a tragedy, sloping endlessly outward and downward. To see that face was always to recall the adolescent I first met in the spring of 1968 in New Haven, Connecticut, and to see that body was to imagine one more time the indescribable distance traveled since.

I received my B.A. from Yale in 1966 and stayed on to work with the historian Harry Long. He had fought at Guadalcanal and was the preeminent progressive historian of his day. Without his work, the new social history would have been unimaginable. What mattered most to me, however, was that this vet who was my father's age took me so seriously.

He used to plead with me not to let momentary passions sweep me away. "There's work to be done," he would say, "and it can't be done without the past in mind." I was flattered that he would speak to me this way, but did I grasp what he was saying? Not in my heart. He feared that someday, just beyond the upsets of the moment, we would all be afloat in a historyless world. He wanted to forge anchors for the future. I was eager to be afloat.

A people without an operative set of explanations for the way they reached the present, he used to tell his students, are prey to every sort of folly, every kind of predator. It wasn't that I thought he was wrong. I just thought he was so old (though he was younger than I am today) that he wouldn't have known history if it bit him on the leg. History, Harry's kind anyway, seemed to me—and this was typical of the moment—beside the point. Why study it, when you could rush directly into it?

I was involved with the Resistance, as one part of the antiwar movement then called itself. I was floundering and organizing— not as contradictory as it now sounds. It was the spring of 1968, the time of Tet. Demonstrations were commonplace. I was living in a polyglot commune in a rundown, three-story frame house on Elm Street, right next to DiCiccio's Funeral Parlor, with Miriam Levy, two history graduate students whose names I've forgotten, the SDS organizer Rob DuVeen, and various "politicos," as we called them.

I was "close to" SDS, as others within SDS were "close to" PL. (Students for a Democratic Society and the Progressive Labor Party for those too young to recognize the radical acronyms of that era.) It was a phrase often used then. In the intensity of the moment, it seemed unbearably important to define the exact degree of distance between you, or your tendency, or your group, and others who were remarkably similar to yourself. Larry was re-markably different.

Rob DuVeen brought him to dinner one night. In the chaos of that house, for a boy like me who had never done more than scramble an egg, being a chef to ten or twelve people could be overwhelming. I was standing amid piles of uncut vegetables and a scattering of dirty dishes when Rob ushered him in.

He was striking. If his jeans and blue work shirt were standard issue, that startling baby face lightly spackled with freckles and the sandy hair in a brush cut were not. Thanks to the strictures of Party discipline, PL members and those close to PL wore their hair short. It was part of a plan to blend in with the proletariat in what they wishfully dubbed a "worker-student alliance." But recogniz-able as they were among the longhairs of SDS, none of them faintly resembled him. He looked for all the world like one of those G.I. Joe dolls still popular then, despite the war.

Rob introduced him as an SDS Traveler and mentioned that he would be staying a few days, which meant nothing in a house where bodies were always sacked out on sagging couches and un-known faces often appeared at the dinner table. His name, how-ever, rang a bell. I had read the position paper he wrote for *New Left Notes* in response to Jerry Farber's pamphlet *The Student as Nigger.* Farber had struck a chord on campus by claiming a position of victimization for students solely on the basis of the analogy in his title. "If I eat in the student cafeteria," the Cal State professor had written, "I become known as the educational equivalent of a nigger-lover. In at least one building there are even restrooms which students may not use."

Larry had responded by describing how blacks, forced to be-come students of their enslavers, had gained an intimate knowl-edge of the deeper workings of power in America (or "Amerika," as it was then beginning to be called, with up to three Ks if you wanted to emphasize the country's Ku Klux Klan heritage). Whites, he pointed out, always had the luxury of ignoring or romanticizing such matters, but it was the ultimate humiliation when your theoretical allies stole your history of oppression solely for organizing purposes and self-glorification. Students had enough genuine issues without falsely claiming slavery and segregation as theirs.

"If," he added, "we are serious about organizing the technocratic class which will someday run American society"—and indeed that boy from Iowa and his Midwestern comrades, a faction dubbed "Prairie Power" in SDS, were utterly serious on the subject—"then we should recognize that they are by no means 'niggers,' and to call them that does not enhance our chances of changing the nature of this country."

With that edgy wit of his, he suggested others who might benefit from the same analogy until he had created a world in which every group had its own version of "oppression"; and yet, among all the "analogous niggers," blacks were still the only actual ones. In two sentences whose absurdity amused us then, but three decades later seem prescient indeed, he wrote, "If considered in the right light, the foremost group of 'niggers' in Amerika would be the white ruling class. Lashed to the wheel of power for centuries, cursed and demeaned by those they rule in our internal colonies and the neo-colonies of the Third World, they need only grasp their situation correctly to become the *primus inter pares* among Amerika's many niggers."

In that passage, you can catch the self-confidence, intelligence, and combativeness of those young men who led SDS. You would not have wanted to meet any of them in a verbal dark alley. Still, the particular brain that launched that assault was lodged in the body of a twenty-year-old college dropout, a farm boy from Iowa. You'll have to excuse my New York prejudices here, but it seemed so unlikely. Yet that young Iowan proved unnervingly himself. His freckled, patently welcoming American face was . . . I can't think of another word for it . . . *deceitful,* fronting as it did for such a powerful and powerfully defended brain.

Among those outsized young egos, power-tripping and guilt-tripping each other and whoever else wandered by, those boys who might have gone on to the CIA or the State Department or some top law firm, who might have made it to a state house or Congress, or a cabinet post, or the Presidency if only the bomb hadn't dropped, Chuck Berry hadn't been born, the war in Asia had never begun—among them, he was probably the only one who would have taught me how to cook a decent meal. We made pasta primavera that night, though he called it "spaghetti sauté." And it tasted amazingly good.

In the process, he solicited my views on the differences between the middle-class students I counseled at the local draft resistance center and the working-class kids who sometimes stumbled in off the street, confused, angry, and unreachable. He lost interest only when I began to confide in him about Miriam Levy. All I learned in return was that he grew up on a farm and spent two years at Iowa State before heading for Chicago.

He refused the toke that passed around the table that night, stayed with us for three weeks, slept alone, managed to talk rather than dance his way through several parties, fascinated some, put off others, and, as I've said, repelled Miriam Levy.

Take sex, drugs, and rock 'n' roll, throw in radical politics, that desire to turn a mess of a world inside out, and you have a credo for an era or a cliché for a moment. In either case, he didn't fit. His mind couldn't have been bolder and work didn't scare him in the least, but he was interiorized, someone you came to love, if at all, helplessly and with frustration. Whatever questions you had about him, you just knew you couldn't ask.

On that absurd November day some three decades later, with the temperature climbing into the mid-sixties, Larry slipped his arm through mine and we began to walk slowly south on First Avenue. That was strange in itself. I could not remember touching or being touched by him. You didn't hug him. No one kissed him.

You didn't put your hand on his shoulder or slap him on the back or tap him on the knee. It was undoubtedly something about sexuality, but who knew what.

I only said, "What now?"

"Now, ve valk, Herr Doktor."

I looked at him and laughed. "You're in a good mood." His face glistened from the heat and perhaps the exertion, though we were proceeding at a languid pace, two middle-aged men on a mission to nowhere. "At least I've got time," I added. "Our production meeting was canceled."

"What I've got," he said, "is aces over eights, the proverbial dead man's hand. It's what you get dealt when you're sitting with your back to the door."

"I know what the dead man's hand is."

"No," he said quietly, "I don't think so." We fell silent for part of a block, then he picked up again in the same odd manner. "Remember when Harcourt Brace chose between books and whales, the ones in their theme parks, and the whales won?"

"Sure," I said, unsure whether to laugh.

"You know," he added as we waited for a light, "we may be the last of our kind."

"And what kind is that?"

As the light changed, I felt the tug of his arm. It was almost— but not quite—as if he were relying on me for balance.

"Do you ever edit while you shit?"

I laughed uncomfortably.

"It's one of the seven signs of the true editor. I can edit while I walk."

Given our slow processional down First Avenue, it wasn't an easy image to take in. "The stages of the cross-out," I said lightly.

Another half-block and he picked up again. "My parents waited their whole lives for time to end. But, being good Americans, they didn't have a clue about what was really ending or why, otherwise they would have dropped to their knees and prayed for deliverance."

For a moment I tried to conjure up his parents about whom I knew nothing on that farm about which I knew nothing. Iowa was a place you flew over on your way to the coast.

"Larry," I said, "do you realize how strange this conversation is?"

"Do you know, my father once took a small, green dinosaur I'd been given and threw it in the fireplace? I still recall the smell of burning rubber, a scent not common in the southwestern corner of my state. My father was a born scientist. He knew more about the natural world than you can imagine, but he believed dinosaurs had been created in the minds of godless atheists and he never doubted that playing with such toys would make me one. Like many people it's stylish to laugh at, he wasn't as wrong as you might imagine."

I took a breath. "This certainly is a postmodern conversation."

"Premodern would be more like it. You should have been born a Christian in Iowa, Herr Doktor. It would have done you a world of bad."

"Larry . . . ," I began.

"You put the puzzle pieces together and they make sense, but not under an Iowa night sky. Horizon to horizon, it doesn't mean a damn thing."

There are moments, I want to say, when you feel generically inadequate. This was one. Everything Larry said looks stranger—and so, oddly enough, less unsettling—in print than it felt at the time. Maybe I'm not skillful enough to re-create the uninflected way he spoke or give a sense of all the uninflected years that lay behind his words. Here was a man I felt I knew in every aspect that was knowable, with whom I talked on the phone every day, whom I consulted on submissions of the most confidential sort though he was at a rival house. He had never lost his sardonic wit or the reputation for not sparing a listener his thoughts; and there was about him, as three decades before, something, if not impersonal, then not personal in any usual way. In a business in which gossip traveled at the speed of sound, he was someone with whom you couldn't gossip. He treated the manuscripts he admired with a respect that crossed all boundaries and their authors with an editorial version of tough love; and they were loyal to him for that. He was driven to uncover what makes the world tick—as the books he published (and the honors they won) indicated—but who knew what made him tick?

He was eager to consider the contradictions inherent in a situation. But of his own contradictions nothing could be said. He was surrounded by prohibitions, which, among other things, prohibited discussion of them. You did not, for instance, call him at home, and this was not discussed. I have no idea how you knew, but if you had the urge to dial a number at nine at night, his was not the number you dialed.

The heat of his curiosity drove you along, and when he was done with you, you were clearer on the world you lived in and your own surprisingly small place in it. He was like one of his Iowa skies. If it didn't bother you to feel dwarfed, then he could be remarkable company, but his was a style that never endeared him to management. He was not a man to be managed, and he was notoriously without a profile in a business where heightening one's profile was on the agenda.

Unfortunately, that day I felt dwarfed in a way I didn't care for. A pattern of relating had inexplicably vanished. It was like not being able to catch your breath, and I had the urge to flee. Undoubtedly, this reflected my style. I find a certain passivity—the ability to be subsumed, if you will—appropriate to an editor's role. Off the page, I'm a listener. Sometimes that's all the help a person needs. Silence, sympathy, the nod of a head, a sense of attention can often lead you where it turns out you want to go. But I'm uncomfortable editing people. If you want someone to step into your life, interpret, organize, rearrange your problems, I'll disappoint you.

I can sense a problem in the quietness of the page and offer an author a way out. But there's no reason such a skill should translate into the noise and confusion of everyday life. I absorb situations slowly. Paper implies time. With Larry, that day, everything happened as in a horror movie, unexpectedly and with the intent to scare. I sensed—I would have been insensate not to— that he had been shaken. And I wondered why he was shaking me.

To know your limits may be the essence of editing. Otherwise, how could you imagine the limits of another mind and work within them? But to know your limits in life can be disabling. Certainly, whatever was puzzling to me then still puzzles me. And yet there were a few things I did understand about Larry and the publishing moment in which we found ourselves. According to the gospel of publishing's new managerial class, there were to be no more turnstile jumpers in the book trade due to an editor's passing fancy or the curiosities of an author who insisted on pursuing what seemed like a less than hopeful subject. Every editorial choice, every gesture to an author, every gesture by an author, now had to pay its own way.

Larry and I were "midlist editors" in a business desperate not to publish midlist books. Once, when the sale of five thousand hardcovers wasn't counted a failure, these would simply have been called "books." Larry's skill was in finding books that sold in the eight-to-twenty-thousand range in hardcover and then steadily into college courses in paperback. But backlist paperbacks, so long a guarantee of predictable cash flow in a business otherwise akin to a lottery, were sinking fast. Any assistant professor could now produce his or her own "anthology" at Kinko's for the cost of permissions.

Authors capable of creating and then re-creating best-sellers were the hard currency of the moment. I had one and a half of them, if you counted the television journalist J. Boyle MacMurphy for his never-to-be-repeated success with *Into the Tall Grass*. Larry now had none, as the *New York Times* obituary page had made clear about a month earlier. With three best-sellers to his name, Martin G. Dillard, creator of *Dillard's Global Dollar*, a successful part of National Public Radio's *Marketplace*, had dropped dead of a heart attack at the age of fifty-two without bothering to deliver his next book.

It didn't help that Larry was incapable of adjusting to decisions based on numbers crunched in the offices of people whose activities, in publishing terms, possibly in any terms, he found incomprehensible. He did not care to take orders that ran against his intellectual impulses. "This," he had said to me not long before, "is by no one's definition a life."

And yet, to the best of my knowledge, there was no other life. No wife, no "friend," no live-in lover, only publishing. It had been his world since, in 1969, he attempted to step out of the madness of SDS's disintegration without stepping away from the urge to change society. He joined an "underground press" loosely connected to *The Chicago Seed,* an alternative newspaper. The Press, as it was known, produced strike posters, antiwar materials, and pamphlets for local radical organizations. But as the movement dried up, work dwindled and the staff factionalized. To Larry fell the task of salvaging what there was to save by transforming the Press into a distributor of radical literature, whose audience was not drying up. The pamphlet *Our Bodies, Ourselves,* Dorfman and Matellart's *How to Read Donald Duck,* Rius's *Cuba for Beginners,* Franz Fanon's writings, Mao's *Little Red Book,* a series on labor history, and Marge Piercy's "Grand Coolie Damn" were typical of the "literature program" he developed.

Not too many years earlier, a few New York book editors had noticed that the movement was spinning off more than its share of fine writers, whose work in paperback attracted younger Americans in more than ordinary numbers. It was as if the news that hit the music world in the 1950s—teenagers would buy 45s unsettling to adults—had just made its way to publishing, which began looking to tiny, radical presses for new authors. In 1972, someone at Simon & Schuster stumbled across Larry, who had been left with a literature program and no presses. Those had been transported across town to a new entity, the Liberated Press, which proved too liberated to last. In a state of reduced irony, Larry dubbed his rump organization—three people and a pile of pamphlets he had no way of reprinting—Unity Press.

He was soon combining those pamphlets with essays he commissioned from local writers into "liberationist teaching packets." He typeset them himself and shopped the results out to a "straight" print shop desperate enough to take a serious young man without resources on credit. These proto-anthologies (under titles like *Dominant Amerika, An Imperial History,* and *Subject Minorities, Race and Class in Amerikan History*) found an audience in the universities. As the radical movement withered, sales soared and, to Larry's surprise, profits followed.

By 1977, when Simon & Schuster, which had been distributing selected titles from his list, purchased Unity, Larry was editing a political economist at the University of Chicago named Martin G. Dillard who produced a best-selling book on, of all things, the global economy and the transnational corporation. That same year, my then-wife, my only wife, Connie Burian, who would soon become a prominent figure in publishing, answered our phone. I remember her cupping the receiver, rolling her eyes, and whispering, "Larry something, who says he's planning to stay with us awhile." A strange month that was. They studiously ignored each other for reasons neither would discuss with me. At month's end, both moved out: she into the apartment of a reasonably well-known novelist, and he into a small flat on Prince Street, after which our lunches began. Three years later, Simon & Schuster closed Unity Press but Larry remained.

You might say, then, that I knew what I needed to know about Larry's situation, and yet, that day, my sense of surprise proved boundless.

As we proceeded, I asked, somewhat sullenly, "Are we walking or eating?"

"A block down there's a Vietnamese restaurant worth a try." He paused. "In honor of old times."

"I'm glad you think there's still honor in them."

"Well, the Vietnamese part of them anyway."

I snorted. "I'll bet the owner's some minor war criminal we air-lifted out, gold bars and all." Why I said that I don't know, but I'm not proud of much I said or did that day.

"Certainly, the odds are he was on our side."

"I wouldn't call it *ours*."

Larry laughed loudly enough for a young couple, also arm in arm, to glance at us. "Where do you think you've been working these last years?"

"I don't follow."

"Re: sides? Herr Doktor, take a memo. You're a Jew working for the Germans. It's a new new world we're sailing off the edge of, and I'm not betting on sides any more."

He was, of course, referring to the fact that Desmond & Dickinson had become German property—if nationality means anything in such circumstances—when David Marsden's Multimedia Entertainment, the American wing of Bruno Hindemann's global fiefdom, swallowed it in one medium-sized gulp.

"Look on the bright side," he said. "The chef is supposed to cook a wicked duck. You know, there's German *ente* and Vietnamese *vit* and French *canard* and good old American mallard grilled over coals by the lakeside. There's just no way to go wrong with a duck."

I had an image, then, of his father and him shouldering rifles in a brilliant yellow wheat field as black ribbons of ducks passed overhead. But on further consideration, the field came from van Gogh, the birds were his ragged crows, and the guns from any TV show you want to name. I've never been to Iowa.

I felt the pressure of Larry's arm on mine. "Here we are, then," he said.

I looked up into the elegant if modest window of Le Pékin, its beige curtains half drawn back. In its muted interior I could just make out the nearest tables, tiny, tastefully set, and empty. A menu in the window listed "Chef Special Dishes." I noted General Hua's Chicken and Ants Climbing Trees.

"Look." Larry pointed to a small boxed area, ornately outlined in red, which announced Sichuan Province Original Tea-Smoked Duck as the Specialité de la Maison.

"It's Chinese," I said, as if someone were trying to cheat me.

"Yes, but the chef isn't. Anyway, do you know how hard it is to find decent tea-smoked duck in New York?"

"The chef, I suppose, is Vietnamese?"

"Exactly."

"And you know this because . . . ?"

"The name, it's a giveaway."

"The Peking Restaurant?"

"It's not the city, it's the French. A Chinese-run restaurant would call itself The Beijing. But for Vietnamese of a certain class, French retains a cachet, and Chinese food rendered by a Vietnamese chef has a delicacy all its own."

Inside I could see no one. I glanced at my watch. One thirty-seven. Past the midtown lunch rush but hardly an explanation. I felt Larry's hand on my shoulder. "Shall we, Herr Doktor?"

"I could do without the 'Herr Doktors,'" I muttered.

"Of course, Herr Doktor. Of course, you could."

He opened the door and we both stepped into the confines of Le Pékin. It held perhaps fifteen small tables: three central ones large enough for groups of four, the rest for twos and threes. To my surprise, along the left wall three were occupied. Dishes pushed back, a young man was working at a laptop computer. On either side were couples, also young, each nearing the end of a meal. Two men at a table by the back wall jumped to their feet as we entered, the smaller one in a black jacket advanced on us, the taller in a white shirt disappeared.

A head shorter than Larry, the maître d', menus in hand, motioned us to the only empty table along the occupied wall. His wispy goatee brought to mind the one Vietnamese face still

lodged in my head after all those years, Ho Chi Minh's. He was—
for I took a closer look—about my age. The resemblance to Ho
proved passing, for he had a large mole under his right eye and a
jagged laceration, an old scar, that ran like lightning down one
cheek.

I wondered if he had been an officer in the South Vietnamese
army, and thoughts of torture floated through my brain, then images of troops hanging from the skids of helicopters, and of that
implacable police general Loan delivering his on-camera coup de
grâce to the head of a Vietcong suspect in Tet-torn Saigon. Suddenly, I felt a shiver of guilt as it struck me that my own war experience was the sum of many images seen on a black-and-white TV
in a commune in New Haven.

All this and more, swift and dreamlike, passed through my
mind while Larry insisted on being seated far from the other diners. I noticed the way the maître d' froze, then forced a smile, not
friendly but a surrender nonetheless, and led us graciously enough
to an empty table for three across the room. We faced each other,
the third chair between us. This, at least, felt familiar. Larry always
chose space over intimacy.

I glanced again at my watch. Only four minutes had passed.

"In a hurry?"

"Not at all," I said a touch too quickly.

"Then we should plan our meal."

"You order for us."

"*Jawohl*, Herr Doktor—"

"Larry," I burst out. "What's this 'Herr Doktor' stuff, some
weird reference to my being Jewish?"

He laughed, loudly enough for the young man at the computer
to look our way. "Jews," he said, also in a loud voice. "In Celine,
the nearest town to our farm, do you know how many Jews there
were, Herr Doktor? I'm reminded of the chapter on owls in a book
on the birds of Iceland. 'There are,' it reads in full, 'no owls in
Iceland.'"

He picked up the menu. The maître d' reappeared, his head slightly bowed.

"Two Vietnamese beers," Larry said.

"No Vietnamese beer. Chinese. American."

"Do you have Tsingtao?" I asked.

"Yes, Tsingtao." He nodded encouragingly.

"Two Tsingtaos, then."

"A Heineken for me," Larry said. "Chinese beer tastes like water."

The couple nearest the door stood up. The maître d' moved toward them and they shook hands all around. Except for the soft clacking of laptop keys, the place was so quiet I could hear the young woman say in a near-whisper, "Thanks, Mister Trinh. We'll see you Friday."

"I'm done," Larry said.

I said nothing.

"As in done for. Kaput. Remaindered, Herr Doktor."

I understood, of course, and there were many ways I might have reacted based on loyalty, on friendship, on decency alone. But that afternoon unfolded like one of those nightmares where you sense an intruder in your room and you're paralyzed to act.

Larry signaled the maître d'. "We'll have your tea-smoked duck."

"Sorry, no tea-smoke duck." There was in his voice a lilting hint of a tonal language, and where his stress marks fell a hint as well of the disorientation that comes when you learn a language too late.

"You don't believe in truth in advertising?" said Larry.

"Sorry."

There was no way to know whether he was apologizing for the missing duck or signaling confusion.

"If you can't serve your *specialité,* shouldn't you indicate that in your window?"

"We have run out."

"Then we'll take any duck dish you have."

"No duck today."

Impatiently, Larry motioned the maitre d' away. He grabbed the menu in disgust but, instead of opening it, glared at me. In his own way, he was waiting.

"What do you mean, remaindered?" I asked.

He squinted, perhaps to consider me in a different light, and then responded as if I were a stranger who knew nothing of this island Earth. "Management called." He spaced his words carefully. "They're without the inclination to read books. Not in the job description. They summoned me and gave me the ax."

"They fired you?"

"That would be too expensive. They suggested I become a contract editor, details to follow. I suppose there would be a stipend and an override royalty on books I brought in, and of course no health care, never mind the fact that they could can me any time without cost. It's bound to be a good deal for someone."

Undoubtedly, he wanted me to edit him. We endured an awkward silence until he said, not so much to me as to the universe, "Marty picked the wrong moment to die. You can't blame the poor bastard. He just should have put a bullet in my heart first."

With a sense of relief, I noticed the maître d'—Mr. Trinh, the woman had said—approaching. He had the feel of a man who had once been something more. He placed a bottle of Tsingtao and a frosted glass in front of each of us.

"Not Tsingtao!" Larry's voice rose in anger.

"Tsingtao was good for you."

Larry seemed about to rise. I felt a pulse of fear. There was something of that war, of some war anyway, in the room with us. "Larry . . . ," I said, alarmed.

Both hands pressed to the table, he glared at Mr. Trinh. "Then, we'll have ants climbing trees."

"No ants today."

Perhaps it was the muffled mid-afternoon light in that cloistered room, but the scar on Mr. Trinh's cheek seemed to be subtly reddening.

"Then what do you have?"

"Cashew chicken. Spring roll and cashew chicken. Very tasty."

"Make it General Hua's chicken."

Mr. Trinh did not respond. This man, I felt sure, had seen killing.

"I will bring you," he said and abruptly departed.

"Larry, we could walk out now, no harm done."

"Believe me, the harm's been done and I'm considering two courses of action, quitting or suicide."

I felt a flutter, as of my heart. "You're not serious?" It was the first question to which I did not know the answer.

Larry smiled.

The other couple was rising. To my surprise, the woman, a petite redhead in a beige slacks suit walked over. She looked desperately young, like a child in her mother's dress-up clothing. Behind her, his body curving in like a scimitar, lurked her dining partner, also unbearably young.

As she leaned toward us, I noted that she had used eyeliner to highlight the astonished quality of her eyes and that she wore a tiny gold stud in her left nostril. "Angela Mueller," she said to Larry. "We met at your office once. Jane Landes introduced us."

Larry cocked his head and stared up at her.

"I'm with Excel." Her edgy voice faltered slightly. "The literary agency?"

Larry still said nothing.

"I thought I might take this opportunity to introduce a wonderful writer, Pete Marlowe—"

"This is not an opportunity," Larry said.

She took a step back as if rocked by a punch.

Marlowe stepped forward. He was anxious. I'd seen it so often in young authors who felt their futures on the line. "You should try the tea-smoked duck," he said. "It's superb."

I was touched. He was taking a chance, defending his agent or, for all I knew, his lover who happened to be dealing his books.

I said, "Unfortunately, by the time we arrived there was no tea-smoked duck."

"Really?" His enthusiasm cracked his voice.

Larry stared at him. "How's your heart?"

He looked befuddled, as well he should have.

"These days I'm giving all my authors physicals before I sign them up. On the sports model."

Angela Mueller tittered slightly. "I know we really shouldn't interrupt, but if you don't mind, I'd like to call you sometime. I think Pete might be—"

"Call as often as you want," Larry's voice was a growl, "but you're speaking to a dead man."

"I beg your pardon?"

He raised his voice as if English were not her native language. "A dead man. You're passing idle words with a dead man."

Marlowe put his arm around her shoulder and with the barest of formal good-byes they left.

"They're like lice," Larry said by way of cheery conclusion. "They swarm over midtown at lunchtime."

I poured my beer and picked up the glass. None of its chill remained.

"Are you in the mood for a toast?" He peered at his beerless glass. "I've been running on empty for a while." He laughed. "To hell and back!" he exclaimed, clinking my glass hard. "A great movie if you were ten and it was the nineteen fifties."

An image came to mind—of freckle-faced Audie Murphy leaping off a burning tank, tommy gun spitting.

"The most decorated infantryman of World War Two and America could bestow no greater honor than letting him wipe out the Germans again on screen. My brother and I must have gone three, four times, and believe me, when you travel twenty-odd miles to town over dirt roads in the back of a pickup, that's a lot."

"I didn't know you had a brother."

"Technically, my older brother. Made it to land three minutes ahead of me. I've been unable not to think about him lately."

That double negative may read ruefully, but it was said with aggressive force.

I felt a wave of sympathy for Mr. Trinh, and Angela Mueller, too, but mostly for myself. Whatever I felt that afternoon, I couldn't seem to feel it for him. Perhaps the slow unraveling of the sixties had finally washed us both ashore exhausted at Le Pékin. At least in the end I asked a question I sensed he wanted. Maybe it doesn't matter what you think as long as you do what needs to be done. "You're not in touch much then?" I said mildly.

"Not much."

"When did you last see him?"

"Nineteen sixty-seven."

"Nineteen sixty-seven," I repeated dumbly. Even when you sense that you're entering an ambush, being ambushed is quite a different matter. For a few moments we sat in silence and then I asked the next question, "What happened between you?"

"He died."

"He died." I repeated that, too.

"In the Mekong Delta. A second lieutenant shot sometime during Tet by a man from the side I supported back home."

Under other circumstances I might have argued about whom exactly we had been supporting, but I was stunned. We had shared so much of publishing for so long, and yet here was a fact without which knowing him undoubtedly made almost no sense. How many former campus radicals, after all, could have found the names of relatives on the Vietnam Wall?

Larry was undoubtedly thinking along more personal lines. After a moment he said, "I left home on the fly. He stayed until the Army took him, poor bastard. He was going to run the farm. I mouthed off about the war but he thought about it. And even though it made no sense to him, when duty called, he couldn't imagine not responding. So some farmer in the Mekong Delta shot him dead."

Mr. Trinh materialized then, carrying a tray with two red rice bowls, two pairs of elegantly tapered red chopsticks, an order of spring rolls, and a reddish platter, fringed with lettuce leaves, shreds of carrots, thinly sliced cucumbers, and what could only have been cashew chicken.

Larry looked at the dish as Mr. Trinh set it on the table and then smiled. It was a charming smile. Like the summer sun in Iowa. Like an idea exploding. "Please," he said, as Mr. Trinh lowered the empty tray to his side. He motioned to the third chair. "Sit with us a minute."

"No, no." Mr. Trinh shook his head.

"Really." Half rising, Larry reached across the table and pulled out the chair.

I wasn't surprised. Somehow I sensed our group was incomplete. That chair had been empty only because a body was missing, that of a Vietnamese man of about our age with a jagged scar on his cheek. Mr. Trinh was our third man.

He continued to resist.

Larry rose to his full height. Set beside Mr. Trinh's thin body, his bulk was impressive. "I do insist," he said. He glanced over at the young man with the laptop. "Excuse me."

The young man looked up. "Me?" he asked in the foolish way people do when the obvious seems unbelievable.

"Yes, you. Do you have any further use for our friend, Mister . . . ?" And he looked questioningly at Mr. Trinh. "Mister . . . ?" he repeated. "Mister Mister." And he laughed. "No problem, right?"

"I'm okay. I'm fine," replied the young man hurriedly.

Larry then seated Mr. Trinh, pushing his chair in with a grace striking in someone so lacking the look of grace. He seemed, for the first time that day, alive, his face young and strangely unscarred.

"You do not want to eat?" asked Mr. Trinh.

"No, feel free. Take a taste and tell me what you think. But I'm curious, you are Vietnamese?"

Mr. Trinh nodded.

"And you come from the South."

"From Da Nang, center of our country."

"And how did you get out? Did they fly you out with your gold bars?"

Mr. Trinh cocked his head, though whether he didn't understand or understood too well was impossible to tell.

"It was a complicated war in your country, no?"

"Many wars in my country."

"And you fought in how many of them?"

He held up two fingers, the back of his hand facing out in what could have been a peace sign.

Larry smiled again. "My friend here is curious whether you're some kind of criminal."

It was a bludgeoning and the bludgeon was mine. I had the feeling Larry might be bludgeoning me or, for that matter, himself. I glanced at Mr. Trinh, expecting anger, but he maintained a pose of stiff dignity.

"You are American," was all he said, whether as a statement of fact or a curse.

"I come from the center of my country, too," said Larry, and from his mouth it did not seem a compliment to either of them.

Mr. Trinh evidently saw no need to say more. I fingered my chopsticks, idly snatched a piece of chicken off the platter, ate it, and smiled in an ingratiating manner. It occurred to me that in all those years when images of Vietnamese were everywhere, I never sat with or spoke to a Vietnamese, and that doing so now seemed hardly different from not doing so then. I couldn't help feeling this was a reunion, though what was being reunited I couldn't have said.

Larry was poised like a predator, searching for something to crack open, perhaps because something had cracked open in him.

"Did you ever fight in the Mekong Delta?" he said suddenly.

Mr. Trinh tilted his head as if for the first time considering this adversary, this interrogator. For it was, of course, an interrogation. Not taking his eyes off Larry, he replied, "Two years."

"And which years were those, Mister Mister?"

"My sister live in Tra Tho."

"Where's that?"

"Not where."

"You mean not in the Mekong Delta."

"Not where," he said stubbornly. "There is not Tra Tho. It is not."

I noticed that the man in white had reseated himself at a table at the far end of the room and was staring at us.

I said, nodding in his direction, "Is he your cook?"

"My son. Born in Tra Ton."

"What would you say," Larry responded, "if I told you that my brother died in the Mekong Delta?"

"Many everywhere."

"For Christ's sake, what the hell does that mean?"

Mr. Trinh continued to study Larry's face from a certain angle. Frustration, resentment, violence, death, a thirty-year-old stew— or so it seemed to me then—was at our table along with a tepid dish of cashew chicken and some wilting spring rolls.

Larry leaned close to Mr. Trinh, well inside any culture's zone of comfort, and said, "My brother died in the damn Delta. Someone you knew could have shot him."

Mr. Trinh shifted slightly, then turned toward his son. A stream of Vietnamese flowed into the air, like poetry from another planet. The son rose and headed toward us with, it seemed, a certain reluctance. He had dark eyebrows, a small mustache, and a tattoo of some sort on his left arm. He said, "What's the matter, Dad?"

Mr. Trinh turned back to us. "My son is translate." Then his voice, freed from its prison, began to speak. There's something about being bathed in another language. First, you lean forward as if to offer meaning to sound, but soon enough you relax—strange to say, even then I felt it happening—and the sounds, not meaningless at all, enfold you. It is, if you think about it, the ultimate anti-editing experience.

A kind of calmness came over me. I had the sense that in our presence an ancient war was dwindling. Sunk in his chair, Larry stared blankly at the ceiling. Mr. Trinh's son placed a hand protectively on his father's shoulder. It was a sweetly unselfconscious gesture. Mr. Trinh spoke for a minute or more.

"My father says, he's sorry for your son, but this is his restaurant and it's not sly to dis him here."

Mr. Trinh spoke again, at greater length and with obvious emotion.

"My father says, it's time to pay and get the hell out."

Larry snapped to attention. "We didn't order cashew chicken. We won't pay for cashew chicken!"

"He ate chicken!" Mr. Trinh responded fiercely, pointing at me.

"That wasn't the chicken we ordered and no one asked for spring rolls!"

I took out my Amex card and offered it to the son.

"Visa or Mastercard only."

It was well past time to be gone. There was no bill, but accountings weren't to be expected. I laid a twenty and a five by my plate.

"If you pay, it's for yourself," Larry said fiercely.

"It's okay. I'll cover it."

"Not mine you won't. I won't pay them a cent."

"My father says, get out or my son will kick your ass." His father, of course, had said nothing.

Strangely enough, any fear that we might come to blows had left me. We were, after all, in a small restaurant at the edge of America. We were already by the ocean.

The son stepped aside as Larry rose. At the door, he turned and the rest of us, including the young man at the computer, froze, but after a moment he simply walked out.

I, too, turned at the door, thinking an apology in order. The son had bent close to his father, their faces practically touching as they talked. For them, I was already gone, so I opened the door and left.

Probably no war ever quite ends. I found Larry outside, his anger still white hot. Perhaps at that moment his brother was alive in him. Perhaps he had been reburying him and felt it for the violation it was. Where, after all, could a lost vet from, as we once called it, "the war at home" go to reclaim a dead brother if not to a Chinese restaurant in New York run by Vietnamese?

I shouldn't have said a thing, but of course I did. "Larry, that man didn't kill your brother."

His eyes seemed to focus. A heartbeat passed and then he said, "I never doubted who killed my brother, Herr Doktor. The United States of God-Bless-America killed my brother."

At the return of my Doktorhood, my heart sank.

Just then, Le Pékin's last customer emerged, his computer in a black carrying case slung over his shoulder. It was evident from his lowered head and averted eyes that he was intensely aware of us.

"You!" said Larry.

The young man looked up like a small animal caught in blinding headlights.

"Maybe your father killed my brother."

The poor boy.

I waved my hand at him. "Go on, the show's over."

It was all the bidding he needed.

"Or your uncle!" Larry called after him, laughing. "Or," he said more quietly, "thought about another way, maybe I did it." He paused a moment. "Thought about another *way*, that is." And then he turned back to me. "Your analysis, Herr Doktor? You've seen the case, you've examined the patient, but the prognosis?" He looked at me and winked. "In your professional opinion, Herr Doktor, doesn't guilt do a remarkable job of making the world spin?"

And with that he left me. For a few minutes I watched his slow progress downtown, away from his office, and then caught a cab, a mistake I paid for with an eight-dollar, twenty-minute crawl through traffic. In frustration I jumped out at Fifth Avenue and ran the last long, crosstown blocks. About three and a half hours had elapsed by the time I passed Joy, grabbing for the pink message slips she held out. "*She* called," I heard her say.

I dropped my jacket on the minicouch and shuffled quickly through the slips until I found the one with exclamation points. One o'clock was checked off, and under "Comments" Joy had written, "ASAP!! Margo needs info, Sylvie Dash submission! Best offer, 72 hrs! Where ARE you anyway? Wants to know!!!" Joy is not especially emphatic, merely a good reporter. Margo Deare was emphatic. I buzzed Joy. What was the Dash proposal about?

"I wasn't sure you'd want me to look," she replied, which meant she'd read it and had no opinion she cared to offer. "But I put it front and center on your desk."

And there it was, the cover letter highlighting the three-day curfew, the first few hours of which had already run their course. It was the sort of thing Sylvie, one of the more aggressive literary agents in the business, reveled in.

My phone lit up immediately. I had no doubt who it was.

"Where were you?" Margo was not a woman to waste words on a subordinate. "You know we're trying to cut down on the publishing lunch bullshit. In any case, I've been talking with Bill Ferguson"—our head of sales—"he's faxed parts of the proposal to key salespeople, and they think it could move in the chains. Where are you on this?"

Where was I? A proposal submitted to me had already been scattered through the organization. "Hold on a sec," I said, glancing down at Sylvie's signature emerald-green folder. A photo of a ruggedly handsome young man fronted the left-hand pocket, backed by a wad of publicity material. Shuffling through the right-hand side I came across the proposal itself, only four pages long. It had something to do with the Vietnam War; unsurprising from

Sylvie, given our mutual success with J. Boyle MacMurphy's *Into the Tall Grass.*

"Margo," I said, "Let's talk in the morning. There's something I want to check out first."

"Listen, this is hot. With sales behind us, let's move before we're preempted."

"What makes you think anybody's preempting anybody?"

"She hinted at it this morning when we talked."

I shuffled quickly through the rest of my message slips, but Sylvie hadn't called me. Evidently I was the last person anyone bothered to talk to. It caught something of the quandary of an old-style editor in a new-style publishing combine.

I managed to put off Margo and read the four-page proposal: Air Force pilot shot down over Haiphong, five years in captivity; author/son plans to retrace steps of imprisonment and explore childhood of embattled absence. It was the sort of book about which four pages told you absolutely nothing. The hook—what had grabbed Margo, Bill, and the salespeople—was Sylvie's note that the author would soon join National Public Radio's *All Things Considered* as a regular commentator. Throw in the heat generated by youthful memoirs, add the unending second run of the Vietnam War as an American tragedy, stir in a televisable face for the book tour, and everybody's enthusiasm made sense to me, the same sense it would make at six or eight other houses, for Sylvie Dash had undoubtedly seeded New York with copies. Who cared what might actually fit between the covers when you could already imagine the look of the package, the publicity, and the tour, when the author himself could already promise a reasonable public performance of his work? All across town, energized people would be looking at that same green folder and dreaming the same dreams.

I put it aside. There was nothing to do that hadn't already been done. We would bid and the bidder would not be me. If we got it, it would be "my" book, a classic lose-lose situation. I told Joy I wasn't to be disturbed, sat down, and let the phones blink. I didn't answer correspondence, or check my e-mail, or look at review clips, or reject submissions. For half an hour I leaned back and watched tiny orange-and-red-striped *T. rexes* chase khaki triceratops across my computer screen.

Only late that night, when Sarah was asleep and I was lying beside her, too awake for words, did I feel embarrassed by the way Larry had disappeared from my thoughts. I felt a modicum of guilt. But as various radical factions discovered in the sixties, guilt takes you a remarkably short way, and when it does manage to goad you somewhere, it's likely to be off the sharp edge of a flat Earth. Still, as a word, as Larry's word, it had its place. It was, at least, a place to stop.

The mind is nothing if not an editing machine. It constantly elides, discards, buries, and reshapes, automatically following the path of the story it wants to hear or tell. So much must be subsumed in recreating the contours of a life. Finishing this account I suddenly recalled a different moment when Larry said, apropos of I don't know what, "Thank god no one at this table is writing a book." And I knew exactly what he meant, even though I already had this one vaguely in mind.

I feel somewhat guilty for portraying Larry in such a fashion. Much of what's appealing about him isn't here, perhaps because I was searching for the shape of something else in the publishing world we once inhabited together. I've recorded what I know of him without trying to make much sense of it. The tidiness of interpretation is a luxury for historians, therapists, novelists, and perhaps readers, but not for an editor. On checking my daily calendar for 1998, I find jotted down, "lunch w. Larry, claus c." on Wednesday, November 11, right next to the official notation: "Veteran's Day (Remembrance Day, Canada)." Though I wasn't aware of it then, it seems appropriate.

Larry refused Simon & Schuster's offer and now works freelance out of a small rented office on Leroy Street. He's one of a crowd of editors who have been pushed from the publishing plane without parachutes. He calls them the "lumpeneditoriate." Hardly a week passes that one doesn't call me, curious about job possibilities in the Multimedia complex. I always chat politely and sound sympathetic, as indeed I am. For the most part, publishing being what it is today, they expect no more.

Larry and I still talk about once a week. I always call. Most of his authors remain loyal, which ensures work, even if the money seldom comes from a publishing house. When asked how he spends his time, his responses are flip. Recently he said, "I rent movies about aberrant editors." But once, to my surprise, he said, "I'm writing."

"Really? What about?"

He laughed. "Don't sound so startled. Someone's memoirs, and before I'm done, it might even be mine."

The last time I called, a sleepy male voice answered. After a moment, Larry came on offering no explanation. I leaped for one anyway. I would wish someone for him, though maybe that's guilt, too.

At one point I remember him saying, "Think of me as the editorial flea shaken loose from the publishing dog's back." He was, I noted, growing more efflorescent by the week. "You and I," he went on, "are like monkish illuminators at the dawn of printing, and I'm living evidence that if you want your book published decently these days, you'd better pay for it yourself."

When I asked what he was working on, he chuckled and said, "Once you're out here we can discuss it." He interpreted my silence in his own way, for he added reassuringly, "Don't worry, you won't have long to wait."

Though every editor approaches a manuscript differently, for each, I believe, there's only one way to do so. The skilled author, however unwittingly, always lays down a path just for you. The question is how to find it. Imprecise though our craft might seem, the experience on that path is so precise as to seem foreordained.

Interpretation is a quagmire. Editing is the opposite. I've avoided interpretation where possible. You may have noted, for instance, that two women I've cared about, my former wife and Miriam Levy, both disliked Larry. But Larry was not, in my experience, disliked by women. When my mind comes upon this, it disturbs me but I have no explanation to offer. There is, it seems, so much not to say and so little time left not to say it.

During a recent phone call Larry asked, "Do you remember when Odysseus travels to the mouth of the river Ocean to enter the underworld and a piteous mass of shades almost overwhelms him?"

As I hadn't read *The Odyssey* in decades, I merely *mm-hmm*ed.

"Well, you should consider what the shade of Achilles tells him: 'To be great among the dead is nothing.' Out here, my friend, we're all ghosts."

If he's a ghost, then he is, I believe, the ghost of the last SDS man in publishing, unless, of course, you count me and I was only "close to" SDS. When I tried to make a little joke of it, he said, "The sixties? Somebody told me that was thirty years ago."

I've since been to Washington and indeed on the Vietnam Wall is someone with Larry's surname who died during the Tet offensive. Larry remains exceedingly alive, of course. And yet who's to say that something in him didn't die that winter three decades gone when we first met? No Vietnam Wall encompasses his—our—experiences or, for that matter, Mr. Trinh's, and Larry has now passed out of publishing unnoted, as he assures me I will in good time. We have not scheduled a lunch since November 11, 1998.

There is, when you think about it, so little that we actually possess and we possess it for such a short time. So much we imagine we possess actually possesses us. About Mr. Trinh I know nothing more. Perhaps he, too, was a ghost. As for myself,

I often feel, when not entangled in the web of someone else's words, less than real.

Sometime the following spring, when I was in that part of town again, I found myself walking by the former Le Pékin. The spot was occupied by a café called Les Trois Soeurs Anglaise. It was, at least, in French.

# Chapter 4
## UNDERGROUND

Mel Sawyer arrived at the West End with a shaggy dog of indeterminate breed and the ABC reporter J. Boyle MacMurphy, author of *Into the Tall Grass,* which I had published reluctantly but to remarkable success in 1987.

"I'd think you'd take your writers to something better than this," Boyle said as we shook hands.

I nodded toward the dog. "If I'd known it was coming, I would have chosen Petland."

Sawyer was a wiry runt of a man with burned-out fuses for eyes and he was no author of mine. He had once been known for *Tears of Blood.* I read it around the time of Tet and I still see it next to dog-eared copies of *Fire in the Lake,* Chomsky's wartime essays, Falk's book on war crimes, or Roszak's *The Making of a Counterculture* on the tables and blankets where the nomadic sell their third-hand wares. Someone's sixties library chucked out for reasons easy enough to guess. I tossed most of mine in the midst of some move, thinking, why would I look at these again?

The author you don't find there is Hunter Thompson. People seldom let go of him. I still have my paperback of *Fear and Loathing in Las Vegas*. A riffle through its pages reveals a riot of marginal notes, the sort you squint at in embarrassment, knowing that a megalomaniac claiming to be yourself wrote them hoping someday they would be admired by a person like you. "Ah, Koppes's Hunter Thompson from sixty-nine, a critical moment in his life and so a collector's item!" I thought no less then, imagining a fame so vast that future biographers would check out my scribblings. Grandiosity may be a charmless trait, but it wasn't rare among restless white boys surfing the crest of imperial wealth into the tumult of that moment.

Mel Sawyer shouldn't, however, be compared with Hunter Thompson. After all, *Tears of Blood* came first. Premature gonzo journalism, it was a whacked out Paul Revere's ride through America by a former foot soldier in the civil rights movement. Travelogue, cautionary tale, head trip rolled into one, it achieved cult status or, as we would have said then, an underground rep. Everything was underground in the sixties. There were underground presses and papers and publishers and the weird thing was that, until decade's end, everything was so unbearably aboveground and out in the open.

*Tears* blew me away. "They dragged me down the stairs by my heels the way Christopher Robin did Pooh, my head banging on each step. I felt nothing. Fear was a drug. My body shook like a Chihuahua's in heat. Nothing I ever took would give me such a high." That was from chapter one, a description of his arrest at an antiwar protest in Ann Arbor back in 1965. The book was over-the-top lush, a nonstop, three-hundred-page mixed metaphor filled with throbbing energy and a passion that would be characteristic of the best writing of the time, even in the hands of as restrained and un-Sawyeresque a reporter as Jonathan Schell. Those of us who remember *Tears* treasure that moment, or maybe the fantasy jailbreak with the giant, farting fruit bat. Adolescent, yes, but what wasn't then? At least, when we tentatively smoked dope, it made us laugh. Straight and scared, we quoted Sawyer to each other and took heart. You could feel the freedom bordering on license in his language and, of course, I still remember those few lines thirty-odd years later. Maybe if someone offered me a toke of weed, I'd remember more.

Then there was that memorable cover: Sawyer, black-bearded, sporting shades, a tiny, upside-down American flag flying from his chopper, and on his button-down Oxford shirt, what looked like a bullet hole and a splattering of blood, a hint of martyrdom that would soon be less startling. *Tears,* after all, was published in 1967, a year before the King and second Kennedy assassinations, two years before the final scene in *Easy Rider* made such an image a cliché, and don't forget his smile. He was almost as young as we were and he had the smile of an angel.

He seemed in those years to fear much but stop at nothing. He had been jailed, beaten, and driven off the highway on his cycle (leaving him in the hospital for months). Yet he continued to take to the road and he brought us along between the covers. He had the courage of his words, which went a long way then.

*Napalmolive,* subtitled *Vietnam in America,* appeared sometime in 1971, and *Styles of Grief* in April 1976, the first anniversary of the fall of Saigon. Hunter Thompson, in his only book review for the *New York Times,* described it thusly—this, too, sticks in my brain—"a stoned anthropologist takes a perfervid look at his own tribe." By then, the tribe had shrunk considerably.

In 1977, before President Carter's amnesty program was in place, he came back from Canada where he had gone into exile to protest the war in the only way he still found meaningful. *Styles of Grief* was his account of a final cross-continental trip through shattered communities of exiles and draft dodgers, deserters and protesters. It was a beautiful work, quieter, sadder, more disciplined, more novelistic in tone, the voice of a man who had lost hope for his country and possibly himself, yet was far from hopeless. It was about what happens to protesters after their moment has passed. Its centerpiece was his own experience in exile, part of a great unreported story of that era, the largest exodus from our land since the Tories split during the Revolution.

And then this traveler moved into a rundown, two-room apartment not far from Columbia University on Manhattan's Upper West Side and didn't stir again for two decades. Initially, he signed a contract with Ted Solataroff at Harper & Brothers. As Solataroff recalled it in an essay in *The New Republic,* "Writers Who Can't Write," Sawyer was determined to produce the great American novel of his generation. Solataroff did, in fact, publish a story of his—"At Home away from Home"—in *New American Review,* the paperback-sized magazine he edited into the 1980s. But I suspect it had been written before Sawyer left Canada. That, in any case, was the last thing he published.

I remember noting with regret that Sawyer had been signed up; and then, a few years later, that he moved his novel to Atheneum. It wasn't a good omen. Solataroff was known for his patience. In 1991, J. Boyle MacMurphy brought him to me.

No small part of Boyle's book is mine, even if the modest thanks in his acknowledgments (". . . whose keen eye proved so helpful in the final stages of preparation . . .") suggests otherwise. Though an editor shouldn't do such a thing, I find myself eager to speak here of what he refused to see in print, for he had ruthlessly excised everything that most appealed to me in his tale. It was a rare—and brutal—editing experience that left me feeling like an embittered author. You can, as a start, search his book in vain for the name Mel Sawyer. Yet he must have told me a hundred times that they both came from Detroit, that he had read *Tears* while still the commander of a junior version of ROTC in his working-class high school. I think he was surprised I even knew who Sawyer was.

One night over drinks, with my tape recorder on, he swore that

*Tears* had changed his life. "Mel Sawyer made me dream about a world I couldn't have imagined." Reading *Tears* had led him to "put down the sword and pick at the key." He meant the type-writer key, of course. The image amused me enough to put it in my version of his book, even if he cut it and the section on Sawyer from his version of my book. "Who's going to read that sort of crap?" he said.

Still, you couldn't ask for a better example of a book influencing a life. Thanks to Sawyer, he didn't follow his father into an auto factory or visit Vietnam by the more usual working-class route. Without Sawyer, he might have returned in no shape to live or in no shape at all. Instead, thanks to *Tears*—"You can't imagine what else I read in those years!"—he decided to be a writer and, in his own way, set off in search of Sawyer to tell him so.

It took him two and a half years at Wayne State and a lot of luck to make it to Vietnam without a weapon. He arrived as a stringer for Reuters. To my mind, the story of how that came about was riveting. But like many people who learn later in life to think ex-ceedingly well of themselves, he valued least what was most valu-able in him. If he had had his way, that story—involving a profes-sor of sociology studying Asian police departments, a long boat ride, and twelve bagels—would never have made it into the book. "You can't ask people who see me in two-minute blips to sit through *that!*" he insisted. It was the only time I threatened him; so, buried in the third chapter is a rare tale of cross-class jumping that, in the end, took him a lot farther than Vietnam.

He arrived in-country early in 1972, determined to be "a global Sawyer." It was late for the American war. Our guys were largely in the air by then, but like Sawyer, Boyle wasn't short on nerve. He left Saigon for the boonies, spending the better part of four months with various South Vietnamese units in the Mekong Delta and the Central Highlands. Reuters moved him on quickly, though. By the end of 1972, he was in Thailand, then—faster than you can say "gecko"—Israel just in time for the Yom Kippur War.

There, he leaped off the page and, via *ABC News,* into your living room.

Who would have guessed that the boy barking commands in a concrete schoolyard under the gaze of a retired major would have the look of a TV personality—just the sort of handsome face, weathered from childhood, people expected to see in Beirut or Sarajevo or Kinshasa while the fighting was going on? A Marlboro man from Detroit, he emerged from the tall grass sporting the very cowboy face he had gone in with, and a voice that on screen radiated a calm curiosity about others, even if it spoke of self in person.

Still—and this was touching—television wasn't enough. He wanted to write a book, and not about his life as a TV newsman, but about those months "in the tall grass." He wanted, I suspect, to do something of which Sawyer might be proud.

By the time he—and I—sat down to do so, Michael Herr and a hundred other ex-soldiers and journalists had entered that patch of grassland and he had, I think, read them all. So, where Sawyer created a form from scratch, Boyle re-created one with my help; and his manuscript—our manuscript—barring only chapter three, read that way.

What is it about books that anybody still wants to write one or have one written in his or her name? How to explain an object that inspires such residual awe and resists so many reports of its own imminent demise? Here was a man known to millions. Why would he care if some part of his life made it into the hands of pitiful tens of thousands, many of whom would buy it but not read it or, when done, turn on the TV? But perhaps I should just drop to my knees and thank the gods of the postvellum world that this half-millennium-old space between boards reserved for pulped tree detritus and marks made from vegetable products or mineral derivatives should still be venerated in any way.

Why Boyle's agent, Silvie Dash, came to me in 1984 with his partial manuscript is a story best left for my memoirs; that is, for oblivion. Back then—and one might as well be speaking of the Middle Ages—I had only intermittent contact with literary agents of any sort, and none of her sort. In an industry still emerging from tweeds even as it was being gobbled up by the new entertainment conglomerates, Sylvie was brash indeed. She acted as if her mission was to bring the antediluvian creatures of publishing up to speed. "Author loyalty," she said to me once—this was years later, of course—"tell that to George Steinbrenner!" And she let go with that roar of hers that, if you weren't the butt of it, gave "belly laugh" a good name. Who knew then that she was an actress of consummate skill, that she had put in time in her own version of the tall grass and unlike Boyle had no desire to write about it? Were I to publish just one more memoir, hers would top my list, but I would have to write it myself.

The first of many agents to rise up from the authorial id and challenge the new barons of publishing, she was sharper than the people she dealt with in a business notoriously filled with the second-rate—and she didn't try to hide it. That she was a woman who felt no need to stroke male egos or speak in quiet, collusive tones had a shock value all its own. When my assistant interrupted an editorial meeting to announce that Sylvie insisted on speaking to me, I felt anxiety, distaste, curiosity, and fear. But I came running, as most people did when she rang.

Two years previously, when Desmond & Dickinson purchased Byzantium, its then-CEO offered copious expressions of respect for "the cultural treasure now in our hands." He promised, of course, to change nothing. "Never touch a machine that isn't broken" was the inelegant way he put it. But whatever one may say, when entities like D&D buy midgets like Byzantium, sooner or later they engulf them in a homogenizing embrace. It took almost to the moment of Sylvie's call for D&D's management to cast aside its pledges and lean its full weight on managing director John Percy III. Undoubtedly, someone from D&D finally took a careful look at Byzantium's books and discovered to his horror what niche marketeering in publishing really meant. By the time Multimedia swallowed up D&D, such promises sounded far mealier. Today, they aren't mouthed at all.

Hand Silvie Dash this: She had fabulous timing. I went directly from the first editorial meeting at which a D&D representative discussed the "popularizing" of our list on to the telephone with her. "I've had you on my mind," she said. I did little more than mentally gulp. That's the way it works with powerhouse agents. Their reputation kicks in the door and all that's left is to take possession of the premises. "I've come across the perfect proposal for you. Do you know the ABC reporter Boyle MacMurphy?" I was able to say I did.

In translation she meant, I've dug you out of the ground after every other editor in New York refused to put ludicrous amounts of work into a hopeless half-manuscript. But I was ridiculously flattered to be unearthed. After all, we had just been told our books should fly down market and so out of D&D's spacious new warehousing complex in Atlanta. Everyone knew that Sylvie's projects cost previously unheard of sums but sometimes made back astounding amounts. It was as if she had put a sniperscope to my eye and there in the crosshairs, right in the tall grass of publishing, was J. Boyle MacMurphy.

I generally don't care to watch authors perform their work. Your options are limited, however, with an author who constantly performs himself in a business where successful books now first appear, one might say, in translation. "Out there in the tall grass, my totemic animal was the owl," Boyle wrote in his neo-Sawyeresque style. "I would have given everything I possessed, which wasn't much then, for the ability to turn my head one hundred eighty degrees and watch my own back." Not a bad line, actually, though I didn't believe it for a second. I doubt he had ever seen an owl, forget for a moment that they can't turn their heads in a half circle. I did my damnedest to cut it. But it turned out he knew better than I what was acceptable in the oeuvre of J. Boyle MacMurphy.

His was a TV book, full of material predigested by others. And yet, here's the touching part—and there always is one, isn't there?—he was a decent and determined reporter. After all, with admirable single-mindedness he ran Sawyer to earth in New York and, five years after his book briefly made it onto the best-seller list, brought him to me.

I was seated at a banquette at Louvain, my restaurant of choice, when they arrived. Sawyer was half Boyle's size, so much smaller than the young man who had once filled out the cover of *Tears of Blood*. And so much older. Beardless, gray-haired, face worn to an edge, eyes behind black, industrial-style glasses fried to a crisp. Wearing an ancient pea jacket, ratty black slacks, and old sneakers, he brought to mind a Vietnam vet. Had I spotted him on the street, I would have reached anxiously for change.

My disappointment was palpable. He looked ill fed and in poor health. He scared me. Without Boyle's assurance, I wouldn't have known that he *was* Mel Sawyer. He shook hands politely and we exchanged a few modest comments—about the weather, actually—his eyes never meeting mine. He ordered *poulet louvain,* but hardly took a bite.

By the evidence of his writing, he'd been an indiscriminant gatherer of people, his sympathy for any sign of rebelliousness sparking it even, as with Boyle, at a distance. At that table, though, no sparks flew. It was eerie and unsettling, as if—I don't know how else to describe it—he were there but we were not. He sat surrounded by a zone of deadness that passed for silence. I knew then why Ted Solataroff had let him go.

I didn't recoil, not visibly, but I did fall silent, which, under other circumstances, might not have been strange. Publishing is a reactive business, and editing a chameleonlike activity. Your job, after all, is to slither inside someone else, untangling knots of words in ways a mind not yours would have, had it been able. Silence is one opening through which an editor slips. At a publishing lunch it can be flattering—an implicit sign of support, an indication of admiration, an encouragement to exposure. Facing him, however, I felt a body sagging inside my own.

Boyle felt the strain, too. He worked at conversation with a terrifying energy. Effortlessness was his trademark, yet he was trying so hard. No civil war had put him out half as much. He seemed in the process of stripping himself down to the awkward adolescent who set out from Detroit those long years ago. That boy deserved credit. He had done so much to get here. I should have offered him a hand.

Finally, like a translator wrung out by an intractable language, Boyle, too, fell silent. Had he wept, I wouldn't have been shocked. The meal was winding into entropy when Sawyer suddenly spoke. His subject proved to be dead novelists. He began with Dreiser. "Our loneliest writer," he called him. Stephen Crane he labeled "the creator of a cult of glory under the guise of cowardice," which still strikes me as outrageous; of Henry James he said, "Imagine what he might have done on a motorcycle." These few phrases I jotted down afterward, though the drift of his lecture—and it was a lecture—now escapes me.

Never did he mention what he wrote or might be writing, or the sixties. Perhaps he was describing himself when he brought up the isolation so many American writers suffered. His speech was filled with flat, Midwestern *a*'s, a reminder of what he and Boyle once held in common. At one point—this, too, I noted later—he spoke of "Ida, Link, and John" (Ida Tarbell, Lincoln Steffens, and John Reed), and of the way words in our country had so often been directed toward changing, not conjuring, reality. There was a chilly immodesty to his disquisition. He was a man who regularly found himself in good company—and we were not it.

I parted from him without shaking hands, more depressed than if he had never spoken. Boyle insisted on walking me back to the office. Perhaps to lift his own spirits, he told a story about Leslie Stahl, Barbara Walters, and a star-crossed telex he sent from Tegucigalpa, whose punch line I still remember: "But Leslie, it wasn't

'Streisand,' it was 'stressed out'!" One was meant to be impressed as well as amused, and in my way I was, which only added to my gloom.

He was eager, he assured me, to discuss his next book, the one both of us knew he would never write, in part because I would never write it for him. In the meantime, he sprawled on my mini-couch, entertaining whoever stumbled in. People with better things to do lingered while he tried out pseudo-war stories that might have gone far to fill out a sequel to *Tall Grass*.

The brusque Margo Deare stuck her head in to remind me of a meeting. While he described a scrape with an IRA bomb meant for Prince Charles, she drew ever closer. Before my eyes, her hair lost its luster; her mouth gained a smile as sheepish yet greedy as any schoolgirl's. I watched her divest herself of her corporate being until only a mouse of a girl remained. She even claimed I wasn't needed at the meeting, which was like having your wife tell you not to turn up at the hospital for childbirth. It was another of the day's surprise performances, a touching revelation I would have given the world to miss. Then again, who should be mesmerized by such a godling, if not a Margo Deare? Delphi, after all, wasn't run by Scythians. And what of Boyle, so eager to prostrate himself before the inscrutable, unpalatable Mel Sawyer?

"Amazing, isn't he?" Boyle said, as if his task in life were reading my idle thoughts. My silence was evidently taken for agreement, since he promptly shut the door and insisted I give Sawyer a contract for "his chef d'oeuvre." This was how he spoke sometimes, as if in a bad novel. I sat there in a daze. That he and Sawyer were close made no sense at all—or all the sense in the world.

"Have you seen it?" I asked.

"Mel Sawyer has nothing to prove to me." His voice was surprisingly belligerent.

"But how do you know"—I heard my voice softening a bit—"that he's writing anything after all these years?"

"On what damn basis are you busting my chops? I'm doing *you* a favor, for crap's sake!"

I sensed his desperation even if I didn't understand it. But I sensed mine as well, even if I didn't understand it either. They frightened me, the two of them. I didn't want their next books, but mostly I didn't want to spend another lunch with either of them.

"He won't show me his work, but someday he'll show it to you. Trust me on this." He was wheedling now.

For the second time that day I felt a body sagging inside my own. "You know what publishing's like now . . . ," I began halfheartedly.

"What's the problem? You've read *Tears of Blood,* you've read *Napalmolive!*"

I felt a surge of anger. "That was a lifetime ago!" I practically shouted. "In case you hadn't noticed, the world's turned upside down since!"

"I hate to tell you, Rick"—he pronounced my name with a certain distaste—"but the world was upside down then. Its closer to right side up now."

"It doesn't matter. The days of supporting an author that way are over."

He offered me a condescending smile.

"Maybe Byzantium would have done it once, but we would have known who he was. We would have read his books. I *have* read his books. D and D's people would rather watch *you* on television." I banged on every other word as if I were banging on him. "If I tell them I have a *possible* book by a *former* sixties radical whose audience in the *best* of times—and they *were* the best of times— was limited—"

"If I called David Marsden at Multimedia, you'd sign Mel in a nanosecond." He paused. "We could run a little test, if you'd like."

I collapsed, of course. I couldn't afford to let him go. Forget that he wouldn't produce a book and that, given the contracts littered behind Sawyer like roadkill, neither would he. I took a quiet breath and agreed to see what I could do, never doubting I could indeed do much. The D&D people were suckers for blackmail. Faith in celebrities and the celebrity agent had hit them hard. It was a form of transnational masochism. All they wanted was for Sylvie Dash to call and demand more money for Boyle's next book than any book could bear. If they tolerated me, it was because I was one path along which they could hope to abase themselves.

Margo was thrilled to learn that, for Boyle's sake, we had to offer a hopeless author a few thousand dollars. She would have offered more. But I settled for an option agreement, assuring Byzantium first right of refusal on his next book. It was as close to a slap in the face as I could think up.

On the way home I stopped at the first rundown bar I saw. Its black bartender spoke in a lilting island accent to a Latin clientele. Ordering a rum and whatever, I fell into conversation with a guy who had "Lucky" tattooed on one bicep. Discovering I was an editor, he filled me in on the book he meant to write about his life, a cross, he said, between *Top Gun* and *Predator 2*. I was unenthusiastic. When it came to publishing, he told me, I had my head up my ass. At least I had a head, I responded, whereupon he flexed a muscle imprinted "Madre" and knocked me off my stool.

The fall hurt more than the movies might lead you to believe. I felt the bone bruise on my hip for a week and a couple of trips to a physical therapist didn't quite sort out what I'd done to my back. Still, I felt satisfied with my imitation of Boyle's imitation of Sawyer and limped to the subway with a sense that I had put them behind me.

I'm aware that I've yet to reach the meal that began this account, but perhaps an editor who's never imagined himself a writer can be forgiven. Philip Roth once vividly demonstrated the difference between the two to me. He had been summoned from Connecticut on business and called me, wondering if we could grab a sandwich—an uncharacteristic gesture for a man whose schedule is as carefully controlled as his fiction. It was that pre-glasnost period when he was still editing his Eastern European series for Penguin and he wanted to discuss a novel by Danilo Kiš we were both considering but that Harcourt Brace finally published.

He was fuming about a review of *Zuckerman Unbound*—he does, in fact, read everything written about him—which claimed he had reached into the well of autobiography once too often. "To imagine that I write autobiography!" I recall him saying. "I could give anyone, even you, a counterlife." And he laughed. "If I wanted, I could write this lunch, which neither of us will remember, and you wouldn't recognize yourself. I could run you through the rabbit hole, pull you up by the ears, and they would still say it was Philip Roth doing himself. But if they want Philip Roth, I'll give him to them in more sizes than they'll know what to do with." Not being Philip Roth, I can only give you myself in one size. Make of that what you will.

Like the famed cat of song, of course, Mel Sawyer came back. Boyle made sure of that. "He holds you in the highest regard," he said to me once. "He trusts your opinion more than his own."

Sawyer himself never called or wrote, and at our infrequent lunches never really acknowledged my presence or alluded to his past. Each meal ended with another chilly, eerie performance. No surprise then that my restaurant choices wound their way down market and into my neighborhood so that I could plead personal business, avoiding postlunch tristesse with Boyle. The whole complicated charade wore on me, yet I couldn't seem to bring the thing to an end.

It was Sylvie Dash who offered me a way out. In 1993, she brought me Walter Groth's gestalt memoir, *The Heart of a Man,* and so made Boyle superfluous to my survival. Rejected by ten publishers, it unexpectedly moved me. His analysis of "presence and the male crisis," so much written about thereafter, struck me as goodhearted, but what touched me deeply—what, in his terms, I "recognized"—was his portrait of his father, a vulnerable bully in a crumbling patriarchal system. I don't mind admitting that I wept as I read those pages and felt a sympathy for my own father I had never before experienced.

Convincing D&D to publish his book was a trickier matter. I finally billed it as "an *Iron John* for the rest of us," though Groth hated Bly almost as much as he hated the woods, mud, and drums. On making our modest offer to Sylvie, I said, "You owe me one." She had a fit of laughter before replying, "Believe me, you'll owe me several times over."

I took Walter out to lunch and warned him to lower his expectations. Significant sales were unlikely. We talked fathers for the rest of the meal. That my assessment of his book's potential was utterly mistaken only endeared me to him. I proved to be his "obverse object of desire," a term *Heart's* readers will understand, and my "stance" sealed our relationship. His "presence" had long been "ego reinforced," so he was charmed but unfazed by my warning. Twelve weeks on the *Times* best-seller list, topping out at number eight, did nothing to change that.

So I owed Silvie several times over, especially since Walter was in love with writing. Only two years later we published *The Masculine Mode.* With a surprise plug from Oprah, it soared to number three. It was like taking out an insurance policy—an author who couldn't help producing best-sellers and insisted everywhere he went that I had saved his life. That was an editor's dream. Still, somehow I couldn't bring myself to say no to Boyle, which was why I found myself at the West End.

I suggested Sawyer tie his dog, a gray cur, to a nearby fire hydrant.

"Forget it," Boyle said and led us through the door.

A hostess blocked our way, but in midprotest she recognized him. Grasping for an excuse, she asked timidly of Sawyer, "Is he blind?"

The dog did seem to be leading him to an empty booth.

"Well," Boyle whispered, "let's just say he has his problems."

"Do you mind," she asked, hurrying to keep up, "that that's the smoking section?" She looked like a tiny wren, hopping at Boyle's side.

He placed a hand gently on her shoulder as if he might otherwise crush her and said, "Any place *you* put us is good enough for me."

"I could get in trouble."

"Anyone says anything, you send them here."

Sawyer was already sliding into the booth.

"You *are* . . . ?" she asked Boyle hesitantly.

He bowed his head slightly.

"I admired your book. If only I had my copy. Could I . . . I mean, would you . . . ?" She couldn't complete the sentence.

Not that Boyle missed her meaning. A pen materialized in his hand as he slid in across from Sawyer. "He likes to face the door," he said to me in his role as Sawyer's interpreter. Then he looked back at the hostess. "How about if I sign the menu?"

She hesitated. "They wouldn't let me keep it, but I'll get something before you go." Then, remembering the dog, she added, "You'll keep it close, won't you?"

"I was about to ask my editor—this is Rick Koppes, who was largely responsible for how my book turned out—to tie the dog to the leg of the table."

Which was how I found myself, fully acknowledged at last, on my hands and knees with a dog's tongue in my ear.

Boyle was in his element. In the restaurants we now frequented, people felt freer to approach, unburden themselves of opinions and fears, or just touch him. The pleasure he took in it all never ceased to amaze me. It lent his face such humanity. Sometimes in his damnable innocence he seemed to me like the last American.

I looked at Sawyer. How had I survived, I wondered, and not him? I wanted to shake him. I wanted to shout, *You're done torturing me!* I wanted to say things I didn't know I felt. I hadn't realized I was still in love with him. I refused to accept that this was the person who had roared off the page and into my heart. I felt such a surge of anger—and it wasn't an editor's anger either. Something must have shown because, for the first time, he looked back. Those charcoal eyes looked right into my heart.

And he said, "I can't give it to you."

I said, "I didn't ask for anything."

He said, "You want something that's not mine to give anymore."

I wasn't sure what he was talking about, but for a second, right there in the West End, I thought maybe, just maybe, I was going to burst into tears like the boy I wasn't.

"Do you have a kid?" It was the first question he had ever asked me.

"No."

"You'd be better equipped."

"Better equipped for what, Mel?" It was the first time I had spoken his name, even in disgust.

"For what we have to do."

I turned to Boyle. "What's he talking about? Give me a hand here." But Boyle looked helpless. "Mel," I said, "you're pissing me off. This is our last meeting. I'm not meeting like this again."

"Of course you're not." His voice wasn't gentle exactly, but it wasn't challenging either. "Think of this as a job application. There's no need to come back because you've got the job."

I didn't even bother to reply.

"It's okay to be mad at me," he continued. "You've got the job anyway because, whether you know it or not, we agree on one thing: We've got to give the kids a little of our luck. People like to say we made history in the sixties, but that's a big, nasty lie. History made us. History was a Harley, a purring hog. All you had to do was climb on. The victors in our world, the people who run the companies that run your companies, they have no use for history. In the emptiness that's left, they've planted their products to feed on us. Kids know they're being fucked. They know their parents couldn't dig anything out of the rubble of those lucky years to help them make sense of things. And they're pissed, Rick, like you are today.

"You should hang out with them sometime. They're braver than we were, even though they're taking out our frustrations on their bodies. You slash your arm and you're defending your life to the death. You're saying, this far, fucker, and no farther. It's what it means today for the political to be personal."

Before he could say another word, Sylvie Dash broke upon us. "Mel, my sweet!" she exclaimed and kissed him smack on the lips. Almost miraculously, he smiled, revealing in that stranger's face a hint of the angelic look once imprinted on the cover of *Tears of Blood*.

Sylvie missed it. "Ricky," she said, appropriating a name I allowed few to use, "I hope you're finally discussing *Up His Tall Ass*, volume two, with his majesty here, and must we have this mutt at lunch, Mel, sweetie pie? Couldn't you have left it home, wherever your home is?" She turned back to me. "And has he given you his manuscript or did you wait for me, Mel?"

"What manuscript?" I said.

"Ah, an answer, however confused. Thank you."

"Are *you* his agent, Sylvie?" I asked.

"Are you his editor?" That truly broke her up.

"Sylvie, sometimes you can be a—"

"A bitch?" she laughed again, with genuine pleasure. "You're not the first to say so."

"It wasn't the word I was about to use."

"But you were thinking it, and Ricky, my sweet, you're such an innocent. If you really want to meet a bitch, you should spend twenty minutes with Rupert Murdoch."

I was suddenly aware that the dog had sidled up to me, its wet muzzle uncomfortably near my pants. When I looked down, gazing out of that ragged face were two piercingly blue and sexy eyes. I swiped at the beast with my hand, then looked up at Silvie. An astoundingly luxurious frizz of red hair burst from her head and cascaded onto her shoulders, framing the kind of face Renoir might have appreciated. I was aware—and not for the first time—that she was a woman whose every gesture turned genuine heft into flamboyant clout.

She had, in fact, set our table aroil. The dog was yipping quietly, the panicked hostess had returned, Boyle was mediating, and Sawyer, well, he had come alive, and yet Sylvie's brown eyes stared back at me as if from a distant galaxy.

I'm afraid there's one more meal I need to mention, a meal with Sylvie. We had been drinking hard for a long time when she suddenly reached into her bag, pulled out a cardholder, and let its innards unravel onto the table. All those little squares were clear but one. She was leaning so close I could feel her hair against my cheek. She slipped the photo out and slid it over to me. In it she was young, wearing shorts and a halter, her hair an exuberant Isro, a Pre-Raphaelite halo illuminating that face, familiar yet uncharacteristically open. Her arms enveloped two smaller, darker women, each exhibiting a shy, uneasy smile. To the side, in no one's grasp, a fourth woman stared at the camera without pleasure, a machete pressed to her chest.

It helps to share a frame of reference. I had no doubt where her younger self had been or approximately when the photo had been taken, even though it had never occurred to me that Boyle's Sylvie wasn't Sylvie herself. Many questions came to mind, but all I said was, "You look happy, Sylvie."

"Yes," she whispered. "I was in love with her." She carefully placed the tip of her index finger on the machete.

Another set of questions floated to mind, but I didn't ask them either. Maybe it was the liquor, or the fact that, even in the sixties, that era of putative mergings, I had never had this sense of being inside the aura of another person.

"I should have stayed." She paused to consider the proposition. "Disappearing was amazing. I never felt such joy." And she let out her breath, not exactly a sigh but not quite a laugh either.

I felt myself breathe.

"Go figure. The only time I was completely of this world, I

wasn't in it." And then she offered up a faint version of the laugh I knew. "One look at her and you know it wouldn't have been easy. But even difficult things are easier when you don't exist. I should have had better sense." She paused again. "Or maybe worse sense was what I needed." She picked up the photo and stared at it. "The strangest thing is, *she* still seems real to me, and yet I hardly believe in this girl," and she covered the face of her younger self with her thumb.

"Were you known as Sylvie then?" Why I asked that one question I couldn't tell you.

"You know I wasn't."

And it was true. I had no doubt she had not always been Sylvie.

"Of course, like an idiot I came back, but this is the absurd part: When I turned myself in, they didn't even want me." She carefully reinserted the photo in its casing and stuck the holder deep in her bag.

At that moment I knew something about Sylvie no one in our world knew. Naturally, I know more now, given the way her story was made public, but nothing I've learned since has surprised me. Without asking a reasonable question I had picked up everything necessary, except why she chose to confide in me. My breath catches when I think of that. Why me? But isn't there a question you can't answer in every experience?

An author I worked with for two years by mail, fax, and phone said to me after we met, "You're better in mufti." I knew exactly what he meant. It *is* better to meet me on the page. In my own fashion, I'm an underground man. Tolstoy wrote, "People are taught to speak, but their major concern should be how to keep silent." Not mine. I was underground before the sixties began. I'm still there. Maybe that's the nature of natures that gravitate to editing. It's such a subterranean activity. You need to be an old mole to tunnel under all those words in search of the person who put them there, but when you finally come upon an author, it's the truest meeting of all.

[ 99 ]

Someone uses us, we say. It has such a nasty ring and yet it's beautiful to be made use of, to feel oneself used, and, so, of use. If I held my breath that night, it was because I sensed Sylvie calling on my underground self to hear her underground tale. She was asking me, I think, to edit her life, and for once it felt wonderful. It felt like love. But what led her to me? The books I published at Byzantium said something about my sensibility, but that's only half an explanation. Perhaps it's not possible to account for the small, unexpected miracles that take place between people. Given my years at D&D, I hadn't thought there was much of me left to recognize. Yet there she was, an underground woman who knew an underground man when she saw one.

Watching her across that table at the West End, with her pita pocket melt and iced tea, leaning over to whisper to Sawyer, I sensed how well-matched they were. After all, the real underground decades are still with us and both of them had gone underground in ways meaningless in the sixties. She had fashioned a flamboyant agent out of what was left of whatever she had been. That involved a kind of courage, and yet, for all her panache, something in Sylvie Dash, as in Mel Sawyer, was missing in action.

I reached across the table and touched her hand. She stared back at me without curiosity.

"You obviously know each other." It was a statement hovering at the edge of a question.

"You might say Mel and I share a history."

Sawyer lifted a worn book bag onto his lap, pulled out a manila envelope, and handed it to me. Inside, I had no doubt, were the only words he had offered the world in nearly a quarter century, and yet it was such a modest package.

His eyes met mine and he smiled. The effect was like an unpleasant shock. "Too bad," he said, and when I didn't reply, he added sympathetically, "If you didn't want your present, you shouldn't have chosen your past. We let them take our moment from us. If we ran from anything, it was from that. But what you can't face still faces you. There's a job to be done. I've begun. It's up to you to lend a hand."

It was the damnedest pitch for publishing a book I'd ever heard. At least, I think that's what it was. I had no time to consider the matter. He half rose.

Boyle nudged me immediately. "Untie the dog," he whispered fiercely.

By the time I made it back to my feet, Sawyer was almost at the door. Boyle grabbed the leash and rushed after him.

"Vintage Mel, " Sylvie said. "How long have you been meeting, anyway?"

"Years."

She laughed heartily. "Then you, my dear, were the audience for a very long performance piece. Now it's time to pay for your ticket." She handed me the check the hostess had wedged under her teacup.

"As the man said, Ricky, just do your job. We'll wait for D and D's offer."

As she was about to leave, the hostess intercepted us. In her hand she held a dog-eared paperback of *Into the Tall Grass*, whose cover with its helmeted owl I recognized immediately. "Where is he?"

"He left." I said.

"You got his book just for an autograph?" Silvie asked.

She looked distraught. "I only live a block away . . ."

Sylvie indicated me with a flick of her hand. "Give him your address. He'll get it for you."

The hostess began scribbling madly on the back of a blank check. "I've put it all here, my address and just what I want him to write."

I was left holding her copy of *Into the Tall Grass*, Sawyer's envelope, and the check. I went to the gym and lingered there. It's not that I wasn't curious. I naturally wondered what a traveler who hadn't left the neighborhood in two decades might have written.

Who knows what unexpected voyages a man can take in a room by himself?

Once home, I left the envelope atop the pile of submissions that sat on the small table by my desk. I often wake up between two and four and read submissions. But that night and the next I slept like a drugged man. The third night, I sat down in my study early, thinking, this is absurd. Editing has its own chemistry and resistance can be part of the process. After an hour, I turned on the TV.

Arriving at Byzantium on the morning of the fourth day, I told Joy not to put through any calls from Boyle or Sylvie Dash. On the fifth day, Boyle called. "He sounded odd," Joy said. The next day he called four times before I took the subway down to the Film Forum and sat through a Japanese animation festival, watching endless armies of cyber-robots destroy cityscapes galore.

Around 10:30 that night the doorbell rang. I assumed it was Sarah without her keys. We were no longer communicating much. When I opened the door, Boyle almost fell into my arms. The sour-sweet smell of liquor clung to him. He said politely, "Can I come in?"

"You are in," I replied. He was disheveled. We stood there, eyeing each other. Finally, I said, "You want a cup of coffee?"

"You didn't call me back." It was a growl.

I tried to take him lightly by the arm, but he jerked free, strode in, and slumped onto the couch. "Well, what do you think of it?" He was glaring at me.

"What do *you* think?"

"You know he didn't show it to me." He inched up to a sitting position.

"And you know I can't discuss manuscripts I'm considering. I wouldn't have discussed your book with Mel." The difference being, I had read his manuscript.

"Just tell me this then: Where is he?"

"Excuse me?"

"If you know what's good for you, you'll tell me what's going on."

"If I knew that, I wouldn't have let you in. Maybe you'd better go and we'll talk in the morning."

"Like we talked today?"

I started to rise, but he rose more swiftly. I had never noticed what a genuinely big man he was. In one fluid motion he grabbed me by my collar, his fist bunched at my Adam's apple, and pulled me up. His face, convulsed with emotion, was on top of mine and it was a large face that stunk of liquor.

"Nobody gives you his manuscript and disappears!"

"I don't know what you're talking about," I managed to say.

"Ah, you fucking intellectuals. They should have sent *you* to Vietnam."

Time stretched out and I discovered one of the advantages of being an underground man. He had hold of my shirt, but that was all. He, too, had ceased to speak. I hung there, like so much meat on a hook, toes barely touching the ground. I saw confusion on his face. The remarkable thing was, having come this far he had no idea what to do.

There was a scraping sound outside, probably our neighbor letting herself in. "It must be Sarah," I said, and like the polite boy he actually was, he lowered me carefully into my chair. Then he sat back down, placed the heels of his hands over his eyes, and began to weep. This I considered unjust.

Finally, he sobbed out, "You really don't know where he is?"

"I don't even know *who* he is."

"Mel. He's gone."

"For god's sake, Boyle, go home! He probably took off for a week."

"He never goes anywhere. We talk every day."

"You talk to him every day?"

"Every day I'm in New York and often when I'm not."

It took me a moment to absorb this. Finally I said, "Maybe he's not answering the phone. After all, the man finished a book."

He shook his head.

In the silence that followed, the Sylvie Dash question came to mind—why me? And then a more obvious question grabbed me by the throat. "What did you talk about?"

His body drooped, a mass of disturbed flesh on my couch. "I talked to him about myself. He was the only person I could talk to about me."

"And what did he talk to you about? Himself?"

He paused. "Not really," he said, surprise in his voice.

"Have you asked Sylvie Dash where he is?"

"She doesn't know."

"Look, a man doesn't just finish a manuscript and disappear."

"There's someone else in his apartment," he replied in a whisper, "and he claims he's never heard of Mel Sawyer."

I heard doors clanking shut, like an archive closing, like your shrink dying. To my surprise, I felt sorry for him, not a noble emotion but there it was. I'd like to say I made a gesture, but I sat awaiting further developments, not truly believing that Mel Sawyer was—could have—gone.

Boyle, too, lapsed into silence, and had Sarah not come home, I can't imagine how the evening would have ended. I turned at the sound of the key. It was past eleven. Exhaustion was visible on her face along with a familiar flicker of annoyance. Then recognition dawned. She wasn't sure whom she'd recognized, only that he was someone to recognize.

And, to my amazement, the person standing there—for he had risen—was the personality known by sight to millions. He had smoothed his hair, but that was hardly it. Somehow he had reassumed his Boyle-dom. A godling graced our living room, unrelated to the man who had passed the last half hour in my company.

He stepped forward to greet Sarah with a polite handshake and murmured words of introduction. I had many times discussed Boyle with her, never in flattering terms, but there was still a hint of awe in her look. You could feel the phrase "and in our living room" hanging in the air.

While she was asking him if he would care for a glass of wine,

I hurried into my study to find the hostess's copy of *Into the Tall Grass*. "Here," I said, proffering a pen, "could you put your name to this?"

He looked puzzled.

"For the waitress at the West End who rushed up with it just after you left."

He smiled, charmingly, inquired after her name, and signed extravagantly on the title page. "It's late," he said. Tilting his head to Sarah, he shook my hand with gusto and took his leave. "Let me know the minute you decide, or hear anything."

Sarah lifted an eyebrow as I closed the door. "What was *that?*"

"Believe me, it's too complicated to go into."

"That's okay, I'm too tired to listen. But I have to say, he wasn't what I expected."

"No," I agreed, "he wasn't what I expected either." And that was all we had to say to each other, which was something of a relief.

About 2:30, chased out of a nightmare, I sat up in bed with a start. I won't bother you with the details. As an editor, I automatically cut dreams from manuscripts. We haven't discovered the form that can carry the dream beyond the self. The novel, the story, the memoir are already dreams of the waking world. How could there be space in them for the uncontrolled creativity of sleep?

I forced my legs over the side of the bed and sat numbly in the darkness. I could sense Sarah, enveloped in quietness. I had an urge to touch her but that, too, was no more than a dream. Outside, I heard the faint wail of a saxophone.

I stood shakily and made my way into the kitchen. Flicking on the light, I crushed three roaches with my palm, lit the flame under the kettle, washed my hands, and sat dumbly at the table waiting for the first sharp hiss of steam. Then I made myself a cup of coffee. I turned off the light and let the warm, caffeinated mist drift up my nostrils. I listened for a siren or the sound of breaking glass or a truck thumping down the avenue or the blast of Metallica and the screech of tires. But the world was muffled.

[ 105 ]

There was nothing to do, other than the obvious. About 3:30, I groped my way into my study, wearing only my underpants. I unhooked the hasp of the envelope and let the manuscript slip out. It was typewritten on onionskin paper of a kind I hadn't seen in years and was evidently the original copy. I flipped to the last page, 189.

Sarah regularly starts a book by reading the last paragraph. She wants to be sure, she claims, that it's going to be worth the effort. This time I did the same. I read the only four lines on that page. They went:

> If, while walking, you see a leaf on a path and turn it over, whether you find a millipede or a ring has everything to do with the history of the place and nothing to do with the history of you. But if, while walking on the path of fiction, you see a leaf and turn it over, whether you find a millipede or a ring has only to do with the history of you. In the fiction of our lives, the leaves we turn over are our responsibility because they're the history of us. If you can't face that, walker, pass by.

The passage, twenty years updated, was him. I quote it here because it manages to give away nothing about the 188 preceding pages and yet calls to mind the nature of the manuscript. It turns out to be a fable for our times and Sawyer, I realize now, is as he always was (as perhaps many of us were), a fabulist, which is to say a moralist.

It had been decades since I last read a word of his. But I felt a little shiver just to have his pages in my hands. I propped my feet on the computer table and leaned back, resting the manuscript on my bare knees. Then I looked at the first page, which read, "Warning: I am not Mel Sawyer. You are not a reader. This is not a memoir." The title page followed. It read, *Out of the Tall Grass: The Life and Times of J. Boyle MacMurphy* by Rick Koppes, edited by Mel Sawyer."

Were this a story, I would end it on that line. It has a bit of mystery and the satisfying element of surprise. I was surprised anyway. But it seems unfair, for the sake of shapeliness, to emphasize a moment that was only part of the winding down of an episode in my publishing life, a moment whose effect on me was hardly transformative. Thanks to D&D, I'm beyond transformation by book.

Still, I admit I was a little flattered by my "authorship." Boyle, on the other hand, was outraged. We talked only once, after Sylvie showed him the manuscript. He threatened an injunction or worse if Byzantium decided to publish. He saw himself as badly used, proving that one of us, at least, still believed in the book's transformative powers.

Looked at less personally, *Out of the Tall Grass* is a paean to a new style of persistence. It has everything to do with the sort of courage—if that's what it is—that allows one to navigate the world of the victors in this millennial age; and in his own way Boyle is painted as a kind of postmodern hero. It's also remarkably funny, but that's easy for me to say. I wasn't the one who spilled my guts to Mel Sawyer and found some version of it on the page. As for the appropriation of my name, he's welcome to it.

By the way, in this account I think I've done a reasonable job of answering the who, what, when, and where questions. As for the why—why me, for one—I doubt that's mine to deal with. I had a certain access to the lived history of my moment, those years we call the sixties that melted us down, and to the more recent transformations of my own small world of publishing. As to the whys of individuals floating in that history but not fully bounded by it, that should perhaps be left to others. My "characters," after all, live on in all their confusion.

*Out of the Tall Grass* will undoubtedly be published someday, even if not by Byzantium. Boyle seems, irrationally enough, to have settled on me as the cause of his troubles. Sylvie assures me he won't follow through on his legal threats, a guarantee hardly likely to impress D&D's lawyers. At the moment, however, everything's in abeyance due to the lack of an author—other than "myself," of course.

About Mel Sawyer's disappearance, I have little to offer. Was he acting out the return to the road of our last bard of change or something more personal? No note or letter was left behind and the minimal instructions he passed on to Sylvie are hardly adequate to the situation. Yet there's no indication that he's not alive and well somewhere. For all I know, he waged a long campaign to recruit me as his chronicler, not his editor, and then left me behind to tell this tale. But if so, and I hardly think it likely, why did he choose me?

# Chapter 5

## THE PALEONTOLOGICAL
## IS POLITICAL

The day Jerry Golden contacted me, Ellen Stakowicz, senior editor at Desmond & Dickinson, was fired. When she called me from home, she was weeping. That morning she had been sent down to personnel. "I thought it had to do with changes in our pension plan," she told me. She was directed to the office of a Personnel Communications Manager on a floor she had no idea D&D occupied. "I had never heard the title before."

The PCM told her she was being let go. She would be escorted upstairs by a "communications retainer" ("a sweet-looking blond boy of about twenty," Ellen said meekly); she could gather only what she had brought with her that morning; she could communicate with no other employees; she must be off the premises within forty-five minutes. Later, her PCM would arrange for her to collect the rest of her "personal possessions."

"She wasn't cold," Ellen said. "She was sympathetic in a distant way. She wanted to talk about something called 'environmental transference' and what the company, in light of my eighteen years of service, would do to ease it. I think she was offering me a severance package. I can't remember anything else except that I began to cry, which was *so* humiliating, and she didn't offer me a Kleenex. She just sat there with a sympathetic look on her face. After a few minutes she suggested the retainer take me upstairs and we talk again when, as she put it, 'you're a little calmer.' And he was nice, actually. He was hardly older than my son. He called me 'ma'am' and let me go to the ladies' room to clean myself up. But I was so embarrassed. I was just so embarrassed and, Rick, I'm so worried about my authors!"

A lot could be written about those last words. There was history there. There was a deep love of writers. And yet of Ellen, I fear, hardly an imprint will remain. This is another thing that being subsumed can mean.

Here, you might say, lies Ellen Stakowicz, who began as an assistant at Viking in 1977, came to D&D as a junior editor in 1981, and (although almost a decade younger than I am) was gone in the spring of 1999. I mention her only as prologue to and, after a fashion, explanation for what follows.

Of all species ever to inhabit this earth, ninety-nine percent are now extinct, an overwhelming majority that, in Leninist terms, voted with their fins, paws, or pseudopodia. Thanks initially to the atomic bomb, extinction, once a minor note in scientific and popular discourse, has stepped front and center. We now dream ceaselessly of obliteration, while on the many screens of our lives comets head unerringly for earth, megalopolises sink beneath the waves, civilizations are pummeled by oversized dinosaurs, and planets are blasted to smithereens. Nuclear winter, global warming, ozone depletion, rising oceans, population explosions, decimating plagues—all the sexiest, scariest horror stories now begin with the phrase The End.

But when we dream of our nonexistence, we tend to forget how long this planet has been a haven for opportunistic species that thrive on disasters. Take the mammals—take us—all those shrew and ratlike things that scuttled through the dusk until 65 million years ago an asteroid hit, volcanoes erupted, something cataclysmic happened that sent the dinosaurs down for the count, and left us to seize our main chance.

Consider publishing's last decade in evolutionary terms and imagine Jerry Golden as a publishing mammal. A packager of minor cookbooks, he took as his model John Brockman, who ran the hottest sci-tech literary agency in town and conducted auctions famed for leaving publishers with remarkably emptier pockets. Spotting an unoccupied niche in a stress-fractured landscape, Golden began packaging illustrated science books to fit onrushing entertainment fads. For an editor, he solved so many problems. A book arrived in your office mercifully ready to go, and he always gave you an obvious hook on which to hang your publicity—the latest space flick, alien craze, or PBS science series. His products were guaranteed to be "high concept," which meant you could sum them up in a single cover illustration, usually with shock value.

That most of them were not successes was beside the point. By the time the results came in, everybody involved had usually moved on, leaving no one to connect the dots. The successes he did have, however, were noticed. He made sure of that. And then he added on a line of self-help texts by new-age scientists and burrowed in for the long haul. It was no zanier, I suppose, than getting basketball coaches to advise businessmen on winning in the corporate world.

Don't think this is just my way of calling Jerry Golden a rodent, a rat, a low-life mammal. After all, he was only scratching itches publishers had. Still, I didn't care for him, and so was mildly surprised that morning to find an e-mail from einsteinjg@ior.com. Awaiting me was an "imprtant, if unorthodox," thoroughly downloadable book proposal. There were also directions to a chatty website filled with news about Jerry Golden Enterprises. This, too, was a Brockmanesque touch. Representing so many experts on our high-tech future, he was the first agent to make that future his own, even shrugging off onto publishers the task of printing out his book proposals. If you were the sort of agent an editor couldn't ignore, the savings were small but real. It said something about Golden that he had the nerve to follow suit and that, without thinking twice, I downloaded his attachment, printed it out, and reproduce it here in all its rushed and error-laden splendor.

"Hey, Rick," the cover letter began (for if you alone haven't noticed, e-mail allows a previously inconceivable tone of intimacy among strangers),

Guess what! Michael Crichton is working on the next sequel to *Jurassic Park,* this time for a Dreamworks animated film tentatively called *King of Creation.* HarperCollins has Crichton sewed up, but right now, you and I, the only book people in New York who know its happeng!

Next month I'll be made official literary agent for American Museum of Natural History's Department of Paleontology, a publishing Godzila. You probably remember the exhibits the museum mounted for both Crichton's dino-movies. Museum peoplescared of turning themselves v into afreak show, but their *Jurassic Park* was a smashing success. Ditto *Lost World* with Universla Pictures, Amblin Entertainment, Don Lessem of Dinosaur Exhibitions, and Mercedes-Bens, the vehicle franchisee, which supports fossil-hunting expeditions in the Gobi. Third time around— another billion-plus $ global property.

news flash 2: Wendell Moore. New head curator of the Paleontology Department. Not yet announced. a gutsy move on the museum's part. No one in the field other than

Robert Bakker, raised preaching in the streets by creationist parents, more controversial. Moore's the rocker Bakkerl: garageband in San Bernatino, 15, touring with ur-dino band Rex, 17, in the badlands of Argentina turning paleontology on its head, 22—and without even a B.A.!!! That was 1969, a vintage year for controversy!

You have chance to be in on the creation of a cultural juggernaut. Our *King of* companion volume—the ultimate illustrated dino-book, authored by beloved dino-rebel and TV personality. Hardcover sales #s on *Earth Dynasty,* Moore's previous book, 135,000, he's a carnivore in the chains.

Surprised I'm contacting you? Well, the promise of a classy publishing house *and* editor is bound to sooth Museum focussed on rep issue. You're a soothin' sort of fella, and I know, as Museum doesn't, that behind yr rep lurks all the marketing weight Multimedia can bring to bear.

May be I'm not your cuppa Oolong, but as project mates, couldn't we prosper?

And, oh yes, you mentioned once yr childhood love of dinos. Find me, 1 p.m. Wenesday, the giant canoe, Museum's 77th street entrance. Meet Wendell Moore, get 1st shot at a book that can only take a load off yr publishing fcct and I guarantee you a few minutes alone with the skull of an allosaurus. No need to confirm, I know you'll make it.

Sayonara,

Jerry

I remembered no conversation about dinosaurs, but my livelihood didn't depend on scoping out my opponents' lives. In theory, an editor has no opponents. When I started in the business, editors existed in a blurry no-man's land. We were in-house representatives of the author and a kind of peace offering from the publisher. Of course, all that's changed. My livelihood now depended on

bending the will of the author to the needs of a marketing schedule. I was, you might say, the publisher's literary agent. It should
have given me a sneaking sympathy for Jerry Golden.

As an editor, my skills were supposed to lie in reading texts. I
could have read much on chutzpah and empty promises in his
typo-ridden proposal. You didn't have to be a genius to sense that
he was juggling a number of things, none of which was guaranteed to come down in his hands. But before I was an editor, I was
one of those boys who spent his time in school staring out the window, dreaming of dinosaurs.

Enter the American Museum of Natural History from the 78th
Street side and you immediately come upon the sixty-three-foot-
long Haida war canoe. Made from a single red cedar log, it lies
athwart the vast entrance hall. The sixteen figures that fill it in-
clude a bear-headed shaman with glowing red eyes, slaves with
poles, rowers with paddles, and a chief in full regalia. They seem
to be passing into life as if out of a dream, not as traditional
wooden Indians but as Indians transmuted into wood, the human
equivalent of a petrified forest. A caption affixed to the rail that
surrounds the vessel reads in part,

> After this museum purchased the canoe from the Haida in
> 1883, Haida paddlers took it from the Queen Charlotte Is-
> lands to Victoria. A ship then carried it to Panama. . . . The
> long arduous journey ended when a horse-drawn wagon
> brought the canoe from the dock to the museum.

It notes that the canoe was collected by I. W. Powell with funds
donated by Herbert Bishop, impressive proof that financial gen-
erosity can have long-term publicity rewards.

Undoubtedly, the Haida canoe had a caption back in the late
1940s when I first saw it, but in those days, even holding a parental

hand, I would not have approached it. Those sixteen mannequins, those Ishis created by unknown craftsmen in the bowels of the museum, took my boyish breath away. They promised the child who ventured too close a trip into a never-never land from which no return was guaranteed.

Back then, they seemed darker and more mysterious. It was easy to imagine that they had just paddled, stroke by stroke, out of the gaping maw, the vagina dentata, of the Hall of Northwest Coast Indians where Claude Lévi-Strauss spent so many hours separating the raw from the cooked, and from whose totemically stuffed interior untold numbers of children, myself included, burst in terror trailed by a lifetime of savage nightmares. The hall throbbed in a forbidding semidarkness, which predated the oil lamp, the gas lamp, and the lightbulb. There, the natural world reached its brutish evolutionary peak in beak-faced wooden poles, sharpened axes, and intricately woven baskets. There, the long path upward from single-celled life found its penultimate destination in the scalper, the headhunter, the cannibal; while in museums across town, the artifacts of the final stage of human evolution held forth a bit boringly in brightly lit surroundings that did not speak of savagery or death.

On that afternoon, amid groups of schoolchildren lining up for an IMAX showing of *Siberia: The White Desert,* I slowly circled the canoe. High-pitched chatter ricocheted off the marble walls, a cacophony of little raptors from a Crichton film. The effect was unexpectedly peaceful.

"Mister Koppes?" A melodic whisper.

I turned to face a face that had glided into that vast hall as if off a movie screen. Its owner wore, as far as I could tell, no makeup, was in her early twenties, and was very, very white, which is not how I would normally describe anyone, especially as she had a complexion so clear and corn-fed it seemed a special-effects miracle.

There's no way I can capture this if you haven't met someone who has the look of a screen star without the support of the screen. Sharon Stone filmed a scene in the lobby of our building and I once was seated next to Madonna in a very loud SoHo restaurant. Both were presences, but each bore only a diminished resemblance to her screen self. Neither glowed. This young woman did. She was the seventeenth figure from that canoe, the sha-woman of shamen.

"I'm Antonia Marwell from the public information office," she said and offered me a smile that lit her already glowing face to bursting.

I believe I blushed.

To blush in the lobby of the American Museum of Natural History at the age of fifty-five while standing near such a woman was no less humiliating than finding yourself with an erection in a high school hallway.

Undoubtedly she understood my confusion for what it was—in a burned-down stub of a balding editor, nothing very pleasant. Nonetheless, she said with practiced good humor, "Mr. Golden wanted you to know he'd be delayed for half an hour or more. I'm here to save you." She offered me a second smile that staggered me. "I'll take you up to our offices where the other publishers are waiting and we can ply you with coffee."

I felt like Ray Bradbury's time-traveler who, on crushing a butterfly in the distant past, returns to a present altered in every way. "Other publishers?" I said, dazed.

"You're the last to arrive."

I felt like the last to arrive. I felt out of breath. "What other publishers?"

"There's a Mr. Green from Knopf and a man whose name I didn't catch from Norton."

"I'm sorry," I said, "but why are they here?" My stupidity was dazzling.

"For the same reason you are."

I did everything but cry out, what reason is that? but what came out was, "There are three of us here?"

"Yes," she replied patiently and, as if summarizing for a child, added, "The meeting will involve the representatives of three publishers, the museum, and of course, Mister Golden."

My brain hadn't died exactly, but my thoughts were making their way back to me excruciatingly slowly. Perhaps she was used to men so stunned they were incapable of intelligence.

She cocked her head slightly as if to say, Well?

I knew with a certainty born of desire that I wouldn't—couldn't—go up to those offices. I felt shabby beyond belief. Survival, Darwinians assure us, is a wonderfully powerful and complex drive. My response came straight from the gut. "Jerry promised me a few minutes with an allosaurus skull. He said whoever met me would take care of the matter." It came out so naturally that for the first time I was able to look at her as if I weren't looking at her.

"Oh," she exclaimed in a hushed voice, "I think I know the skull he means, but—" She bit the word off and paused.

"It's okay. Believe me, it won't be a problem. Anyway, I'm just a small-time fossil thief." And I smiled.

I could feel her relax. Desperation makes you cunning. In a second, I had lifted the barrier to sight. I could look at her and immediately felt less worn, less shabby. I could sense my mind on its way back. I could hear it wondering about the way men of a certain age fall to dreaming of young women. I touched her arm tentatively with my fingertips and said, "Lead on."

I felt like a celebrity beside her. She parted a Red Sea of children with ease, glided by the gift shop, and entered a large elevator alongside a paunchy man and his two boys. He pushed the button for the fourth floor. Dinosaurs, of course. The older child leaped at the younger, chanting, "*T. rex! T. rex!*"

The man paid no attention. His eyes were locked on Antonia Marwell as she took a key from her pocket, twisted it in the button board, and pressed five. He stared at her without shame. I felt an urge to whack him. As the doors were opening on four, he leaned close to her and whispered something.

At five, we stepped off into a cul-de-sac. "What I think we should do . . . ," she began and her voice faltered. She walked forward, hands at her sides, head bowed into the space where two walls came together, and began to sob quietly.

I searched my pockets, finding only a soiled Kleenex. I was overwhelmed by a fatherly desire to comfort her that felt completely bogus. It seemed unreasonable that her body, even up against that wall shivering slightly, could be breathing the same air as mine. Somewhere, of course, she had parents, brothers, sisters, a dog, a pony for all I knew. She had gone to college, had roommates, taken Psych 101, laughed at bad jokes, felt depressed. But none of this seemed possible.

After a moment, her fingers searched out her clothes, straightening and smoothing. Under that harsh, fluorescent light, her face held a transcendent irreality, a prelapsarian sensuality. Even the tears on her cheeks glittered like jewels and shining within them were the tiniest of rainbows. Laugh if you will, but I swear this was so.

I was in a movie. That was my conviction. I took a step toward her. "Are you okay?" I asked, and held out that soiled Kleenex.

She began to laugh, wiping at her eyes with the back of one hand, like a child or a kitten; then she reached out and gently took the scrap of tissue.

"That pig," she said, dabbing at her cheeks. It was a word I hadn't heard in years.

"What did he say?" I sounded solicitous but my curiosity appalled me. To be a good editor has, I suppose, nothing more to do with being a good person than saying "Polly wants a cracker" does with being a good parrot. Sometimes we're possessed by ourselves in surprising ways. I had done nothing but look, react, touch an arm with my fingertips, feel a chill, ask a question, sound concerned. Yet thoughts I didn't recognize crowded my brain. I felt histrionic in a B-film sort of way.

She smiled at me, somewhat shyly. "I'm sorry. I just lost it.

Please . . . " She ducked her head and began again. "I don't mean to . . . " And then again, "I don't want to put you in an awkward position, but if there's any way you could not say anything about . . . " She faltered for the third time. "It's just that I'm new enough to be on probation here and I wouldn't want . . . " Her voice trailed off into silence.

She hadn't managed to finish a thought but I was transfixed. Perhaps she meant me to be. You can't serve a life sentence inside such a face, such a body, and not make some use of them. Who would blame you for wielding them to save your job? Extreme beauty is, if you think about it, a kind of deformity. How else to explain her presence here and not in a lingerie catalog, on a fashion runway, or, for that matter, on screen?

"I understand why you want to be near that skull," she said in a hushed voice. "I went on a dig this summer with Paul Sereno of the University of Chicago. You can't imagine what it felt like to pull hadrosaur bones from the earth!"

I had an unbearable desire to embrace her, an urge so strong my face was burning. I was not too far gone to note, however, that when it came to dinosaurs her voice did not falter.

"Sereno's a dream and I brought home a bit of hadrosaur rib!" She smiled in a confiding way, raising her thumb and forefinger to eye level. "About that big."

"It must have been a baby."

That made her laugh. She rested a hand on my shoulder. She smelled of spring flowers. I could almost feel her hair. It was the single most unsettling sexual moment of my life.

"Come on," she said.

My heart leaped.

She had maneuvered us out of the cul-de-sac. "The amazing thing here is being so close to the fossils." She made a soft, whinnying sound. "Did you read the *Times* story about the first tyrannosaur fetus? I guess I should say, possible tyrannosaur fetus."

Shop talk, I thought, she's practicing shop talk on me.

[ 119 ]

"When Doctor Novick, who led our Mongolian expedition, got up at the press conference, he handed it to me. The most valuable fossil in the world in an open box and I was holding it!"

Her enthusiasm was infectious and I asked, with a curiosity I could finally abide, "Did you see the fetus?"

She looked into my face and blushed. A fabulous cardinal red, a Technicolor flush that spread slowly across her pink cheeks. It was like a Hallmark card, ethereal yet commercial, the sort of colors that brought halos to mind. "Not at first," she said, sadly. "I thought I saw it, but Dr. Novick showed me I'd been focusing on the wrong thing."

We had, while talking, followed a shabby corridor to a stairwell, climbed a steep flight of stairs, and emerged on a longer, shabbier corridor, which turned into an aisle running through a warren of ripple-fronted half-offices with dirty, white half-walls. Six stories up, we were in the bowels of the greatest natural history museum on earth, winding our way toward the skull of a gigantic carnivore, and none of this meant anything to me, nothing, at least, that lay beyond the presence of this young woman.

She waved a hand casually, "Here's where we house our design department."

We passed sinks. There were piles of bottles and plastic containers that might once have held chemicals. There were artifacts, none of which I took in.

Suddenly, she yelped with joy and steered me into a cubicle. A woman with a mass of black hair, thick and rich and pulled into a ponytail that twisted like a lanyard down the back of her chair, was bent over a desk. On a stained wall hung two tiny Inuit prints in a harshly modernist style: a polar bear in shades of blinding white and a hovering eagle, its glaring eye on prey below.

The woman, who had been poking at something with what looked like a knitting needle, laid the instrument aside and half-turned. I had an impression of an eye no less penetrating than the eagle's.

With an easy grace, Antonia Marwell placed a hand on her shoulder. "This is Katrina, Kathy . . ."

But I missed her last name. I was distracted by a row of stones no larger than acorns, propped on the desktop, from which the shapes of animals seemed to be emerging as in a fairy tale.

" . . . our wonderful designer. This is Rick Koppes. He's . . . ," but here she faltered.

The woman's bronze-tinged face seemed itself to be emerging from monumentally stony flesh. She stared at me in silence, then offered a grin that, were she a man, I might have called a leer. She looked well used. She might have been in her early forties, but I wouldn't have bet the ranch on it. There was something sharply defined yet ageless about her, attractive in an abstract way.

She nodded and flung out a hand in a limply dismissive gesture of greeting.

"He's in publishing and the rest's too complicated."

The awkward conjunction of her seated body and my standing one meant that her hand simply sat in mine, inert yet surprisingly warm.

"What publisher?"

"Byzantium Press," I said.

"I was married to a man in publishing once. Ever heard of Grazia?"

"No."

"Well, it was specialized and he's dead."

"She's just finished working on the new dinosaur halls," Antonia Marwell interjected. "She did the gulls circling the tyrannosaurus."

For some reason, I brought my other hand up to hers. She glanced at her hand now encased in mine. Then she considered me as you might examine an insect and the same unnerving smile spread across her face. She had no doubt why I was with Antonia Marwell.

"Kathy's putting the finishing touches on our rain forest diorama, the centerpiece of our new Hall of Biodiversity."

[ 121 ]

Kathy offered up a laugh, sardonic in the extreme. "To hear our Antonia tell it, I've created the exhibit vine by vine."

The "our" caught my attention.

"But look," Antonia Marwell cried out, "this is what I wanted to show you!"

"And I thought it was me," the designer said dryly.

"I always show you off! You can't deny it!" Her voice rose to charming heights of excitability. "But this is you, too. It's your beautiful taste!" And she directed my gaze to a sandy-gray slab of stone on a desktop mount, her finger caressingly outlining chambers of fossilized shell like so many rooms in an Italo Calvino high-rise.

I said, "My god."

"It's the daddy and mommy of nautiluses," commented the designer.

When, for reasons of our own, we each fell silent, my gaze dropped to the desktop. There, a grotesque water bug squatted by a penholder and row of books. Grabbing a volume entitled *Avian Morphology* from a knee-high stack of books, I brought it down on the bug with a satisfyingly smack.

Antonia Marwell gasped.

"Oh my god, Kathy, I'm so sorry. He had no idea . . . "

The designer's face softened. "It's okay, Antonia, it's perfectly okay." She reached out and touched her cheek lightly. They looked at each other with fondness and began to giggle.

"I don't . . . ," I began.

The designer lifted the book. Underneath lay a spray of tiny legs and purplish-black body pieces jagged at the edges.

"Kathy made it," Antonia Marwell said. "Here," she pulled out books, one after another, revealing a series of small roaches frozen in place. "And here." She carefully turned the nautilus fossil to reveal another water bug. "And there." She pointed under the desk where a lifelike rat, crouched in a dark recess.

The designer laid a hand on my shoulder. "Smashing that was a kind of tribute." She inspected me with curiosity. "In any case,

[ 122 ]

they were in a box in the supply closet when I came. I just fell in love with them."

"Who made them?"

"I can tell you the names of the men who mounted the mountain gorillas in the turn-of-the-century diorama downstairs, but the makers of things like this are as anonymous as the things they made. Whoever she was, she had a beautiful soul."

"She?"

"Without a doubt."

"Beautiful?"

"Gorgeous. As you showed us so vividly, you can't help but imagine one of these bugs scurrying away. That nautilus, it's just a pattern in stone that once was life. Artistically speaking, what interest can the formerly real hold? Hyper-reality, art that's fanatically lifelike, now that's beautiful."

Her hand was moving almost imperceptibly on my shoulder. Flexing or creeping or pulsing. Her voice lowered to a hush. "I've taken some of her work home. On loan. Water bugs terrified me until I began to think of them as moving pieces in apartment dioramas."

I said nothing. That hand edging toward my neck had a paralyzing effect.

"People have the same potential, but on the human level the museum fails dismally. Look at the Chukchis, Yakuts, and Ainu in the Asian halls, or old peg-legged Peter Stuyvesant in the basement, or Lucy and her protopal in the new biology hall. They're visual dead meat. You'd never smash a book over their heads. But is human reality too hyper for art? That's what I want Antonia to help me find out."

"You know I won't do that, Kathy." And she blushed.

Watching it happen again was like stumbling into a clearing just in time to catch a sunset, then plunging on, only, at the next opening, to catch it again.

The designer offered another of her sly smiles. "The museum's planning an exhibit on the early years of paleontology. To give women some representation they're putting in Mary Anning." We must have looked blank because she added, "You know, she sells sea shells by the sea shore. Anyway, it's mine to do and I want our Antonia for my model."

"Never," said Antonia quietly but firmly and the designer's hand left my shoulder.

I felt freed. "Perhaps we should go," I said.

"Oh," Antonia muttered, "I'm such a fuck-up! They must already be wondering . . ." With pleading eyes, she turned to the designer. "That big dinosaur skull they're repairing, I'm supposed to show it to him. Take us, *please!*"

The designer bowed her head in amused agreement, then swept the remains of the water bug into a manila envelope and without a trace of a smile handed it to me. "A souvenir of your visit."

We followed her to a stairwell, descended a floor, and after several abrupt turns, found ourselves in a well-worn office area indistinguishable from the one we'd left. It was hard to imagine this warren of ratty offices, peeling walls, and industrial stairways as part of the lopsided horseshoe of buildings that rose monumentally in bumps and turreted spirals over Central Park. In one of those bumps, two editors and an agent, stand-ins for a way of life I called my own, were still waiting.

A Giacomettiesque man in a white lab coat materialized down a distant corridor and drifted toward us, seeming to rise as he advanced. In a novel from another continent, such an effect might have made for a remarkable passage, but in our world it lacked the flare of ET dying, a car crashing through a plate-glass window, or a planet exploding. His was but a minor mirage, like a puddle of water on a bone-dry highway.

He proved on closer inspection to be a razor-thin, exceedingly handsome black man wearing a dirty white smock. Antonia Marwell took a step toward him and I thought I heard her whisper,

"Hugh, I am your dream," or possibly "cream," or as it was said so softly, something else entirely.

They met as if in slow motion. Her face tilted up microseconds before his hand came to rest in a gentle fist under her chin. His face decelerated and their heads adjusted imperceptibly so that their lips might touch without interference from their noses. This I had seen innumerable times in movies. Her mouth opened to meet his and his tongue, a pinkish flash, entered it.

He turned then and took me in. "We call that an Olduvai," he said. And he might have winked. At least his eyebrow, a single, slashing, black V, moved.

The designer laughed, uncomfortably I thought.

Antonia Marwell held his hand, her fingers loosely entwined in his. In my left hand I held an envelope inside which was the crushed model of a water bug.

"This," she said, "is Hugh Brown."

Actually, Brown's color struck me as amber, though only perhaps because somewhere in this museum a host of ancient creatures were trapped in bits of golden Haitian resin. He was over six feet tall and his head was shaved, which gave the fragile structure of his face, overwhelmed by that pitch-black exclamation point, a skeletal feel.

"And Hugh," she continued with a politeness that hinted at upbringing, "this is Rick Koppes. He's a publisher. We're taking him to see the dinosaur skull they're restoring."

"You're . . . ," I began and stopped, for race has an awkward way of making itself known even in Wonderland. I felt the designer's hand on my shoulder, whether as warning or goad I wasn't sure.

" . . . a paleontologist," Antonia Marwell said immediately.

" . . . a paleontologist?"

"No," he said, monotonally. "I'm one of the museum's sanitation engineers."

I hadn't thought janitor. I couldn't have accepted a janitor's tongue inside the on-screen mouth of Antonia Marwell.

"That's not fair, Hugh. It's a reasonable question. You *are* out of the ordinary."

I hadn't actually asked a question; it had simply reared its ugly head. But I did then ask, "How many African American paleontologists are there?"

He looked at me through tired young eyes. "I am them, Doctor Livingston."

Around us, telephones rang, a fax beeped madly, hushed voices spoke. I felt as lacking in responsibility as any minor character in a Hollywood film. I stared at the two of them helplessly. They looked perfectly black and white to me, an exquisite contrast.

"What kind of dinosaurs do you work on?" I asked.

"What makes you think I work on dinosaurs?"

I gestured at our nondescript surroundings as if the answer were self-evident.

"Big, ugly, uninteresting things. The last great imperial line before white men." He said this in an uninflected voice as if offering information of no interest. "You would think your sympathies might run to what's small and underfoot, what's in the blood, so to speak."

"What," I asked, nonplussed, "are you a paleontologist of?"

"Of a world that begins and ends with me."

"What about her?" I indicated Antonia Marwell.

"Everything indicates that she, too, comes from a line of creatures who were once underfoot." And he smiled, perhaps at the conceit of her.

Antonia Marwell turned to the designer. "Who makes men enter testosterone hell?"

"You," she replied, releasing my shoulder. "And you," she said to Hugh Brown, "get us out of here now."

"I'll be happy to leave him with that brute. But what can he do with something he's so ignorant of, except worship it?" The fluorescent light gleamed brightly off his pate as he turned his back on us. We followed him until he came to an unobtrusive white door, which he opened for me.

"We'll wait," Antonia Marwell said. "Come out when you're done."

"Or don't," Hugh Brown added quietly.

I found myself in a white-walled room with two opposing doors. In a corner on a large table on wheels sat a double row of yellowed teeth in a vast scimitar of a jaw, imposingly narrow at the snout, above which a number of dark, empty orbs seemed to track me. I was alone with evolution's ultimate antique. A faint, briny odor lingered in the air. A light mist of white powder covered everything. My shoes were already splotched white and leading back to the door were traces of footsteps larger and lonelier than Lucy's but distinctly in the line she had begun by an ash-covered African lakeside aeons ago.

As it seemed incumbent upon me to do something, I placed the envelope in the giant mouth. I wondered whether an intelligent water bug might someday make such an offering to a skull like mine, once, that is, the last human head had been laid into sediment not so far above where Hugh Brown undoubtedly searched for evidence of how we began.

I bent close, cocked my index finger the way you would to send a marble across a floor, and pinged one of its enormous incisors. It sounded a tiny thud, flat and dead. I moved to the next tooth with same result.

"Disappointed?"

It was the second unexpected voice of the day. In the silence of that room, I whirled and found myself looking up into a weathered, thin-beaked face set on a six-foot frame topped by a Colorado Rockies cap. It was a face not unlike that of an intelligent dinosaur (as I was hardly the first to note).

Wendell Moore, who evidently took recognition for granted, cocked his head in a birdlike way. "Were you disappointed then?"

"I suppose so," I replied glumly.

"No wonder. You don't mind if I remove this?" He handed me the envelope and gave one of the lower incisors a ping. Though I couldn't describe the difference, it would be accurate to say that it rang true. "You were banging on the plaster of paris ones. Necessary dental work after eighty million years. It's one big mother, isn't it?"

"Was this a female allosaurus then?"

"Actually, it's an albertosaurus, kind of a junior tyrannosaur. It could have been female but we'll never know. Paleontologically speaking, sex is the most evanescent of soft tissue activities. By the way, if I don't seem too curious, who are you?"

"Rick Koppes," I said reluctantly. "An editor from Byzantium Press, here for a meeting with you. Jerry Golden arranged it."

"Ah, Jerry Golden . . ." He let the name drift off into space, then added with a certain good humor, "He told you to meet me near the albertosaurus skull?"

I managed an *"Mmm."*

"Look," he pointed to a section of the jaw. "See how dark it is? Barnum Brown found this specimen along the Red Deer River in nineteen thirteen. They probably assembled it in the nineteen twenties using gum arabic to attach it and shellac to preserve the mineralized bone, which is more fragile than you might imagine. Both darken radically with age. The restorers evidently decided it was too fragile here to dismantle. Everywhere else—look how much lighter it is—they've dissolved the old gum joints and reserviced the thing. But this is not your everyday fossil and here they got anxious." Then, without breaking verbal stride he said, "So you edit science books?"

"No."

He looked at me quizzically.

I shrugged. "You'll have to ask Jerry Golden to explain."

He stared down with a kind of predatory amusement. "I've needed an editor. It's a good sign to find one staring at a skull."

I had, right then, no desire to edit anyone. "I didn't know scientists believed in signs."

He smiled. "Nonscientists have such ridiculous ideas about us!

When you're on an eroding landscape in the broiling sun and every way looks the same, you don't think twice about letting the rawest intuition guide you."

To my mind, you don't choose an editor by discussing gum arabic. But he wasn't, I sensed, a man who cared to be contradicted.

"Contingency," he said, "is everything in our trade. Imagine if John Ostrom had walked down the wrong incline in Montana in nineteen sixty-four and missed that glinting raptor toenail, the one that would turn our field upside down, or if he had appeared a couple of years earlier, when it hadn't eroded out, or a couple of years later when it might have been dust! There was a lot of talk of revolution in those years, but this *was* one. Everything we thought we understood was overturned by a bird of a man and a toenail, or are you," he said, leaping elsewhere like one of the dancing dinosaurs he had done so much to bring back to life, "implying that you're a poor editor?"

"No, I'm not."

"Then let's get out of here. Establishment institutions have a way of cutting off the air."

It was like a small explosion on a distant horizon. "Establishment" rang so oddly unless, I suppose, you had spent the previous decades largely in the eroding badlands of the world and many millions of years in the past.

"I've been at this museum a week and already it feels oppressive."

I thought then of the two editors and Jerry Golden anxiously awaiting this paleocelebrity, and felt a ridiculous pang of pleasure even as I said, "Jerry Golden's expecting us."

His laugh echoed as if off steep canyon walls. "You're interested in a book about cartoon dinosaurs?"

It wasn't actually a question.

"Have you ever noticed," he went on—for this man, who had spent so many years alone in inhospitable landscapes, clearly preferred the sound of his own voice to silence—"that in dinosaur fiction creatures like this one have unbearably bad breath?"

"I've never read dinosaur fiction."

"Human beings have dreamed of tyrannosaurs breathing down their necks for most of this century and never has their breath been described as less than grotesquely rancid. Yet vultures don't smell vile unless they've just fed on dead flesh. Vultures will reject meat that's truly rancid. Why should dinosaurs have been different?"

"You've read a lot of . . . "—I hesitated—"dinosaur fiction?"

"All of it," he replied with pride. "Do you know, there are now novels where advanced dinosaurs have sex with humans and it's good sex? I assume, since I find you here, that you have an interest in dinosaurs?"

"As a kid."

"I was one of those. Then you must have read Roy Chapman Andrews . . . "

"I don't think I've ever read a book about them."

"Not even mine?"

"Not even yours."

He chuckled. "Well, the adjectives applied to the dinosaurs of our childhood were meant to wound. Sluggish, stupid, oversized, they had their brains in their butts. *T. rex* was Stalin and the rest of the clan were the imperial communists of evolutionary history, which wasn't the best thing to be in the fifties. The first creatures with the inherent ability to open a chain of fast-food restaurants were going to leave them in the dust.

"But here was the irony: We little boys loved them for their awesome clunkiness. It was the purest kind of rebelliousness. Boys like you moved on, but a few of us wanted dino-sex. We just didn't know where the hell the back seat of the car was. Now, we've brought them back from extinction; sleek, smart, warm-blooded, sexy, successful, parental. Thanks to John Ostrom, we revived them as ancestral birds and so ensured their life on earth today. And in the process, we buried the fifties, paleontologically speaking. It was great science and better politics."

"Are you claiming," I asked, amazed, "that there was a pale-ontological SDS in which 'the personal is political' made literal sense?"

"Exactly!" An unbalanced smile spread crookedly up his face. "I knew you'd get it. I find my intuition utterly reliable."

"And while SDS collapsed in the real world, its paleontological equivalent was triumphant?"

"That's undeniable."

"You know," I said suddenly, "I do remember an amazing *Life* magazine—"

He laughed. "September seventh, nineteen fifty-three. The famous dinosaur cover." His face suffused with pleasure.

"I remember a picture of something tearing flesh."

"An allosaurus. Boys are fascinated by the rending of flesh. At three, my son told me he would rather be a carnivore than a herbivore. In my experience, early science centers on the basics. Large or small. Eat or be eaten."

I haven't yet mentioned his voice. Actorly, generous, it wouldn't have been dwarfed in desert expanses. It addressed an intimate audience of many, of whom I felt myself to be the closest and dearest, using a passionate language from a long-gone era. I felt a sudden urge to know him and asked, "Is your wife a paleontologist?"

"My wife is in another city on another continent," he replied acerbically.

Embarrassed I said, perhaps a touch too brightly, "There was a fold-out, I remember . . ."

He chuckled and was again Wendell Moore, dinosaur impresario. "The only truly sexy centerfold I've ever come across. One day we'll drive up to New Haven and I'll show you the Zalinger mural *Life* took it from. A hundred and ten feet of green heaven presiding over the Peabody Museum's Great Hall of Dinosaurs, John Ostrom's room, and under it, his leaping deinonychus. It took Zalinger from World War Two to the brink of the Cold War to get us from the dawn of time to the end of the Cretaceous, and his dinosaurs aren't Russians. They exist with a dignity all their own in a self-enclosed Eden."

I noted that he had, in some fashion, taken possession of me. When I tried to think of Antonia Marwell, only a blurry approximation materialized. And yet, strangely, the designer's face appeared with a hyperclarity she might have appreciated.

Wendell Moore, of course, had not stopped talking. Perhaps all those years alone in sere climes had left him with an uncontrollable urge, or perhaps it was simply in the nature of the celebrated to expect to be listened to.

"If anyone's around a century from now," he was saying when I returned to the confinement of that room, "they'll be laughing at our dinosaurs the way we laugh at the lamebrained reptiles of our childhood."

I had missed something and must have indicated as much.

"Of course, that's just a prediction and a prediction's a projection and most projections arise from fear. Our minds hunt us night and day. That thing up there . . . " He reached over with his index finger and pinged my head.

It stung terribly and I recoiled. "That hurt," I exclaimed.

He laughed. "It wouldn't if you lost the flesh. Stick that prediction machine underground for a few million years and see if you don't need a little dental work from the next intelligent species to come along."

Without the modest knock on the door, I think we might have stayed locked in that room forever. We both looked over. There was a second knock, no less modest. I had the odd impression that the skull, that iconic mass of mineralized bone, was grinning. Then the door opened just a crack and, when there was no response, a little more. It was a lesson in how to open a door diffidently. We watched curiously as Antonia Marwell's tilted head poked through with part of her chin, cheek, and an ear missing. But nothing other than a few million years underground seemed capable of rendering that face less extravagant.

"Rick . . . ," she began. "Oh!" And she slowly eased her way into the room, staring at him exactly the way I might have stared at her. There was no mistaking that Wendell Moore was Antonia Marwell's Antonia Marwell. She swayed slightly, a minute shudder. When I looked at the paleontologist, who had uncharacteristically fallen silent, he, too, seemed possessed of an infinitesimal tremor.

Perhaps it was only the natural movement of the eye, or of a planet on which stillness is more spiritual quest than attainable reality, but they seemed to be vibrating in unison. Another second and I would have missed it. His look was, I would have said, predatory but she did not look preyed upon.

Mating rites, to adapt his words slightly, are among the most evanescent of activities. Future creatures of whatever sort will find no evidence of that slight movement between well-tuned bodies or of the look that, in my presence, passed between them. And unlike leaves drifting to the bottom of some oxygen-deprived lake, this book will never be pressed into sediments; nor will their bones speak of moments that can hardly be preserved upon a page.

The giant skull seemed amused. And why not? In the blinking of a paleontological eye, humans will disappear and intelligence may turn out to be nothing more than a trope of time. I had my own small moment then; for editing, it occurred to me, may be uniquely human exactly because it's meant to leave no trace, no trace at all.

The two of them looked at me as if I were a screen upon which to review what had just passed; then each grinned and Wendell Moore herded me toward her. I said, quite automatically, "Antonia Marwell, Wendell Moore."

"I know," she responded quietly.

He smiled and, of course, began to talk. "The brain, I was just telling Rick, is nothing but a prediction machine meant to trigger the body's neural response system. Fight or flight in a world where neither makes sense most of the time."

"Yes," she said, "I see what you mean."

At that moment, I was certain, neither of them was short on predictions, none of which would trigger fight or flight. But I said nothing. I was, in a sense, no longer there.

"It's the urge to predict that tags us as human, though its use is anybody's guess since we're such lousy guessers." At the door he asked expansively, "Who predicted Pompeii or World War One or the Cultural Revolution or, for that matter, e-mail? We think of ourselves as the ultimate adaptable species, but the truth is we can't stand change, which is why we won't last long."

I was observing one of this planet's stranger mating rituals. He was, of course, wooing her.

"Marx, Lenin, Mao, Ho, none of them could move humanity off its plot of ground. Nature's the only real revolutionary agent. When it acts, you dance or die. That's why I love dinosaurs. They danced for two hundred and thirty million years—two hundred and twenty before I came along."

As a revolutionary, Bruno Bettelheim would have loved him. There was patricide in his voice. His face was radiant. He was singing our death song, a hymn of praise to the species he had brought back to life, and if Freud didn't suggest that death and the sex instinct are entwined, he should have.

If I hadn't reached for the doorknob, no one would have. To my relief, I found the designer and Hugh Brown talking quietly outside. They looked up just as Wendell Moore emerged, a proprietary hand on Antonia Marwell's shoulder.

"Ah," he said, "a convocation." There was no hint of disappointment in his voice. He was a communard at heart.

What can be read on a face is often exaggerated, but Hugh Brown had the look of a man who took in the situation instantly and with dismay. The designer's face was less easy to decipher. Somehow, they, too, reminded me of raptors. That giant skull had infected me.

Antonia Marwell made the necessary introductions. Wendell

Moore sized up the stakes at a glance. Perhaps hunting fossils gives one an eye for erosive situations. "Ah, yes, the young archeologist," he said slyly. "I've read the summary of your Somalian findings in *Science.*"

Brown tipped his head slightly. "I saw your work on television."

Moore laughed. "You don't think a scientist should appear on TV?"

"I think entertaining the public has nothing to do with being a scientist."

Antonia's face clenched.

Wendell Moore turned to me. "Are you Jewish."

"More or less."

"Well, we don't have a minyan but, as Mister Brown is critical, it seems we have a critical mass. I suggest we use it to propel us from this institution."

Antonia hesitated. "I'm not sure I should—"

"Technically speaking, I'll be your boss soon," Wendell Moore said jovially, "so you have little to fear."

"I'm not afraid, but I'm responsible for Mr. Koppes"—I had been returned to my rightful place in the universe—"and I think—"

Moore laughed. "As I understand it, he's here to meet me, and, as I'm here, where else should he be?" Then he gathered us up willy-nilly and we left, a strange enough grouping for the delectation of some future paleontologist.


We skirted the Haida canoe on our way into the glare of that sunny spring afternoon. Taking the small flight of steps up to the sidewalk was like passing from one dimension to another. At the corner of 77th Street, Wendell Moore, as long-legged as a stork, turned up Columbus Avenue. He walked like a man who knew where the bones were buried. In a city whose oldest buildings are plowed under in less than a century, on that wide stretch of pavement with its fruit trees exploding in delicate pinks and whites, every step we took pressed down on a minirecord of life.

Children screamed with joy and nannies complained; elderly couples strolled by; a juggler tossed carrots and mangos; and a group of Andean musicians played haunting airs on panpipes and guitar. It was a panorama of life, of skeletons not yet set in stone. Wendell Moore and Hugh Brown stalked ahead. Antonia Marwell shifted from a fast walk to a ragged hop as they argued above her.

I found myself noting the busses thundering by, the honking of horns, the piercing cries of an infant, the inchoate rumble of the city, my tiny slice of sediment, buzzing and humming and vibrating without regard for time or space not immediately its own; my New York, that heedless sprawl whose imprint would be left on millions of brains, evanescent tissue hardly fit for the span of a life.

The designer dropped back beside me. She wore a tattered, English-style raincoat shaped for a different body. She reminded me of no one, though her hair was of a sort now found only in anthropological photographs. Released from its ponytail, it cascaded down her back. She neither asked for nor repelled my gaze. She was, to the eye, self-contained.

It's an odd thing to fall in love, paleontologically speaking. And yet an indefinable sense of peace is never enough, is it? The mind struggles for definition. The spring sunlight highlighted the bronze cast of her skin, which, given the width of her face, might have been Aztec, or, thinking of those prints on her wall, Inuit, or a mix of Italian and African American, or Salvadoran and Anglo. The urge to classify is overwhelming. Under its pressure, what can love explain, being only a word for whatever lies beyond?

By the time we stopped for the light at 81st, the others were a block ahead, three lithe dinosaurs, two striding, one hopping along a path that would leave no trackways. We passed the win-

[ 136 ]

dows of Maxilla & Mandible, filled with skulls, antlers, giant claws, and gargantuan teeth, freaks of nature set against the wood of upscale commerce.

"Someday," she said, "I wouldn't mind making bones for windows like that."

"Someday, we'll be bones for windows like that."

She looked up at me. "That would be boring. Nature's so artless."

"You don't find bones spooky?"

"No spookier than dead coral and would you really want to put an accretion of calcium in your living room?"

She fell silent as we approached the Tomcat Café. The paleontologists were embroiled. Seeing us, Wendell Moore promptly turned and strode into the Tomcat's interior, where a wall of espresso and latte machines fizzed.

Antonia Marwell whispered something fiercely in Hugh Brown's ear. "I don't give a damn," was all I caught. We took the last booth, Antonia and Wendell Moore facing Hugh Brown and me. The designer sat in the aisle. Reaching deep into the pockets of her trench coat, she began emptying them of small bits of wood, old Popsicle sticks, pieces of colored paper, metallic-looking scraps, pipe cleaners, a pocket knife, and, in a Ziploc bag, a small ball of what looked like blue Silly Putty. Only I seemed to notice. Perhaps Hugh Brown and Antonia were used to such behavior and there were, of course, other things at stake.

When the waitress came for our orders, my last-nameless Kathy asked for a Coke and "five or six straws," which she proceeded to slice into segments with the small blade of her knife. She cut toward her thumb, exactly the way children are taught never to do. Despite her precision, I held my breath.

With an economy of gesture she set to work. Slowly, a miniature Mardi Gras creature began to form. Red and white where the straw bits were, it was jointed in blue, and for a back had a lattice of white pipe cleaners to which she attached an armoring of reflective silver slivers. The creature was squatter than, but no larger than, a mouse with a braided pipe-cleaner tail encased in a bit of straw, and a head of menacingly bony bumps. Its legs were slightly splayed in a defensive stance. A stubby snout protruded from a face in which the eyes, empty shadows, glared malevolently. With each small addition, I thought: Dinosaur? Crocodile? Iguana? Aardvark? Rodent? But in the end, beyond its four-legged body plan, snout, and tail, it resembled nothing I had ever seen.

"How about it, Rick?" Wendell Moore said. "Haddonfield in the morning, then Princeton for the skull Benjamin Waterhouse Hawkins cast almost a hundred and fifty years ago?"

I must have looked dumbfounded, for Antonia attempted to save me. "Wendell"—yes, it was already Wendell—"is going to take us to the marl pit in New Jersey where William Parker Foulke found the first hadrosaur bones in eighteen fifty-eight."

"The first dinosaur bones to be assembled and mounted anywhere in the world."

"*Hadrosaurus foulkii*, Foulke's bulky lizard," his newest student added proudly.

"A drifting mind is not an attribute one prizes in an editor." Moore said mildly. He was a genial man in victory. He rested an easy hand on the booth just behind Antonia's head. "Pay attention. You might get a kick out of the autobiography I'm working on."

"Just what the world needs," muttered Hugh Brown, "your story."

"Actually, it's the autobiography of Foulke's bulky lizard, the first hadrosaur of the dinosaur revival."

The table fell silent, but my editorial heart skipped a beat.

"That," said Brown, "is an absurdity."

"Dinosaurs were long considered absurdities, but thought of another way, we're the absurdities. At the end of this century, maybe we should all be writing and"—he glanced at me—"editing absurdities. I believe I'll call it . . . ," he paused again, a genuine pit-pat of the heart, "'The Two Lives of Foulke's Bulky Lizard,' because *H. foulkii* has had a double existence. Recent breakthroughs in our field have put the earlier of them within our grasp, but its life with us has yet to be fully taken in."

"Hold on to the movie rights," Brown said quietly.

"Hugh . . . !"

"People always doubt me." Moore was magnanimous, as you are in a film where you've just walked away with the girl.

But I didn't doubt him. When it came to books, I evidently had the intuitive confidence of a Wendell Moore.

"Now, there's a plaque in Haddonfield, but nothing was there when a Boy Scout troop led by a dedicated fourth-grade teacher identified the spot. That was nineteen eighty four. Amazing woman. She'll be in the book."

Call it caution, exhaustion, or intuition if you will, but I said, "I'm afraid there's something I can't get out of tomorrow."

He dug two bony fingers into his pocket and came up with a rumpled five-dollar bill, which fluttered onto the table. Antonia Marwell slid out ahead of him. He reached across the designer to shake my hand. He had a solid, satisfying grip. "You'll hear from me." Then he looked at Hugh Brown. "Are you coming tomorrow?"

"I . . . ," Brown began, and stopped dead.

"Hugh's not into dinosaurs," Antonia offered.

"Neither am I," said the designer. "Not in Haddonfield anyway. I was stranded there for a couple of years and couldn't wait to get out."

I looked at her. The Aztecs of Haddonfield. The Inuit of New Jersey. Who ever knew what to expect?

And so the three of us watched the two of them stroll down the Tomcat's long aisle and out into the late spring afternoon. The designer reached over and covered Hugh Brown's hand with hers. "Nice try," she said. He had the look of a man about to burst into tears.

"I suspect one morning she'll wonder who this old man is," I said.

"Antonia has her own agenda and it's not riddled with regrets."

"It's not what you think," Brown said to the designer, his voice packed with emotion. But he did not—in my presence—say what *it* was.

A conversation was waiting to begin. "I'd better be going," I said. Neither of them objected.

As I slid out, she pushed her small animal toward me. "It's yours."

I picked it up. It stared at me balefully from an absentee eye. "What is it?"

"A prototype."

I looked down at her face unabashedly.

She said, "Don't forget your envelope."

I had left the remains of the water bug on the bench. I dutifully picked it up. She smiled. It was the smile I had earlier taken for a leer. It was certainly knowing, but what it knew I couldn't guess. As I walked away, I heard Hugh Brown say something of which I only caught the phrase "immortal white men."


Is the mind a prediction machine? At the risk of disagreeing with Wendell Moore, my vote goes to fantasies. We spin such elaborate ones around such tiny disparities and then blindly pursue them to the ends of the earth. We are, you might say, so overcooked.

It took almost a week for Jerry Golden to call and by then I had been seized by an urge to put the experience behind me.

I didn't reply when he identified himself.

Maybe he took it as a sign of guilt. He said, "We waited for you. Quite a long time."

"You weren't there and two editors you hadn't mentioned were." To my surprise, my voice was shaking.

"And *you* walked off with my author!"

"You're his agent?"

"I represent the museum department of which he's an employee."

"Fuck off, Jerry!"

We both fell into a shocked silence, awkward when you happen to be holding a phone receiver.

"Wendell Moore assured me that—"

But I didn't care what Wendell Moore had said. "Listen, you fucked with me. If the results displease you, tough shit. Now, I'm hanging up." It was a stranger talking.

"Rick," Golden said quickly, "you're a genuine shark."

The admiration in his words calmed me as praise, however unwanted, will.

"Just make me part of the deal."

I caught the tremor in his voice. I felt faintly sorry for him, but the stranger didn't. I heard the stranger say in a tired voice filled with experiences I hadn't had, "There is no deal, Jerry."

His voice was suffering breakdown. "I'll sell you his damn memoirs. What's he going to do, negotiate for himself?"

"I have no idea," I said calmly. "He didn't confide in me." Which was true, but the stranger knew Wendell Moore wouldn't leave a find to the wind and the rain.

Jerry Golden was speechless.

"So long, Jerry," I heard the stranger say in a tone familiar to me from a hundred noir films and I hung up, amazed. I was evolving. I was dancing. It felt something like being edited. I didn't recognize myself, but who was I to quibble when, unlike Ellen Stakowicz, I was not about to be wiped from the face of my Earth?

One afternoon about two weeks later, Joy buzzed and asked me to come out. There was worry in her voice. When I arrived she was standing by her desk, motioning to a small package. I picked it up.

She took a step back. "Be careful."

I held the package level on my palm. Wrapped in plain brown

paper, it was addressed in a tiny hand to "Rick Capps, Byzantium Publishing House."

"I'm not important enough for anyone to blow up."

"You never know how angry an author could get."

I considered the package more carefully. It lacked stamps or a return address.

Joy had no memory of its arrival. "That's what alarmed me. One moment it wasn't there, the next it was, and I don't remember leaving my desk in between. It just weirded me out."

Had my eyes been closed I'm not sure I would have known I was holding anything. "No bomb could be this light. Let's see what it is."

"Open it in your office then. They don't pay me enough to get blown up." As I disappeared, she called out, "Buzz me if you're still alive. Otherwise I'm just going to sit and worry."

I placed the package on my desk, then stared at it as if that might clarify things. Finally, I picked it up and, feeling like a fool, put it to my ear.

The power of suggestion is not to be lightly dismissed. I unwrapped the package at arm's length, my face half turned away. The paper came off excruciatingly slowly to reveal a nondescript white box. I considered that, too, for a while.

"What is it?" Joy called in. She was standing by the door, which was ajar.

"I haven't finished opening it yet, but come in. You're making me jumpy. If someone's going to lose a few fingers, it'll be me."

"Don't kid around," she said and sidled through the door.

The power of a woman to goad a man to act is not to be lightly dismissed either. I forced myself to jiggle the top until it came free and we were left staring at a layer of white Styrofoam peanuts. When I reached in gently, some spilled onto the desktop. Joy gasped. I froze. Then we both laughed. She walked over and slid her hand in next to mine. Under my fingers I could feel something small and sharp-edged. I put my thumb and forefinger around it and lifted it out. She did the same. Each of us held a tiny, armored creature, no larger than a mouse. Mottled, russet-colored backs gleamed unevenly in the light. Baleful, red pin-eyes glared up at us from black cavities.

"Too weird. What are they?"

"That's their parent." I indicated the prototype perched on a bookshelf above my desk.

She looked at me curiously. "It's not a bomb but it gives me the creeps anyway. Here," and she handed hers to me. "Two of them, exactly the same."

"Not exactly," I said, for each was crouching in a subtly different way.

"Aren't you going to read the note?"

I, too, had noticed the yellow paper peeking up among the peanuts. "Not now."

We stood looking at each other. "Don't bother to explain," she said. "I don't even want to know."

I put her creature down on the desk. For a second I was sure it was about to scurry away.

Another moment passed, then Joy said, "Well, this is anticlimactic."

"Under the circumstances I'd think anticlimax was what you were looking for."

"You never know what you're looking for until you find it."

I said nothing.

"Well, we're not exactly the most forthcoming of bosses today, are we?"

I laughed.

"I can take a hint, and *someone* should get some work done here." She smiled to indicate the joking nature of the comment, but of course she meant it. One of us, she felt, worked endlessly for next to nothing; the other did next to nothing but wander around town for enviable sums of money. This inequality of labor made secrets hard to swallow.

At the door she turned back. "By the way, while you were at

lunch a charmer named Wendell Moore called. That box unnerved me and I forgot to tell you."

I must have come to full alert, for she asked with renewed curiosity. "Who is he? His name was familiar. I think I've seen him
on TV."

"He's a dinosaur hunter."

"Yes, I saw him on *Conan O'Brien*." Her voice had gained an
edge of excitement. "Wasn't he Speilberg's adviser on *Jurassic
Park?*"

Touché, Hugh Brown.

"Are we going to publish *him?*" I caught the amazement in her
voice. She often feels her future, which seems already upon her, is
being wasted on an editor out of the publishing loop.

"Not if you don't tell me his message."

"He's leaving town unexpectedly for a month. Something
about Mongolia. Is that possible?"

"Anything's possible."

"He, and Antonia something. I wrote it down."

"Marwell," I said.

"Marvel?" She looked puzzled. "He said you'd hear from him.
Those were his words. 'Tell him he'll hear from me.'"

"He left no number?"

"Ulan Bator calling . . . He said you would hear from him."

I nodded. I wanted to be alone with my two creatures. I wanted
to read that note. But she was thinking something over.

"Rick . . . ," she began, and my name hung in the air.

I could see she was considering possibilities.

"Rick." She invoked my name as if it were a talisman. "If we
publish him, would you let me be his editor?"

I should have expected it. It was exactly what I admired in her.
"That's a big if," I said, stalling.

"I'm serious. Just say you'll consider it."

There was a complex set of factors to take into account in considering whether to consider. Joy was my barometer. Her urge to be

Wendell Moore's editor was a confirmation. His book might be another meal ticket on the pay-as-you-go turnpike of publishing life. I wanted Joy to succeed, even if I doubted the joys of the success she wished for. But I was gripped by a fear—of ending up where Larry was now, where Ellen Stakowicz had only recently found herself. I feared being in tears on the other end of a phone line.

What I finally said was, "If it happened, I'm afraid I would be part of the deal."

"Part of the deal always involves having you as an editor!" she exclaimed in frustration. "What difference can you really make!"

This was what made me so fond of Joy, not her unbridled ambition but her youthful inability to value what I did at any price. It was bracing and strangely familiar. Every time I ran up against it, I felt I was meeting whatever was left of the energy of the sixties.

"Just consider it, that's all I'm asking." She read character better than manuscripts, and she had a good eye for a sharp manuscript. She knew the longer I took, the more hope for her.

"Maybe," was what I finally said.

"Maybe? Maybe you'll consider it? That's your considered answer?"

"That's my best offer on the issue of considering."

She stood there quietly, considering me.

"Don't push too hard," I said. "On a project like this you can't get rid of me completely."

She laughed. "I'm not an assassin, and if you think I'm pushing then you don't know what pushing is."

"Nonetheless—"

She raised her hands in mock surrender. "Okay, I won't say another word."

"You know I wouldn't lie to you."

"No," she said with a certain solemnity. "I know you wouldn't."

From her, this was not a compliment.

"Do me a favor and field my calls for a while?" That was by way of asking her to leave.

"And if Wendell Moore calls back, I swear I'm going to proposition him." She smiled, a self-deprecating, crooked grin without a trace of Hollywood that was unmistakably triumphant.

The two creatures were still crouched on my desk. I reached down hesitantly, as if not to startle them, and extricated the sheet of yellow paper from the Styrofoam peanuts. Toward the top of the page was scrawled in a tiny hand, "Two, in case you feel the urge to smash one . . . " Farther down was this: "Hugh Brown is the one who should write a book." That was all. Not even a signature.

I read it twice, folded it in quarters and slipped it into my breast pocket. Then something possessed me and I reached into the box once more. It was a miracle that I touched the stone. Ash gray with a fine, even grain, it was smooth as a river on one side, while a wolfish snout poked from the contours of the other. She must have assumed I would throw it out. Perhaps it was a sacrifice to gods of whom I knew nothing.

I dropped it in my pocket, then stood, hands on the desk, and spied on her creatures. I was waiting, I think, for them to betray themselves. Suddenly, I snatched one up and set it down next to its prototype, then with a swift, flat-handed slap that sent pain flashing up my arm, I smashed the other to bits.

I pulled open the bottom drawer of my file cabinet. In the back, beyond the metal divider that held in place the layered history of my professional life, lay the manila envelope with the remains of the water bug. What was left of the other creature I swept into a white Byzantium mailer which I placed on top. It felt satisfying to close the drawer.

About three that afternoon, personnel called asking me to come down immediately. I sat in an anteroom on the seventh floor for twenty minutes, my heart pounding. At some point, I drew out her stone and began to rub it. The meeting concerned incorrectly filled out medical reimbursement forms.

That evening, I called the museum and put a message on Hugh Brown's voice mail. I suggested that we meet on a day of his choice by the Haida canoe. That was all. Perhaps he would call. Perhaps she would call. Perhaps all of us, and Joy, too, would paddle into the Hall of Northwest Coast Indians, light a fire, roast a joint of meat, and discuss the chanciness of evolution, the hyper-reality of the Inuit, the origin of our species, and the descent of man.

# Chapter 6
## SUBMISSION

If editing were synonymous with living, wouldn't that be bliss? So many things step between you and another person, while on the page there are only knots of words calling out to be pried apart, each unknotted passage leading you ever closer to the writer. It's so sensual, really. To edit means to draw close, but here's the perverse twist: It also means to be alone, for every obstacle removed brings you closer to manuscript's end. To be a good editor, you have to know when to leap from a manuscript and so from another's life. To do your job, to be subsumed, sooner or later book and author must make their way as if you never existed.

Connie Burian was my only human manuscript. I traveled along her path for two years, unknotting as I went, and then, before I was even done, she left me. She subsumed me. You'd have to judge for yourself what kind of editing job I did.

If editing means drawing close, I never drew closer. Editing your lover, editing your wife, then watching her go into the world as if you never existed, there's beauty in that, commendable denial, distinct perversity. But what's new? We've been observing the universe for aeons and it gets lonelier all the time.

Once we believed the earth lay at the center of the heavens. Then, thanks to a cylinder of lead tubing, lenses, and a mirror, we discovered myriad dazzling things where nothing had been before. The longer the tubing, the finer the lenses, the larger the mirror, the merrier the skies; the more we looked, the more marginal we became, especially when we discovered everything racing away at staggering speeds. Every second, space was an emptier place.

But visible light proved deceptive. Four centuries looking outward and we had seen two percent of what was there. It took a twenty-six-year-old engineer from New Jersey who heard "cosmic static," the hiss of the stars, to set us looking where we couldn't see, directly into a blackness popping with infra and ultra and gamma and X, filled with nebulae upon nebulae, blue shifts and red shifts, dwarves and giants and quasars and pulsars, and let's not forget dark matter, so pervasive it had to be there even though we had no way to detect it. The less you saw, the more there was; the more crowded the skies, the fewer the interactions.

My own small discovery lay in the everyday world of our minor planet. As with nebulae and galaxies, the perverse, too, clusters and whatever may be visible on the surface of life, dark matter reigns.

It's undoubtedly not a writer's impulse to bring up the perverse this way. For an editor, the pathway is all. People imagine I read like they do, but I approach a manuscript the way a blind man might a face. I touch it haltingly, trying to imagine its essential shape. I wait. I dream. I encircle it and refuse to let go. I sit alone and ignore it until I see the path to the book that could be, until I imagine my way to your reading experience, the one I'll never have.

There's hardly a manuscript I can't outwait. With women, my attention span's been shorter. Perhaps the thought of being edited is unbearable.

## MORNING

While I was at a submissions meeting, my ex-wife called. That's a perverse event in my small universe. We run into each other at parties or award ceremonies once or twice a year, bid on the same book once a decade. We've had two brief phone conversations since our marriage straggled to its end in 1978.

Marrying Connie Burian was the most out-of-character act of my life. Even the urge to marry took me by surprise. Nothing led up to it and, once it was over, nothing followed from it.

We married on August 22, 1976, a day so hot that plaster melted. That night, we smoked dope in our apartment, made love on a mattress sopping with sweat, and slept curled on the bedroom floor, a small fan blowing directly on our butts. You have to be young to do that. She stopped calling herself Koppes less than six months later. The only time I asked, she said her name was important to her. Neither of us mentioned it again.

We seemed to be living on the same planet. How could either of us have known that I represented the end of one thing, she the beginning of several more? I had the look of someone up-and-coming in a business prepared for an editor like me, and she . . . well, no one would have said that Connie Burian looked like nothing at all. But based on our vitae, you couldn't have predicted what was coming, or which of us would be where when it arrived. After all, who foresaw that the most important radicals of the sixties would be on the Republican right, or that a communal business of the rich and clubby was teetering at the edge of a conglomeration party, or that the driving force in a largely male cottage industry would fall into the hands of women? I was clueless.

I first ran into Connie in April 1975 at a book party for a radical author. I was new enough to be excited by a rumor that the editor of the *Times Book Review* would show up. That month Saigon fell and Connie turned twenty-three. She had skipped the sixties, passing straight from college into publishing, pedal to the metal. She became an assistant editor at Vintage just as the trade paperback came into its own.

Connie did not spend time alone if anyone on earth was available. She arrived with a male friend. She knew no one, the author least of all. But to an observer—myself—she looked like she was just where she meant to be.

She *was* a striking figure, though why isn't easy to describe. Something like an aura clung to her, a faintly misty, spiritual look I now associate with missing contact lenses. Her hair was long in the style of the moment. She stood at almost my height, so when she approached me, I looked directly into those deceptively mystical eyes. She was wearing faded jeans at a time when fading still came from use. It seemed like a statement in the staid world of publishing, though she was there by mistake, owing to a confusion of invitations. And, of course, she had a stutter that had long ceased to stand between her and anything that interested her.

She was bold enough, upon noticing me noticing her, to introduce herself. I was struck by the force of her attention. It gave the softness of her face a vertiginous depth. Gazing into her eyes was like falling into the dizzying heart of who knew what. I despair of describing the feeling for fear of sounding adolescent. Still, a jolt of energy ran through my body. It wasn't something you forgot, nor was the sense of loss when that look left you.

She said, "I was wondering . . . ," and paused. I paused with her. "I was wondering what in . . . " Amid the chatter, a moment stretched silently between us. I did nothing except imagine ways her sentence might end and watch her launch herself a third time. "I was wondering what in . . . "—there was an elongated beat—"the world this is," and she gestured around the room. "What is the publishing point of this party?" How typical, by the way, that her first question had to do with the mechanics of the business. "And who are . . . ?" She swallowed the "you," but offered me a dazzling smile in its place.

Have you ever been seduced by a stutter? I doubt a noneditor can imagine what it feels like to find yourself in a space filled with such energy, absent only the words to explain it. It was as if she were showing me the path directly into the wilderness of her.

The crucial thing I did, the most natural thing in the world, was nothing at all. Alone with her in that warm, packed, loud room, I trusted my editorial sense. Later she would tell me how much she hated the helpfulness of listeners whose discomfort or impatience masqueraded as kindness. Everywhere she bumped up against an urge to barge into her space, mistaken for emptiness, offering words that could only obliterate hers. Everywhere, it seems, but in me. The impulse to take silence for emptiness is such a human one. Perhaps some impairment—like the nerve-damaged hand that doesn't register the burning stovetop—prevents me from sharing it. Perhaps in some sense I'm a stutterer, too.

Connie's gift to me was the fullness of her hesitations; mine, the urge not to intervene. The truest paths often unfold in silence, not much valued by the nonstutterers of our world. There was something beautiful in that swirl of words lying in all its obdurate mystery just beyond the tip of the tongue. It was like awaiting the touch of a lover.

She had never met someone like me, or at least some human like me. As a girl she talked freely in the company of her dog and two cats. Here, then, is an odd fact to carry away from this book: For reasons that puzzle those who study stutterers, but not me, they do not stutter in the presence of animals. And so that girl, trapped in a Möbius strip of words, besieged by people intent on dragging speech from her, developed her signature machine gun–style delivery in the presence of her pets.

In those two years with me, her stutter lost its hold. I came to miss those swallowed thoughts and to take their absence for what it did indeed represent. Not so long after they left her, she left me. I never doubted the connection. When I look back, I still feel a perverse pride in her. She was, after all, the only person I ever edited. She was my book.

That first moment, I thought, she's the one, and I followed her through the crowd, ran her to ground, made her look at me, stutter for me again. I even began to brag a little. As if I were a figure to be taken seriously. As if my assessment of our business meant a thing.

Did it matter that every assumption I made about her was out of whack? Does it ever matter what impulses send you down a path when it's the only path you'll ever take, when there's no way of editing your own life?

In two years we used each other up. After that it was simple. There was nothing to fight over, nothing, materially speaking, worth a damn. We had been living in a railroad apartment on 114th and Morningside Drive. Two unimpressive salaries, old furniture covered with Indian bedspreads, a large waterbed neither of us cared for, two electric typewriters, and a handsome butcher-block table she ended up with. There was no reason to look back. And given the years, given who Connie Burian had become, there was no one left in publishing to connect us.

When the phone rang while I was staring at the message slip with her name on it, I let Joy take it. She came in immediately. Sarah, she told me with barely suppressed urgency, wanted to discuss the disposition of our joint property. That was Sarah's phrase, of course. Four years together and we hadn't purchased a single major item. At stake wasn't property but time. Baby time. Sarah was forty-four and I was the cusp on which she had so inelegantly impaled herself. Maybe it was tactless to speak to Joy of property matters, but she was angry. She had such high hopes for me once. Then again, it's harder than we admit to float, two to a raft, in this ocean of a world.

I disapprove of the public display of private life. It's dreaming in reverse. Dreams are pyrotechnic, but tell them to a friend, put them on paper, give them to us on screen or at a trial and boredom ensues. There's nothing less interesting, moment by moment, than private life, and yet display it anywhere and crowds gather. I swore I wouldn't let my private life intrude on this account. But that's what happens when you trail your story too closely.

"She's at the apartment," Joy exclaimed, "and she swears if you don't talk to her, she'll take what she wants."

I considered this. I knew what "talk" was likely to mean. Much yelling. Some tears. Paralysis on my part.

"Tell her I'm in a meeting."

"She won't believe me." Joy sounded choked with sympathy that I doubted was for me. "And I hate to lie." The "for you" was implicit. She doesn't object to lying in her own defense in ways transparent enough to amuse us both. But lie for your boss and to-morrow you'll be picking up his dry cleaning.

"Okay, tell her I refused."

"I can't do that!" she practically howled. "She scares me!"

Sarah was angry for wasting so much precious time on me, but she was relieved, too. There was someone else. I could sense him in the wings. I knew she would discover her relief the minute the shouting and weeping subsided. I already felt relieved. To float on that ocean alone seemed like the truth.

And, of course, there was Kathy from the museum. I glanced up at her strange creatures. I hadn't called. I wasn't sure whom to call. But she was on my mind. None of which stopped me from spending enraged nights at home, life being in part a play staged for unknown witnesses.

"Rick," Joy said suddenly. "Do something! She's on the phone and she must be getting suspicious!"

I nodded and picked up the receiver.

"Sarah."

There was a cold silence on the other end.

"Take what you want," I said, motioning Joy out.

But Joy was in no hurry. She was off the hook and a drama, however humdrum, was unfolding. I shooed her away with my free hand. She departed reluctantly, leaving the door suspiciously ajar.

"That's easy for you to say." Sarah spoke in that dead voice of hers.

She was a remarkably decent person. Leave her to split anything and she would take less than half. I might have said many generous things, but in the spirit of the moment I chose, "There's nothing easy about it"—which was a lie. Saying that was far easier than living one more moment together.

There's a rhythm to breaking up so hypnotically familiar that you can't help falling into it. The inexorable way our lives were unraveling was as ancient as Greek tragedy, but in its gracelessness closer to soap opera.

"I want the bureau," she said.

It was an unexceptional piece, the sort of thing you filled with socks and underwear and never thought about again. "Take what you need. I trust you." That was a provocation, but in a relationship what wasn't?

New Yorkers marry, sue, and leave people for apartment space. Sarah wasn't so much moving out as in. When we met she lived in a modest co-op near the New School where she taught. She rented it out after we got together. Thanks to that co-op, we had spent two months experiencing the rhythm of ending without the means to depart. Her tenants were finally leaving. Only now could she end what had already ended.

Whoever you are, you already know what transpired next. And yet just when you think you have it down, there's the twist that surprises. In our calculus of gain and loss, neither of us could afford to hang up first. So we lingered long enough for me to suggest not coming home that evening. "For your sake," I believe I actually said.

"Where will you go?" she asked with unexpected concern.

"I don't know," I replied, which was the unprovocative truth.

"Why don't you just come home and we can talk?"

There was such feeling in her voice that I almost crumbled. I had nowhere to sleep, no place to go. Emotion can be mistaken for anything, even possibility. But we had done a lot of what passed for talking. "I don't think that makes sense," I said, sounding surprisingly teary.

"Sense?" I caught an edge of the edginess I had once loved her for. When I said nothing, she added, "I hope the only child you ever get near is a five-hundred-page one."

And I laughed not just because it was funny, but because the hurt behind it unnerved me.

"You son of a bitch," she said. "If I had been a book, you would have loved me!" And she slammed down the phone.

Maybe I had an urge to get the pain over with as fast as possible because I looked again at that message slip: Connie Burian, with a phone number. Joy had scrawled ASAP across it. I was under no illusions. There was nothing Connie could tell me I wanted to hear.

I buzzed Joy.

"Was she mad?"

"Well, she weren't happy, if you know that old joke." But of course she didn't. "Did Connie Burian leave a message?" It felt odd to say her name.

"Just to call. I hear she's really cool."

I felt a tiny burst of pride as I clicked off.

I stared at that pink slip as if to root out some bit of information that might make sense of the path I would presently plunge down. Then I dialed and was greeted by a young man's baritone. I asked for my former wife, identified myself, and got an "Oh" of recognition.

"You published Boyle MacMurphy. I remember the acknowledgments. In my opinion, it's the best Vietnam memoir we have by a journalist. Other than *Dispatches,* of course."

Of course.

"Have you read W. D. Ehrhart's postwar trilogy?"

"No."

"You'd find it interesting. Vietnam was one of my areas of concentration in grad school."

I said nothing.

"I was a student of Fred," he paused, "Jameson."

Fred Jameson, I thought, and my heart sank. This unknown boy was bullying me.

His voice dropped to a whisper. "Connie's great. Do you know her?"

I would have been noncommittal, but it didn't matter.

"Still, this isn't exactly the place for serious intellectual work. Connie does a lot of fiction and . . . " His voice dropped away, leaving me the task of filling in everything good breeding and job insecurity prevented him from saying.

"Increasingly, I feel like what I publish is fiction," I replied.

He laughed uneasily, though it should have been an appropriately postmodern statement for a former student of Fredric Jameson. That I had been his boss's husband was certainly a fiction of the wildest sort; and this unlikely boy, Connie's own Joy, seemed no less so. He just wasn't my fiction.

"I wonder," he continued, doggedly, "would you catch a cup of coffee with me?"

It shouldn't have taken me aback. "How old are you?" I asked.

"Is there an age limit?"

His boldness amused me. He was indeed Connie's Joy. "There might be."

"Is twenty-four under or over?"

He was Joy's age. "How about . . . "—I began flipping my calendar in the belief that scheduling something far enough away was but another form of fiction—"Wednesday, August seventh?"

"But that would be . . . I know you're busy, but is this evening possible?"

There was no need to glance at my calendar, no reason except the obvious to say no. "Okay, one cup, six o'clock."

"How about the coffee bar in the Virgin Records store halfway between our offices?" I could hear the relief in his voice.

"How will I know you?"

"Six-foot-plus, blond hair, black backpack. My name's Todd Platt, by the way. How will I recognize you?"

I had a thought. "I may bring a friend."

He fell silent.

"I'm about five-six, bald, and I'll be the only person wearing a jacket and tie. She's your age, my size. Short, brown hair, many earrings, and a gold stud in her nose. She's in publishing, so we'll have plenty to talk about."

"Uh . . . ," he began, but, quick as he was, this had not been part of his agenda.

It made me feel like the author of our narrative. "Could I possibly speak to your boss?"

"Oh, I'm sorry." He lingered a few more seconds, then added feebly, "I'll see you both later," and was gone.

I remained a moment in the peaceful emptiness of phone space before Connie arrived, finishing a conversation. "Don't, just *don't* send it out until we've checked." I caught a muffled response. She was, of course, not alone. She had even liked to edit in company. My solitary act had, for her, been a communal experience. Perhaps that's why she was the only person I ever taught to edit. I thought nothing of sitting by her side late into the night working on manuscripts.

Connie read everywhere: in cars, in bed, on the john, in the street. In the company of anyone she read aloud. And if a third or fourth person was in the vicinity, everyone was welcome to squeeze between the covers. I swear she could have run a nationwide food co-op or a worker-operated business or a socialist country. Unfortunately, the only thing available was a book company transmuting into a multimedia entertainment outlet.

"Not until we're absolutely sure." I heard her say. *"Absolutely."* Repeating words like that, banging them on the head for emphasis, was all that remained of her stutter.

"And check the warehouse. Call Bill Barber, for god's sake." In the background were other voices, then hers again, "Sorry to bust in on you with so little warning."

I didn't realize she was speaking to me until she added, "Rick?"

"Yes?" I said, already feeling slow and stupid in her presence.

She paused and I waited. Then she laughed. "I forgot about your silences. How's life?"

"Creeping by."

"And Byzantium?"

"As you might expect."

"That bad?"

I laughed, despite myself.

"I amuse you."

"Surely."

"And you're surprised to hear from me."

"You could say that."

"Yes, of course. I like you sardonic. I always did. Some things should never change. *Never.* I have two matters to discuss. One minor, one not so. Among the various options, meeting is the sanest."

Two matters, no less. Another of that day's clusterings. I won't say I wasn't curious, but curiosity, I knew, wouldn't lead me where I wanted to go.

"Would you catch a drink with an ex-wife? That is," she added quickly, "if I'm not keeping you from something."

"I doubt you'd be keeping me from much," I replied, trying to be sardonic but sounding bedraggled.

"As it happens, the only evening I have is this one."

I hesitated.

"I beg you, say yes. *Please.*"

"Actually, your assistant . . . "

She burst out laughing. "Did Todd proposition you?"

"More or less."

"He's very upward mobile in a downward mobile way. *Very.* And he got you to commit yourself?"

[ 159 ]

"Amazingly, yes, to coffee."

"It's a compliment that you're on his radar screen."

"I suspect he thinks I'm a dirty old man. I told him I would bring someone young—my assistant, in fact—but I didn't make our relationship clear."

"That doesn't make it clear either."

Her amusement on the other end of the line reminded me that ours had not been a successful marriage. "I thought I might introduce them."

"You've taken to playing Cupid?"

"It was a self-protective act."

"Be careful or he'll have your job. No, Byzantium's not quite big enough for him." Then she edited herself. "Not quite fast enough."

"We're a slow bunch here."

"I have a thought. Why don't I come? We'll chaperone them."

Only minutes before, mine had been an evening for one with no end in sight. Now, there were four of us, parents and children from a family that never existed. It sounded like a dream of redemption, like, given the crush of bodies, Connie's dream.

"I'm not sure . . . ," I began.

"Don't be a quince."

"A quince?"

"A sour fruit that makes you pucker up in distaste. It sounded dreary before. Now, we'll have a good time."

Facing Connie's desires I already felt out of breath, and silence had never been protection enough. She was like a riptide against which you struggled at your peril.

"By the way, I've been wondering why your Sarah's calling me."

I could feel my chest tighten. "Sarah Dixon? Why would she call you?"

"I must be the mystery figure in your life." And she laughed genially. Good fortune does that to you. "She seems like a fine soul. Are you sure you want to split up?"

"You were a good soul and it didn't stop us."

"We were ten years old. I don't know about you, but I've done better since."

I knew nothing of her private life and she was on the phone with my lover.

"You might try talking things out," she said, reasonably enough.

But this was not a direction I cared to pursue. Perhaps there were no directions I wished to pursue with Connie Burian. "You know, maybe a drink isn't the best idea."

"I hesitated long and hard before picking up the phone. I won't let you off the hook now."

I took a breath.

"But the kids will make it fun. We'll be like seconds in a duel."

The kids. So be it. "Six o'clock at the Virgin Records coffee bar. Todd's suggestion," I added defensively.

"Let's make it seven fifteen, drinks at Patria. You know it, don't you?"

I knew it. Nuevo Latino food, California style. Plantain chips that soared like druidic rune stones out of red-and-yellow pallets of salsa amid a noise level only imaginable when young stockbrokers belly up to bars.

"Joy can't afford that."

"Neither can Todd. But I'm taking. Then if we're still on speaking terms, you and I can catch dinner."

She was never not in control.

"How romantic," I said dryly.

She laughed. "We deserve a nostalgic moment."

"I doubt Todd had this in mind."

"He's surprisingly flexible. It's you I'd worry about." And she laughed again.

I amused her utterly. It was frightening how harmless I had become.

"I've got another idea. Why don't you ring Sarah, I'll call my Claudio, and we'll make it a foursome once our business is over?"

The critical mass of the meeting threatened to rise again. "Thank you, no, or you won't see me tonight."

"Then we'll reserve that for another time."

For a season in hell, I thought.

"Until seven fifteen, then, *dear.*" It was as if a sharp object had made contact with a fragile rib. And then I was alone.

But not for long. Joy stuck her head in.

"The very person I wanted to see," I said as brightly as I could.

"That woman who—"

"Are you busy tonight?"

She stopped just inside the door, flustered for the second time that morning. "Why?"

"I want you to come to Patria with me."

"You're taking *me* to Patria?" I could hear the panic. "Now that I think about it, I promised a friend . . . " Still, she paused to consider. "This is too weird. A night with my boss."

"There are perks. You get to meet my ex-wife."

"You *have* an ex-wife?"

"Connie Burian."

A stunned look crossed her face. "You . . . ?"

"I find it improbable myself, but that was in another country."

"What country?"

Joy, when flushed, becomes a literalist. "She's bringing her assistant, who's curious about life at Byzantium. Connie's offered him and a second-round draft pick for you."

"I would work for her in a second." She paused again. "But I can't go. Look at me."

I looked at her. She was in exceedingly well-designed jeans and an elegantly tapered blouse. Her face had its normal lopsided charm. Strange loops dangled from one ear. I found her, as always, highly lovable.

"I can't go looking like something the cat dragged in, as my grandma used to say." And she smiled despite herself. It was about as homey as she was likely to get.

"You can go anywhere looking like anything these days."

[ 162 ]

"That's a consoling thought. You're saying I look like shit but it doesn't matter. Not wanting to meet Connie Burian in a job interview–type situation looking like a slob is more than female narcissism."

"Joy, this is not a job interview–type situation."

"Not for you anyway."

"It's more like a date."

"You're getting back with your ex?"

"For you, I mean. Her assistant sounds like some kind of hunk."

"Oh, great. . . . My god!" she said suddenly. "That woman, the one you had me write, Ms. Hiroshima, she's waiting out there!"

I had forgotten about her. "Okay, what's she like?"

"Like? How do I know? I'm stuck on the phone with your . . . your . . . she slouches."

"Useful observation. Give me a minute, then bring her in. Let's take off at six thirty."

"Well . . . ," she began.

For once, Connie-levels of company seemed attractive. I would have taken six, eight, ten assistants to Patria. "Listen, I really want you to come and it doesn't make a bit of difference how you're dressed. Look at me."

"You look the same whatever you're doing."

And on that note, without committing herself, she left.

I felt like a juggler being juggled. A soon-to-be ex-partner, a former wife, and, for a change of pace, the author of *Daughter of the Bomb*. Marissa Kuby was her name and her partial manuscript had arrived in the mail unagented, a sentence that now seems as odd as, "The knight entered the field of battle on foot and without armor or a sword." When I came to Byzantium most manuscripts were unagented and we thought it a good thing. Now none are. It's unappetizing to be too vulnerable in our world. You automatically devalue the manuscript of such a person. And it's not wrong to do so.

When I ripped her package open, out spilled a self-addressed envelope and loose stamps. I felt a jab in my heart. Still, I looked at her title and did the least expectable thing. I closed the door and read the 147 pages, six of twelve projected chapters.

Whoever imagines an editor reading during office hours is an incurable romantic. Nonetheless, I told Joy to hold my calls and rang up an agent to beg off lunch. Two and a half hours later I emerged to a fistful of urgent messages, a scrollful of in-house e-mails, and a managing editor anxious about catalog copy for a book pubbed in January that didn't yet exist. I was also hungry, but I felt an unspeakable urgency re: Marissa Kuby. Like an itch I couldn't scratch. Of course, I could have picked up the phone. She had included her number and she lived on West 85th Street, only a Zip code distant from me.

I stood in my doorway looking at Joy. She was my sixth assistant. My first had been twenty-two. I was twenty-nine then and had no idea what you did with someone meant to assist you. That was the sixties for you. At twenty-four, Joy had aged only two years to my twenty-seven, remaining more or less stationary while I receded at the speed of life. Marissa Kuby, on the other hand, had aged with me and though her partial manuscript ended in May 1979 just as she joined the Reno 7, I sensed that we had been moving toward each other as down a tunnel darkly.

While reading her chapters I experienced regret, an alien emotion for an editor, and was convinced I could have done so much better, the least worthy thought an editor can have. Yet, I felt—I don't know how else to describe it—a kinship with her, and when I finished I only wanted to meet her, though I couldn't have told you why if my life depended on it.

I write my own letters, so when I asked Joy if I could dictate a note to be sent off under her name, she looked at me oddly. I handed her a pad and pen. "Could you write a Ms. Marissa K-U-B-Y?" And I gave her the address. "Something like: Dear Ms. Kuby, Rick Koppes has read the manuscript you submitted and would be happy—"

"You actually want me to write this down?" she asked incredulously.

I nodded. " . . . and would be happy to meet with you. Give me a call at the above number so we can arrange a convenient time. Regards, et cetera."

She looked up at me. "I'm et cetera?"

"Actually, I'm probably et cetera."

She gestured toward the manuscript. "Would you like me to take a look?"

Normally, my attitude is, if it's on my desk, it's yours to read. But I said, "Maybe not. It isn't very good."

The truth has a way of sounding unconvincing. She looked at me oddly. She thought I was holding out on her. "All right," she said, doubtfully, "be weird." And she began spreading message slips in front of me.

I put my hand on hers, sensing her unbounded energy. "It's okay if things go on without me for a day."

"Be even weirder. See if I give a damn." But she sounded less sure of herself, more like a twenty-four-year-old in a world where losing your way is the easiest thing of all.

"Send off that note and don't fret," I said. But I should have been the one to fret. I knew I would never publish the manuscript, and you don't issue invitations under those circumstances unless what you're searching for is a close encounter of the third kind.

Even her title drove me crazy. Who wasn't a "child of the bomb"? And yet there on page seventy was the heading *Sub-Mission*, complete with caps and that bizarre hyphen. It was a title odd enough for the book Rick Koppes would have written. Unfortunately, she wielded it with an obscure literalness, even though a terrifying submission to her father was the theme of her life.

Luther R. Kuby had not faintly "dropped the atomic bomb," though his daughter clung to that claim for dear life. He had been the navigator of *Dan's Baby*, which reconnoitered the city of Nagasaki two days before *Bock's Car* arrived with the second bomb of the atomic age in its scientifically impregnated belly. His was, as she saw it, a "sub" (as in subsidiary) mission in an operation to obliterate a Japanese city in a new and revolutionary way. It was a stretch, though with a weapon that held the future possibility of no future, maybe nothing was a stretch.

Poor Bock, I thought, as I sorted through her memories. The previous pilot of the B-29 that seared Nagasaki, he would find his name forever attached to the world-ending mission he didn't fly simply because the similarity of boxcar to Bock's Car amused him. Poor Bock, I thought, you pissant. The thing was, you couldn't put a fine point on the nuclear act. It could encompass Poor Nagasaki, Poor Bock (who hadn't even been there), and then, without much effort, poor me. It threw the same carbonized shadow onto any wall.

God knows why but that damn manuscript just churned me up. Maybe I felt angry with the young men who carried out the act that cleared the way for Marissa and me. It was a hell of a birthday card to the baby-boomer generation: Welcome to Earth, Marissa Kuby, and kiss off. Yet they were just boys like my father, who was slogging up the boot of Italy watching his friends die, when the 509th Composite Group first began testing their specially fitted B-29s in the Nevada desert.

The day her father's bomb dropped, my father was on a troopship in the rough waters of the Pacific heading for Okinawa. He told me once—and he seldom volunteered anything about his war—that when the ship's loudspeaker announced the obliteration of Nagasaki, they cheered their heads off. It was, he said (and he was not given to overstatement), the happiest day of his life, the first time in three years he felt he would experience the future. We were arguing at the dinner table about another war and I had said something like, We've been committing crimes against Asians since Hiroshima, and if the Vietnamese don't quit we'll nuke them, too (a point on which I was wrong, but not, the history books reveal, by much).

Usually he'd stick his angry face close to mine, my voice rising along with my terror to meet his. But what I said uncharacteristically hushed him, and when he responded, it was about those cheers. That was too disgusting for words, I insisted, and left, slamming the door. The last thing I remember was my father's face, the otherworldly red of early Technicolor movies.

Those who know what the fathers of one war said to the sons of another, and vice versa, will fill in the blanks from memory. I'm the age he was then. Too late can I picture that cheering adolescent facing his death or imagine why others like him turned the weapons of destruction into cheesecake, or lame jokes, or, like the crew of the plane that bombed Hiroshima, scrawled crude curses and bizarre greetings to the Sons of Nippon on the weapon about to descend on the way we imagine forever. If only I could rewind that scene and offer the boy my father once was, not to speak of the boy I was then, the respect needed when you break bread at the edge of an abyss.

That was one of the regrets I brought to Marissa Kuby's manuscript. I should have felt empathy. She was young on the page. For her, 1945 was yesterday and her father, whose bomb still fell, but an exaggerated version of all the vulnerable, despotic fathers we grew up with who wavered ceaselessly between obliterating anger and collapse. Anything less than her literal submission called forth, by her account, a violence, verbal and sometimes physical, that was horrifying.

Her pages could have held such hyphenated music and yet *Sub-Mission* was only a subsidiary mission. Still, there was something I couldn't touch, like a roaring silence where her manuscript lay, and it drove me wild. It took me beyond editing, but maybe that was where I was heading anyway.

Every now and then you would stumble on a striking passage. There was something vivid, for instance, in the way she described coming home from school in the "golden years" of the fifties when her father was an unemployed drunk. She would catch a snatch of Sinatra's voice on the record player and know he was there, sunk in his easy chair, a glass of Johnnie Walker beside him. She wrote of entering the living room and "seeing His face flushed almost the color of the chair. It was the flush of the liquor, but when I was young and didn't know, I imagined it as a reflection of the glow of His bomb over Nagasaki."

She did that kind of capping elsewhere, usually of pronouns connected to her father as if he were God Himself. It might have been curious, had it been a stance rather than an unbearable urge. And she couldn't sustain the best of her writing for more than a few sentences. Yet when chapter six ended as she collected pig's blood from a slaughterhouse for the Reno 7 and a year in prison was mentioned, I was eager to know more. Maybe I just wanted to reassure her that someone else had had such a father, that sometimes he was drunk and sometimes hit me, that even in the golden fifties, he was sometimes without a job. Or maybe it was leaving Sarah Dixon who was never drunk or did a mean thing. Or maybe I just wanted to meet the daughter of the man who had, however indirectly, dropped the bomb. You tell me.

Marissa Kuby took my hand skittishly, then folded herself into a chair as if she had spent years trying to be a much smaller woman. At least six feet tall, she would not have fit comfortably in the cockpit of a B-29. She was dressed in a black skirt and fuzzy, gray sweater that buttoned down the front, and might have come from a fifties thrift shop. Her face, on the other hand, would have been at home in an old Dorothea Lange photo, though her cheeks had an unnatural ruddiness. We exchanged a few polite words before she lapsed into a nervous silence.

Her eyes were like a cat's. She seemed about to bolt from the room. To hold her, I asked what she did.

She said softly, "I teach four-year-olds at a Montessori school." Her voice had a smoker's rasp.

Then she waited, undoubtedly for me. Because the silence was surprisingly painful, I asked, "Is your father still alive?"

"He died of lung cancer in 1986." She leaned forward and added in a harsher whisper, "I was with him to the end." Taking a white envelope from her shoulder bag, she handed it across the desk. It was addressed in a girlish hand to Lt. Luther Kuby in Tokyo and had an oval hand-cancellation mark of a sort I hadn't seen in decades. I checked the date: October 22, 1945. Inside were two photos, no bigger than those you get at a subway photo booth. I gently picked one out. A microscopic man knelt under the nose of a giant plane, a dark shadow over all but the glowing white spot that was his face.

"Here." She drew a magnifying glass from her bag.

As I took it, her fingers brushed mine and a ghostly shiver ran through me. His face leaped to meet me, staggeringly young and glistening like a rajah's. She could have been his mother.

"He was already on Tinian. Of course, they hadn't told him a thing. That's *Dan's Baby* behind him." Her voice had grown stronger.

I moved the lens slightly and there it was, a vast, wavy arc of script across the diaper of a cartoon infant hurling a winged bomb to earth.

"Now, look at the other one." She stood up and came around the desk. Her hands settled on either side of mine. Her shadow spread over me. I could hear her breathing the way I imagine you might hear a horse softly snorting. Her hand reached for the envelope.

And Margo Deare stormed in.

Like a creature from an irradiated Oz, Marissa Kuby shrunk against the bookshelf. Had there been an open window she might have leaped.

Margo tapped her watch. "The reading's in half an hour." She advanced on Marissa Kuby like a tiny, strutting bantam cock.

I stepped between them. "Margo, Ms. Kuby's written a curious memoir."

She turned on me as if we were alone. She looked like hell. "Let's not keep Walter Groth waiting!"

I offered Marissa Kuby a smile. "I'm sorry. I've evidently miscalculated." I held out the magnifying glass.

She grasped it like a lifeline, pressing it to her chest as she took an involuntary step forward, and stumbled into me. Reaching out to steady her, I felt her body too large and tense for this unexpected embrace.

"Listen—" Margo began.

"Be quiet!" I practically shouted.

Marissa Kuby contorted herself into a knot, knelt down, and pulled from her bag a sheaf of papers that promptly slipped through her fingers, fanning what were undoubtedly further chapters of *Daughter of the Bomb* onto the floor.

"Oh, for god's sake!" Margo exclaimed.

Just as I knelt to help, Marissa Kuby lunged for the papers, her shoulder banging into mine. Stunned, I toppled and lay a moment on the rug, studying the fluorescent fixture.

"Oh!" she cried in astonishment.

Scrambling to my knees, I found myself staring into her shivering eyes, azure as the sky on a cloudless summer day. She was panting, practically sobbing, and exuded the faint aroma of cigarette smoke. Remembering when adults gave off that scent, I touched her cheek.

"It's okay," I said.

I called out for Joy; then, realizing the look of the scene, staggered to my feet.

Joy glanced at Marissa Kuby, alone on her knees, and began gathering pages, which she thrust into my shaky hands. I felt tremors passing through my body. For an instant I wondered whether a small earthquake was in progress. But if so, only Marissa Kuby and I were on the fault line.

Margo stalked into our midst, seized the pages and tossed them on my desk. "He'll read them later," she said and turned to Joy. "Now, escort . . . this woman . . . to the elevator."

Marissa Kuby looked back pleadingly.

"Don't worry," I said. "I'll be in touch."

"But . . . ," she began and then, hunching her shoulders, submitted to her fate.

"What the hell was that?" Margo asked.

"I don't know."

"You should."

What could I say? A quarter century of professional experience hadn't stopped me from asking Marissa Kuby in.

As Margo started for the door, I grabbed her arm. She turned, startled—she hardly reached my shoulders—and we looked at each other at remarkably close range. I had never experienced her smallness so intimately. I peered into that uncharacteristically pale face. Under her makeup were the tiny bumps and lines of a life. She looked bad in a way I hadn't noticed before. Neither of us moved. Above the hum of the air-conditioning, the silence was so intense that I had the urge to lean down and kiss those tiny, reddened lips. And then—I don't know why—Sarah came to mind and I was overcome with fear.

Margo cocked her head. "Are you okay?"

"I feel, I don't know, dizzy."

"Listen," she said abruptly, "we got off on the wrong foot, but it doesn't have to be this way. I'm thrilled to meet Walter Groth." Her voice, surprisingly, shook with emotion. "I'm proud Byzantium represents him. I think with backing of a kind you're not used to, you could find more authors like him. We're not enemies. We . . . You and I . . . " She swallowed hard and stopped.

It was my turn to ask, "Are you all right?"

"Why shouldn't I be?" she said.

So I left it at that. I gathered Marissa Kuby's pages, evened them against the desktop, and let them slide into the wastebasket.

"I assume we're not going to publish Ms. Kuby, then. Odd name, Kuby."

"Odd enough," I acknowledged.

This was as close to small talk as we had ever come.

Only then did I notice Marissa Kuby's envelope on my desk.

"We really should go," Margo said, "or Walter Groth will read without us."

"Take my word for it, even by himself he's never alone, but I'm ready."

Of course, the photo was still there, light glinting off the face of the man who had, to believe his daughter, ushered us all into the Atomic Age. I slipped it into the envelope and licked the tip of the flap, catching the faint sourness of glue already a decade and a half stale when Kennedy announced that we might all be toast. My back to Margo, I let it slip into the wastebasket.

"So you think it's safe to leave?" she asked, and while I might not have called her expression impish, she did smile.

As we departed, she took my arm. We were almost to the elevator before I excused myself, rushed back, picked the envelope out of the trash, and placed it securely in my jacket pocket.

## AFTERNOON

You know how, depending on what loose end you pull, you can untie a bow or create an intractable knot? That day, Margo Deare picked up the loose end of me and pulled first.

I found myself mulling over her proposal while we grabbed a cab. Until that moment she hadn't been a person to me. So how was I to know she had a husband to burst into tears about?

It was a typical New York ride. We raced uptown at outrageous speed, zipped past the golden chariot of Remember the *Maine* at park's edge, and turned onto Broadway only to gridlock at 63rd Street, twenty blocks short of our destination. A couple of minutes and Margo was bawling out the cabby.

He looked like a skinhead, had the voice of an angel, and was undoubtedly an actor. "The ball of a crane went through someone's bedroom," he said. "I heard it on the news. The Upper West Side's locked dead."

"Why the hell didn't you tell us?"

"I guess I had my head up my butt. I don't like being here any more than you do."

"Margo, let's take the subway."

"I hate the subway. Let's talk about our future, starting with Walter Groth. When's his next book coming in?"

If this was the first step in her plans for us, disappointment was guaranteed. Start with my only true best-selling author and you can easily imagine me finding five or six more like him. But head out from Bob West's *Senator McCarthy and the End of Innocence* or Eugene Bell's *Bosnian Tales* or Margaret Boisoneau's *Reading the Media,* and the future takes on a different shape. It takes on my shape.

I had once imagined the book as a thoroughly modest object meant to break you into immodest spaces. On a bookshelf it would be forever. I arrived in publishing believing an editor of such a lasting thing ought to last as well. In pursuit of this faith, I had stayed put, like Larry across town or Ellen Stakowicz a few floors below me. Now they were gone, while Margo, who looked to be leaving from the moment she stormed our premises, was still here.

Twenty-two months later, her oversized office remained bare of all but a few book dumps, those inelegantly named, freestanding bookstore ads. Her shelves, of course, were filled with books, a few—like Walter Groth's—face out, the rest arranged by spine color: quadruple shelves of red, a bloc of white, a snatch of blue, a range of greens and yellows, and a quarter shelf of flaring pinks. There was no day I didn't doubt she'd be gone tomorrow. And yet here we were.

In the years since I'd joined Byzantium, Vietnam had ended as a war and revved up as a cultural event; the sixties had become advertising; Ronald Reagan, senile; the Berlin Wall, rubble; Oprah, a book club; the independent bookstore, a memory; the Amazon, a mail-order river; and former publisher, then managing director, later retiree, John Percy III had died of a heart attack while pruning tea roses at his eighteenth-century farmhouse in Westport, Connecticut. He was now turning to dust in the family plot between his grandfather, who made a fortune off a police tabloid, and his father, who founded the press to promote good Protestant fiction.

At Byzantium, Margo had inexplicably lingered. Now, she was looking to me. But you are what you edit. Her request was so simple. It's just that I was incapable of asking Walter Groth when his next book would arrive or what it would be. And since I couldn't figure out what else to do, I said so.

"Why not?" she asked bewildered.

"It's the way he wants it. Anything else would feel like betrayal."

She was looking out the window. I heard a cacophony of beeping horns. Ahead of us, a driver stepped out of his Lexus, stripped off his suit jacket, and flipped open his cell phone.

"Is that how you deal with all your authors?"

I knew she was trying. "No."

"Then why not ask? With a potential best-seller, you have no idea what it means to a sales staff to have a date and hook in place."

I knew what Walter would think of providing a "hook" for his future book. "I don't think so, Margo."

"When's it due?"

"Whenever he gets it in."

"But what does the contract say?"

"I haven't looked and he hasn't given it a second's thought. Have you read *The Heart of a Man*?"

"Of course I have."

"Then you know how he imagines the process of inner unfolding."

"Is it just that you don't like me?"

"No, Margo . . . ," I began.

"I like *him* so much! Every man in America should read him! I find him so inspiring and men are generally such fucks!"

You know how when women wept in old movies their mascara

ran? Well, she turned soundlessly to me, her face dripping wet, and something—mascara, kohl, whatever kind of plant or synthetic face paint made her eyes resemble a Keane orphan's—was running black, the way the ink comes off the *Times* on a boiling summer's day. Her fists were balled up like a child's and her tiny mouth was clenched in a pencil-thin scratch across the smudge that was her face. "That fuck! That son of a bitch left me for someone half our age."

"Who, Margo?" I said.

"My husband, you idiot!" And she began giggling, or that's what I thought until her head dropped to my shoulder and she wept copiously. I hadn't known that the woman had a husband. She might have had children, too, or Scotties, or spent her off-hours tutoring illiterates. I had never asked. Details complicate, especially in a country where every serial killer is loved by his neighbors and anyone can display the sort of pain that's indisputable proof of humanity.

Even with her head on my shoulder and my arm tightening around her—proof that I, too, was human—I had no desire to know more. But I couldn't help looking down in amazement. I had seen her bully others in a distinctly male way, and yet I found her small, shivering body in my undoubtedly male arms.

I might have let the moment pass, but on that topsy-turvy day there never seemed to be less than three of us in the space for one. I had gone years without sprawling on the floor of my office, seeing a tear, or finding Byzantium's managing director in my arms.

"I'm with *you*, lady," the driver said emphatically. "Men are for shit." He slipped a Kleenex through the payment slot. "Two months ago my boyfriend walked out. Like that." He snapped his fingers. "No warning. Nothing. And what was at stake? Just a body younger than mine."

He didn't look twenty-two.

"I cried like you at first and I was so damn pissed off!"

Margo sat up, sniffling, rubbing at her eyes. "What did you do?" she asked in a tiny voice.

"What can you do? It's how they're raised. They lack feeling. By the time you get close, it's too late. The ones with fathers are monsters and the ones without, well, what can you say?"

"Have you read any of Walter Groth's books?"

"I don't read much."

"Write down your address," she said with just a touch of enthusiasm. "I'm sending you *The Heart of a Man*. It'll knock you dead. He's got the father thing so totally down."

I heard him tearing a piece of paper. "How old's your husband?"

"Forty-three."

"And how old's she?"

"Twenty-ish."

"Then he's pursuing a fantasy of a fantasy."

"Yes," she said, "that's exactly what he's doing."

"But you know what? One day that fantasy will wake up, look at the old fart next to her, and ask, How the hell did I get here? And you already know what happens next."

"What?" You could feel her urge to be enlightened.

"She'll walk. By then you'll be with someone better, and when he comes crawling back you'll stomp him good. It's the only damn thing he'll understand. That's what I'm going to do anyway. Here's my name and address." He passed a slip of paper through the slot.

"You're so damn right!" she exclaimed. "I'm going to send you a package of books."

"One's plenty. I probably won't read it anyway. But if you have any free movie tickets . . . "

"You want to see the new Mel Gibson film?"

"You're kidding. It's not even out."

"We work for the company that distributes it. I'll send you preview tickets in the morning."

"That's so cool. You know, I'm stuck here but if you want to make eighty-third, he's right, you should get out. And that guy beside you, he was there when you needed him."

She smiled, found a twenty in her purse, and shoved it through the slot. "Keep the change."

"And you keep your head up."

And so we stepped into a bracing, early summer New York day, the sun's warmth brought to a roil by a humming sea of cars. At every restaurant, tables were out and an audience had formed to watch the spectacle that was the city.

Margo grabbed my arm. "He's right. I should marry you." Whatever my expression was, she added, "It's a joke. Anyway, three husbands would be one too many."

I decided not to ask.

"And you really aren't suitable, but I owe you. He was smarter than half our authors. We probably should have published him." She was stoked. She glanced at her watch. "It's almost two-thirty! We'll never make the reading! I'm starving!" She motioned to Fiorello's. "And we're lucky, it's not bad."

I followed her in. The restaurant, polished gold handrails and plush tomato-red decor, was almost empty. The hostess nonetheless seated us at a distant booth, possibly because Margo's face indicated an emotional moment that might not be over.

I had no urge to eat. Margo ordered minestrone, a linguini with wild mushrooms, and a small Caesar salad. "Let's share a half-bottle of wine."

I held up my hands in the negative.

She turned to the waitress. "Give us your best Chianti and a glass for him," she smiled, "so he can keep me company."

The waitress looked to me.

"Nothing thanks."

"Don't spit on Bruno Hindemann's perfectly good marks! He'll have the pizza with lobster and truffle oil. They make these fabulous paper-thin ones." She raised an eyebrow, which, given the state of her face, lent her a comical look, as a glance at the waitress indicated. Her hand went involuntarily to her cheek. For a second, her mask split open and I saw I don't know what, but it hurt. The waitress lingered as passing motorists do at the sight of an accident.

"I think the lady's hungry," I said

"Oh." She startled as if out of a dream. "I'm so sorry." And she was gone.

"I'm a mess!" Margo exclaimed. "Thank god for work! I'd be lost without it. Have you been married?"

I considered the question carefully.

"You live with someone, right?"

I nodded.

"Then you know what it's like to come home from a day at Byzantium. He works for a dotcom, so he doesn't have the foggiest. Even you don't understand, because you've never actually had to sell Walter Groth, no less that woman writing about television—"

"Margaret Boisoneau."

"Exactly. Just try to explain to the Barnes and Noble buyer why she should stock an obscure critic of TV with David Duchovny's memoirs—"

"It's not just television . . . "

"—a book that won't be reviewed in any place larger than the *Nation*. Then figure out how to make any store display it face out without a cent of co-op money. Just try getting a book like that noticed against the me-me-me of a trillion infinitely glitzier products. It can give you a migraine in thirty seconds. You wouldn't expect him to understand, but he's such a jerk about it. I stagger through the door, I haven't even picked up the phone to order Chinese, and all he wants me to do is go down on him. Now is that reasonable?"

I had an unbearable urge to look around that empty restaurant in case someone was listening.

"Do you call that a relationship? *She* probably does, but she's too young for a work permit. I should take a lover to spite him," and she looked at me appraisingly. "No one would call you good-looking, but still . . . well, never mind." And she touched her face again with no less startling effect. It was as if someone had hit the zapper. It was like the twilight zone.

"Let me sort myself out before our meal arrives," she said, excusing herself.

I sat there, surprisingly bereft.

As it turned out, watching that tiny woman devour a meal was inspiring. An appetite's an infectious thing. It wasn't long before I found myself gorging on pizza washed down with Chianti followed by tiramisu and brandy. Something like well-being swept over me.

Holding a spoon dripping with zabaglione, Margo said, "Do you mind if I speak candidly?"

I was feeling a certain glow. "Please, I treasure candidness."

"You're like some valuable, outmoded machine that needs a retrofit. I'm not knocking you, but you're an archive on how publishing used to be. My interest is in selling now. Let's face it, books are dicey products. If you're young, whatever you'll be reading in twenty years, it won't be a book. Still, you brought in Walter Groth and J. Boyle MacMurphy, so you're doing something right. The question is how to harness you to the moment. Have you noticed how noisy it is?"

I looked around.

"Not here! The selling environment."

I smiled, wafted aloft on food and wine.

"When they assigned me to Byzantium, they might as well have said Siberia. But you look for the positive. You say, can do. And so I thought, Margo, you sell these books and you can sell sno-cones to Eskimos. Succeed and you'll prove yourself to David Marsden. In the end that's all that matters at Multimedia. I took it as a life test. But I can't do it alone."

I smiled even more broadly. Life was wonderful.

"Let me tutor you in the business and, I swear, I'll free you to do the work you're capable of. We could start with Boyle MacMurphy. Do you have any idea how big he is now? A new book from him and we could write our own ticket!"

It was touching, really, a wonderful dream, and I felt so pumped in a woozy way that I could almost imagine myself part of it.

Suddenly she glanced at her watch. "Oh my god, look at the time! Put it on your expense account. And tomorrow, let's launch Byzantium into a new era." She leaned over, bussed me on the cheek, and ran for the door.

Half an hour later, the last pizza crust finished along with whatever brandy remained in my glass and hers, I stepped into the glare of the afternoon sun. In front of the restaurant, gridlocked cars still purred. Vendors were selling flowers and newspapers window to window. Heat rose from the sidewalk. My mind was blown clear of thought. It was a New York–style satori.

When I made it back to the office, Joy was not at her desk. On mine sat a small pile of message slips. Two were from Sarah. I tried her without luck at work and home. There was the normal traffic from anxious authors and would-be authors, frantic sales people and harried copyeditors. There was a message from Walter Groth: "Regrets missing you. Tomorrow Lake Como. No nuns, therapists, or e-mails. Catch you in the next world." Joy had scribbled, "His words exactly!" There was nothing from my ex-wife or Marissa Kuby.

I almost missed the last slip: "Katrina Adlebat" followed by parenthetical question marks. That brought me to my feet. Joy was by the Xerox machine sipping coffee and talking to another assistant. I waved the slip in front of her. "There's no phone number on it!"

She glanced at it disdainfully. "She didn't leave one, but she called me 'babe,' which I didn't adore and gave me her name too fast. That's an approximation. Who is she?"

I looked at my watch. "I'm locking myself in for an hour. See you then."

Before she could reply, I headed down the corridor. I was relieved that Katrina Adlebat, if that was her name, hadn't left a number. Not today. I stood in my office, hemmed in by books. My legs felt shaky. It was—I looked at my watch—only 4:45. I jammed a chair under the doorknob just as I had seen done in a million detective movies, folded my jacket so as not to crush Marissa Kuby's photos, laid my head on it, and passed out.

## EVENING

The subway ride downtown had not brought us to Patria early, yet Joy and I had been in a swirl of waiters balancing Rothko- and Riveraesque trays of Nuevo Latino food for twenty minutes before Connie and Todd stepped out of a cab. Joy was anxious. She doubted her judgment in coming and so made sardonic comments at my expense. Outside, stretch limos and beemers disgorged preening men and power-suited women, many hardly older than Joy. Money floated in the air. High-toned pheromones jostled with well-toned bodies. The atmosphere was feral. Joy undoubtedly wished she were with anyone but a guy old enough to be her father.

"Jesus," she muttered, "what if they don't come?" It never crossed her mind that I might be anxious, too. I kept glancing at that gorgeous, spindly, jittery youth, the only thing between me and a woman who did not have my best interests at heart. She stood tall in platform heels, flaring black slacks with huge flapped pockets, and a silky blouse of the most intense green— where any of them had come from I had no idea. The four holes that ran up her right earlobe held an arsenal of dangling metal. I felt immensely proud of her. I was a younger, better person in her presence.

"Here they are," I said softly.

Even amid that din I heard her little intake of breath, which made mine superfluous. Backpack dangling, cowboy booted and bejeaned, blond and rugged in a river-runs-through-it way, Todd strode in. The sleeves of his blue Oxford shirt were rolled high.

Joy leaned close and whispered, "Don't I feel the fool."

I gave her a paternal squeeze. "You look beautiful." I felt like a father about to give his daughter away.

And then he was upon us. He took my worth in a single amused glance as we shook hands.

I noticed—you weren't likely to miss them—the dark-brown Chinese characters running up his arm and under his sleeve. "What's the tattoo mean?"

"Gone fishing. Back in a billion years."

I couldn't help laughing at his self-assurance. From his right ear, too, dangled a modest arsenal.

"Joy," I said, "Todd."

From the heights he took her in appraisingly. She stepped up to him and they shook toughly like opponents before a boxing match.

He nodded toward me. "What's he like to work for?"

"You should be so lucky," she said angrily.

But before my heart could warm to the way she guarded her turf, Connie was kissing me lightly on the cheek and Joy, the tough girl of Patria, was melting. She lowered her gaze as she shook Connie's hand and, possibly for the only time in her life, said nothing.

My ex-wife held me at arm's length and considered me. It was such a hackneyed gesture, as she meant it to be. Ah, yes, after all these years, how *is* he?

What surprised me was my relief. Sarah Dixon was not with her. That had been my deepest fear, the kind you only recognize when it rears up and bites you in the face.

Grasping my shoulders, she said dramatically, "I could have done worse for a husband." Joy was visibly impressed. I said nothing. It was a statement meant for others. Somewhere an invisible audience was being seated. Her eyes slid past me to scope out the room. Age and success had filled out her face. Those dark-rimmed eyes had a certain hardness to them only an ex-husband might have noticed. She lifted a hand in distant greeting and was about to speak, perhaps to one of us, when something ate her words.

Let it be said again, the universe is a perverse place. Until that moment I was considering Connie Burian critically and with a certain self-satisfaction. But when that face came to bewildered life, I knew I still loved her, and in that second I gasped, a gargling of air no less unexpected than her missing words.

All those years I had been facing her and her alone. It was like discovering at the heart of a manuscript the pathetic openness of your own heart. I stood dumbstruck in the chaos of Patria. How could I have loved poor Sarah Dixon when it was this woman I was waiting for? I felt an oceanic longing, a sympathy for whatever I had never understood about her. There were wonders in her world. I simply couldn't see them.

We all journey unedited along the paths open to us. She had plunged down the only one available. Who could have guessed that it led directly to the new entertainment universe? I had been on a wider path leading, as it turned out, to a junkyard. But we go where we can. Isn't that the point? Isn't that history?

In the din, Joy said softly, "Are you all right?" Connie, too, was looking at me, confusion on her face. Then, unexpectedly, she smiled, a radiant burst of energy, and kissed me tenderly on the lips.

A moment later, the maitre d' greeted her by name and ushered us to a booth looking out on Park Avenue South. I was about to slide in next to her when Joy slipped in first.

Todd said, "Show Joy your newest toy."

Connie extracted a sleek, steno pad–sized object from her purse and passed it across the table. He flipped its top up and its gray surface burst to life, a flickering jewel of light and color. One-handedly he reversed the machine and presented it to Joy.

"Awesome!" she hissed.

"That's a selection from an old Kingsley Amis novel we control."

Her fingers were already moving on the microkeyboard. "What else can it call up?"

"Not much. It's only a prototype. Some Shakespeare, the Amis, bits of a few other books. But someday it'll hold a universal library and you'll be able to talk with an author, catch scenes from the movie, access any newspaper on earth, plan your trip to Tibet, or check out a friend on screen, and that probably won't be the half of it."

He retrieved the machine from Joy with a proprietary gentleness and handed it to me. "Meet Q," he said. "Officially it's the Q-Print, product of an alliance among MIT's Media Lab, Dell, AOL, and us. It's the closest anyone's come to the feel of a book in the electronic universe."

I balanced the shimmering object on my palm. I was in the presence of a wonder from Connie's world. Surprisingly light, it throbbed in my hand. "What's Q stand for?"

"Quasar," Todd said. "They undoubtedly wanted to associate it with the primordial power of the universe."

"An excessive claim can reveal the fears behind it," I said.

Todd threw his head back and laughed.

"He doesn't believe in computers," Joy said, embarrassed.

I looked at Connie. "I just can't imagine one of these things replacing a book."

She sighed. "Decades pass and I still know what you're going to say. Boo-hoo, we're taking the book down with us. But answer me this: Could a medieval illuminator have imagined Gutenberg's effect on the word?"

She narrowed her eyes slightly and considered me. I said nothing.

"That Gothic typeface of his was so fucking unreadable! This thing's revolutionary, but like his press it's got a long way to go. Take a look at Q! Read it. Yes, by all means, *read* it. It won't bite. It doesn't *bite*." Joy and Todd were staring. The coolest woman in the business was losing it. "As a matter of fact, it should thrill you. If this works, a trillion kids younger than they are may actually read something without a tree being lost."

Icons dripped from the screen, evidence of a new technology intent on organizing the book in unknown ways. The shimmering words riveted themselves to my brain. There were no words to describe them or any question of not looking, but read? I couldn't.

"I can tell you hate it," she said angrily. "I don't know why I bothered."

At that moment, the waiter announced himself as Eduardo-who-was-to-serve-us-tonight, and asked if we would care to order drinks.

Struggling to master her irritation, Connie picked up the menu. On its cover was an immodestly elegant image of a fluted bronze leaf.

"It's a Fili," she said to Todd.

"She can do more with a menu than anyone on earth."

Joy would normally have rolled her eyes and said something sarcastic. Instead she shot a warning glance my way.

"Bring us a guacamole," Connie said. "And I'll have a Kir to calm myself."

I ordered a Sam Adams, Joy and Todd, scotches. He insisted on Macallan's single malt and a smile passed between them.

The surprising thing was, I could no longer imagine what I had to fear. Sooner or later we would be alone. I would take her news like the man I was in the process of becoming. I would wait for a path to open and, as an editor of life, head down it with panache.

I was still holding the Q-Print. Connie smiled encouragingly. "I'm trying to remind myself that you're not used to Q. Just think to yourself, this may remind me of a book but it's something else entirely." She spoke as if to a child.

"They should make it with a faux cover," Todd said. "Then old-fashioned readers would feel more comfortable."

"If they perfect electronic ink, he'll be happy because it'll be so totally p-bookish," Joy added brightly.

Connie turned to her. "Unfortunately, e-ink doesn't work when millions of pixels are at stake, but even Q, crude as it is, tells us things about the book we've had no way of grasping for the last half millennium."

"Like what?" The sarcasm in my voice surprised me.

"As a start, *as a start,* we've thought of the book as a unitary thing, a thing in itself, when it's really the equivalent of a cardboard box, a simple container whose contents, the collected stuff of five hundred years, can be dumped out anywhere."

I sighed and handed Q back. "I can't think of a cardboard box as a book analog."

"The image seems infelicitous to you only because you don't grasp the electronic world."

I shrugged. I was ready to concede.

"But there's a bright side, Rick, even for you. There's hope for the serious book . . . " She edited herself. "The content of the serious book, anyway. After all, what's the basic problem a publisher faces? You're printing seventy-five hundred copies of some book you love. It's not Stephen King, it's not about a celebrity, it's not focused on a hot topic, it's not a new novel by Michael Ondaatje. Still, you want to give it a fair shake in the world. You want to advertise and tour the author. So you crunch the numbers—I've done it a thousand times for editors like you—and the p-and-l statement gives you the chills. If you're honest about what can be done, the answer is nothing. *Nothing.*"

"It's cross your fingers and hope," chimed in Todd.

"You know why only the book can't support itself in companies like Multimedia, Viacom, or Time Warner?"

"Too modest an object?" I said.

"Hardly. *Hardly.* It's lack of advertising. Music, film, TV, DVD, the Internet, magazines, newspapers, comics, sports, everything is ad-driven. Every other form carries its weight in ads." Fervor lit her face. "Why ads haven't made it inside the book I'll never understand. But now they will. Dump its contents into the Q and you can break the book down into chunks suitable for an ad environment. You'll be able to run ads down the sides and in the corners. You'll be able to promote the movie and sell the T-shirt. In the world we're creating, the book will finally be capable of standing alone."

She smiled. Her voice had calmed. "In a future *Middlemarch*, the church will offer public service ads when Casaubon appears, the drug companies will support Lydgate, and architectural firms can pitch their wares while Dorothea reorganizes the housing of the poor." My expression must have told all because she added, "I thought the least I could do was drive you over the edge of our brave new world."

Just then Eduardo reappeared to ask about refills. She said, "Why don't you kids go enjoy yourselves?"

Todd took the hint. "I know a place with fantastic Ecuadorian seviche and afterward the editors of *The Baffler* are reading at the St. Mark's Bookstore." He turned to me. "Do you know *The Baffler*? It specializes in young writers with attitude."

Connie growled, "Todd . . ."

"Okay, okay." He looked at Joy. "*On y va?*"

"Whatever. I guess seviche is okay, but there's a slam at the Nuyorican Café and music down the street. If you dance, that is."

"I can move my feet."

They both got up.

Connie said, "Nice to meet you, Joy."

Shaking her hand, Joy went silent. "But Rick," she said suddenly, "I need to talk to you a sec about tomorrow."

I slipped out of the booth.

Joy grabbed me by the arm as we plunged into a milling mass of waiting diners. "She must think I'm an idiot!"

"Her presence made you shy, and I'll tell her about you anyway."

"You'll tell her I'm a smart-ass numbskull who doesn't read interesting magazines. Todd tried to show me up, didn't he?"

"I think he was mainly out to impress me."

She paused. "There's a theory just weird enough to be right. So you'll say something?"

"I promise."

"Rick, why are we here? What's going on?"

"I think I'll find out once you leave, but you were here to protect me."

"That's a truly weird thing to say."

I smiled at her.

"So, did I?"

"You did your best."

"I can't believe you and she . . . Maybe you'll remarry."

I ignored that. "I suppose I owe you for Todd?"

"He's kind of a jerk, isn't he? But guys usually are, in public. You just have to know how to deal with them. What's seviche, anyway?"

"Marinated raw fish."

"Oh, gross. I hope they eat something else in Ecuador."

Trailing behind us, Todd had grown bored. "Hey, you ready?"

She looked him up and down. "The question is, are you ready?"

We shook hands. "Maybe I'll give you a call," he said. "I could introduce you to a couple of talented young writers at *The Baffler*."

"Have you ever gone out with someone who wanted your job?" Joy asked. Then she kissed me quickly on the cheek. That was a first. "Don't forget your promise."

"Cross my heart."

"So he has a heart," said Todd.

She laughed and gave him a little shove toward the door like the guy she wasn't.

When I returned to the booth, I found a man in a floral shirt seated where Todd had been. He was shouting into a cell phone whose antenna sprouted above a gelled hairline the height of a Mohawk, the width of a flattop, with the peaks of a mountain range. Connie patted the seat next to her. "Mark Rider from Via-com, normally out on the coast, but miraculously here tonight. We've been plotting for a year to turn *When Darkness Falls* into a global blockbuster."

Rider reached over and shook my hand vigorously. "Our focus groups give us uniquely high hopes. Connie's a gem and she tells me you could be a source for us."

"The lowest profile editor in the business, I told Mark, but don't be deceived, *don't* be deceived. He's always had an eye for the long shot." And she offered me a look so intimate it stunned me.

Rider folded the phone into his breast pocket. Though he leaned forward as if to impart private information, his voice boomed across the room. "A story's to a movie what a nuclear reactor is to an atomic sub, and it's editors like you who can put those reactors in our hands. We just picked up Barricade Films, so we're looking for lower profile, higher concept projects. Quirkier, more idiosyn-cratic, like *The Full Monte,* the sort you might run across."

The name Barricade rang a bell. "Isn't that Rob DuVeen's company?"

"DuVeen was legendary. Died this spring. Heart attack, hang-gliding. Came down in Pasadena. It was all over the trade papers. Company's been floundering ever since."

"God," I muttered.

"Lived hard, died on landing. Not a bad epitaph for a producer. He was putting together a Vietnam epic with Oliver Stone, but that's dead in the water now."

"You knew DuVeen?" Connie asked.

I nodded. "We lived together in that commune in New Haven in sixty-eight. Jesus, how bizarre." The truth was I couldn't tell if it meant anything to me. From the perspective of Patria, all those nights we spent talking might as well have been on Mars.

"He was the genuine thing," Rider said. "Very unique. I met him once. Looked like he was answering a casting call for the Elec-tric Kool-Aid Acid Test."

I turned to Connie. "He introduced me to Larry."

"Ah, Larry . . . " She let his name dangle there. "The only editor with a lower profile than yours."

"No profile at all. S and S axed him almost a year ago."

"So I heard."

Rider's shirt burbled. He pulled the phone out, upped the antenna, and began barking away.

Connie leaned close and, in what passed for a whisper in the din of Patria, said, "I wanted you to hear it from me. After all these years, I'm coming over to Multimedia. David Marsden convinced me to take the plunge and I . . . "

For the second time that evening she came up short. She cocked her head slightly. "I'm under so goddamn much stress." She stopped again.

I couldn't say what was going on in my head. I had a dead friend in there, and her news, and then there was love. Someone walks into the crosshairs of your desire, of everything you never imagine is inside you, and there it is. Even if you can't drive a car or read a comic, you can experience love. And evidently it lingers in your system like chickenpox, long after its identifying marks disappear.

We sat within a hair's breadth of each other like two exhausted animals. She got her wind back first. "It's a challenge," she said. "Among other things, Marsden's asked me to oversee the full range of Multimedia's operations in new and electronic media. It's a formula for failure, imagining how a major content-provider should interface with audiences that hardly exist yet."

"I don't see you failing," I said quietly.

"How touching. A vote of confidence from my ex-husband." A tiny smile lit her face, lending it an indescribable vulnerability. Then she touched my cheek, while the world seemed to fall away. "And Rick," she murmured, "there's always the past, isn't there? *Isn't there?*" She looked at me with fondness. "You might say I'm supposed to bring Multimedia's past into the present and prepare for the future. When a company buys small firms profligately with synergy in mind, sometimes it ends up with a pile of rubble. Such is the case here." She laughed almost silently. Perhaps the image pleased her, or maybe she felt a tidal flow of words within. I only know she took away her hand.

"D and D has at least eight separate publishing units, not counting tiny imprints, paperback lines, and floaters like Counterforce or Pegasus. They duplicate, compete with, and bid against each other. A number of them lose money. It's madness, a classically profitless proposition that can't go on. I'm anointed," she smiled. "*Anointed* to turn this unwieldy mess into a well-oiled entertainment machine expected to yield fifteen percent at day's end. Byzantium's not exempt."

As I started to protest, she put an exceedingly cool finger to my lips. "*Shhh.* It's not at the top of my list. It might be months before I get near it. But I will. I wanted you to know that. Your help would mean something to me. And even if Byzantium were to go, you wouldn't. I meant what I said to Mark about how deceptively low profile you are."

"Ah," I said, "Walter Groth."

"Walter Groth indeed."

"At least it isn't just sentiment for an ex-husband."

"Precisely, an ex-husband. *Ex.* The question you and I will have to face isn't a sentimental one. It's practical, like me. What value still lies in the Byzantium name?"

"What's in a name?"

"A question asked since sixteen hundred. Does Byzantium add brand value to a book's spine? Do readers care who publishes a book?" She waited, as if these were real questions we should indeed discuss.

"You're thinking of wiping out almost a century of publishing history," I said. "Most of those units you're supposed to deal with were once independent houses."

"'Were' is the operative word."

"So all history leads to one company?"

"You make me sound like such an idiot, which I most distinctly am not."

This, of course, wasn't the conversation I meant to be having. "Connie," I said, "I think you're anything but an idiot. Still, the impulse lurking here—"

"The impulse I represent, you mean."

" . . . seems to be taking us toward a one-publishing-house world."

"Well, down here at ground level all I can see is a riot of overlapping outfits that make no sense to anybody. No sense at all."

"Shouldn't history still count for something, even when profits are at stake?"

"You and Larry," she snorted. "Neither of you cared for capitalism. But correct me if I'm wrong: It's the only thing we've got. It's what hired me and I'm not complaining."

"What was it with you and Larry anyway?"

She looked at me oddly. "Let's skip Larry."

"Well, I'm not going to help you wipe Byzantium off the face of the earth."

"That sounds so hyperbolic. *Hyperbolic.* I never understood how you could be so quiet and hyperbolic at the same time."

"Without the sixties, without Larry, without you, maybe I would have been quiet and nothing else."

"If a publisher's been reduced to a name the way Byzantium's been, it's already more or less gone, isn't it? You can't think I'm wiping out glorious publishing houses and a hundred years of backstory. I'm not even trying to make you unhappy. What if you had heard about my arrival from a company press release?"

"I'd feel upset. But I'm upset now. You—someone anyway— is going to do away with Byzantium. The process is pretty far along already. You're right about that. And all in the name of something that can't happen. No one's ever going to make fifteen percent off books. Not actual books anyway. They're too strange. Most of the time you just can't tell which will sell. Important ones don't but should be there anyway, or they sell too slowly, or years too late. I took the sainted Dr. Groth's book for ridiculous reasons from a selling point of view, but neither you nor I would ever have picked it for best-sellerdom. Not in a million years."

"I knew it would go like this! That you'd make me feel defensive. I'm proud of what I've done in this business. I'm not a yahoo. I read books, and not just books that work commercially! If someone has to do this, and someone does, it's good it's me. It's *good,* and I'm going to do it, and now you know I'm going to do it. I knew you'd have a problem because it's me. You should be rejoicing. At least, I've been straight with you. Shit happens."

"Talk to Margo Deare. She'll see eye to eye with you."

Connie laughed loud enough for Rider to look over. "I can assure you of one thing. Margo won't be sticking around."

"But why . . . ?"

She looked at me as if I were mad. "Why? You know why. Because I'm a class act and she's not. And why would you care? You hate her. That's a given. I just don't want you to hate me, too."

"What I feel about you I don't begin to understand."

"Rick—" she began plaintively.

But just then Rider pulled out a business card and snapped it between thumb and forefinger. It made a faint popping sound and reappeared two fingers down. He held it out triumphantly. "Lucky man, you've won the lottery. A lot of people would die to work for Connie."

Eduardo returned to run through the night's specials. I took Rider's card and stood up. "I should be going."

"Next time I blow through, let's lunch. If Connie says we've got things to talk about, we'll be in bed before you can blink."

Connie touched my arm gently. "Stay and I swear I'll argue about publishing till we're bleary-eyed." She turned to Rider. "He's like one of those cult films you only appreciate when someone explains it to you."

I shook hands with Rider. "Tonight's probably not my night."

"You don't know," Connie responded brightly. "Maybe you should wait it out." She slipped from the booth, took me by the arm, and leaned close. "You're not angry, are you? After all these years I don't know why I care, but I do."

I felt around inside the way you grope for a light switch in a dark room. "I don't think I'm angry."

"That's great! Then the worst is over and the best's still to come." Her eyes flicked off me one more time, and in that second I felt unbearably alone. Then she smiled that smile I hadn't spent time with in almost a quarter century, said, "See you soon," and sent me spinning out of Patria.

## NIGHT

I was a block up 20th Street when I realized Connie had promised two surprises and only delivered one, another block before I remembered my promise to Joy. It was like waking from a dream to discover you'd missed a meeting. I retraced my steps, but where Patria's light spilled onto the pavement I stopped. I felt normal enough. I just couldn't make myself take another step.

Finally, I headed aimlessly uptown. Despite the city's reputation for unending life, I passed no one until, to my surprise, I was suddenly disgorged into Times Square, that blinking, scrolling, winking ad that climbs the heavens, while buying, touring humanity clogs the sidewalks below. Music hung in the air. Billboards flashed. Sheer cliff sides were consumed by shimmering visions. Theaters glowed like jewels. Brand names loomed like colossi astride the earth. Glass that scaled the heights revealed vistas of toys and dolls, sneakers and T-shirts, CDs and DVDs, Letterman mugs, Calvin Klein underwear, and hip-hop space suits. It was capitalism in a million colors and a river of energy ran through it. I was swept along like a book in the busy entertainment universe.

You could at least pay for the world to stop and so I spun into the Stardust Dine-o-Mat, a simulacrum of a World War II diner. It was just after nine according to a General MacArthur clock with corncob-pipe hands, and tourists were still waiting for booths while ogling photos, news stories, and model planes from my birth-war. I slipped past the line and settled onto an empty stool at an old-fashioned soda fountain. Opposite me was the famed photo of a sailor sweeping a young woman into an extravagant VJ Day kiss on this very square. I opened the Takeoff and Landing Menu and considered the U.S.S. *Enterprise* all-hands-on-board giant grilled-cheese sandwich before settling on a vanilla egg cream and a hot dog. These I ordered from a boy dressed in military khakis, a white apron, and a standard-issue army cap, whose name, Phil, was pinned like a medal to his chest.

Despite the fountain, Phil did not make the egg cream. It arrived from the innards of the Stardust, lacking the edge of intense sweetness that should send shivers through you. Four Japanese men in dark suits occupied a nearby booth. The former enemy on holiday talked with animation as they stared at the icons of someone else's war.

I had the urge to walk south to 42nd Street, where the Disney store now stood, and meet my father, dead these many years. I could almost see him, fedora rakishly cocked, his glistening face, the face I never knew, expectant and vulnerable just as in Marissa Kuby's photograph. The crowds would be breaking up, the victory celebration coming to an end . . . and we would begin again.

I stared at the rippled mustard on my half-eaten hot dog, then out onto the night-lit streets where the crowds surged by. I knew what was missing here: Luther Kuby's mission. I felt just over my heart for his daughter's envelope, gently unhinged the flap, dipped a finger in, and touched the two tiny photos the way you might a talisman.

[ 195 ]

On the day war ended in Europe and a sailor bent over a woman for a kiss, a tiny group of officials in Washington were discussing Japanese cities, one of which would disappear thanks, in small part, to a professionally done job by navigator Kuby. Yet no chain of Dine-o-Mats would ever serve atomic fireball candies or display Day-Glo posters showing off the eerie glory of an atomic explosion. None of the Stardust's dust would settle over the father who left that war closed and bitter, or the daughter who, on page 147 of her uncompleted memoir, was about to join a group arrested and jailed in 1979 for pouring pig's blood on a spot in the Nevada desert where a missile sat targeted on Russia.

Here was the strange thing: I had hardly given a thought to Rob DuVeen, obliterated in the spring, or Marissa Kuby's manuscript, which suffered a similar fate that afternoon, or Margo, who would soon be looking for more than a husband, or my own Sarah. My day, like the Stardust, was missing elements. But I could feel the tears and they seemed humiliatingly real.

As I lurched into the aisle, I had an urge to sweep those Japanese men aside, sit in their booth, and weep. Families waiting for tables parted like the Red Sea in *The Ten Commandments* and I stumbled out, tears streaming down my face as tourists recoiled. Never in my life had my father's face glistened with tears. I wiped furiously at my eyes and staggered on. At Columbus Circle, I struck out for the comforting darkness of the park. I wanted to turn back, but it was too late and there was no doubt where I was going. I had, it seemed, been going there all along.

At 72nd, I cut across to Broadway. Feeling calmer, emptier, I dumped a quarter in a pay phone and dialed our number. Sarah's familiar voice reassured me: We were only momentarily occupied; one of us would get back to me at the earliest possible moment. To believe our machine, Connie hadn't returned, Rob hadn't landed, Margo wasn't gone, and I had a partner to go home to. We had three messages, it confided, in what it still called our mailbox. A man's voice, unknown to me, came on first. "Sarah, dear, I'm running late. My editor called with last-minute changes. But I'll be there by four." The voice, mellow and comforting—I already liked the man who owned it—added something blurry, perhaps "kisses," or "best wishes," or even "missed you." The message, the machine assured me, had arrived at 3:10 P.M., while I was in Fiorello's drinking Chianti and imagining another life.

Next came a woman's voice that quickened my heart. "Oh, so you really are nowhere, not at work, not at home. Truly, you're a man of mystery. I've seen water bugs easier to pin down." She chuckled. "Anyway, this is Kathy Adambak. Have you heard from Wendell Moore yet? Antonia and he—" The message limit kicked in.

Then her voice was back. "Even your machine won't talk to me! Okay, I'll be brief. This is Kathy Adambak. That's A-d-a-m-b-a-k, Katrina, if you want to reach me via the museum's phone system. Hugh Brown and I each have something to discuss with you." That came in at 7:49. It was now, the machine informed me, 10:39. My limitless day seemed to be winding down without an end in sight. I turned my hand palm up and wrote A-d-a-m-b-a-k on my left wrist just above my watchband.

My path took me past the 83rd Street Barnes & Noble. In its window a poster still promoted Walter Groth's afternoon reading. A gift was in order. I walked past display tables laden with books whose presence had largely been determined by the finances of their publishers. At the information desk a young man in a flannel shirt was talking on the telephone. He gave me a friendly smile and went right on.

"Excuse me," I finally said.

He put his hand over the receiver and asked, "How can I help you."

"Well, two things . . ."

He rolled his eyes heavenward.

" . . . I'm Walter Groth's editor and was wondering how his reading went."

"I'm sure it went well."

"Any idea how many books were sold?"

Cradling the receiver he began typing into a computer. "G-r-o-w-t-h?"

"G-r-o-t-h. He was here this afternoon."

"We've had three or four events since, and this damn thing—" He broke off in disgust. "You should call our community representative, Ben Schwartz, in the morning. He knows everything." He grimaced, though perhaps it was meant as a smile, and returned to his conversation.

"Excuse me," I said again.

"Abby, we'd better call it a night . . . Okay . . . Soon." He hung up. "Sorry. It's late and I got lazy. Now, how can I help you?"

"Thanks. I'm looking for a copy of Robert Jay Lifton's *Hiroshima in America*."

"Okay, let's see." And he began typing again. "L-i-f-t-o-n, right? Oh god, I don't know what it is with this system!" And he banged the keyboard in frustration. "This is the gazillionth time the screen's frozen. I'm not sure I can get in."

"Well, where would I find the book if you had it."

"Maybe under Travel on the mezzanine?" he said doubtfully. "What's it about?"

"The atomic bomb's fallout in American society. It's kind of popular history."

"Well, Popular Culture is up on the—Look, the truth is I'm helpless without this," and he gestured at the computer. "When the systems go down, well, look at this place."

And I did so. It was, of course, a palace of books, its elegant wooden shelves rising with the escalator toward the entertainment heavens.

"Just try to find a book here!"

"I get your point. I guess I'll take my chances."

"Good luck," he called after me.

And so I ascended past New Releases, Best-sellers, New Paperback Fiction, New Paperback Nonfiction, bookmarks, mugs, tote bags, calendars, daybooks and audio books, New Hardcover Fiction, Science Fiction, the café, Mystery, Travel and Tourism, Children and Young Adult, Cookbooks, Computer Books, Bargain Books, Paperback Fiction, and somewhere in the far reaches of the top floor amid special tables, discount tables, and Our-Staff-Picks, I found History, American, Twentieth Century, just beyond Psychology, before Sociology, near Popular Culture, this side of Self-Help, across the way from Personality, up the aisle from Reference, and it was there I began to check spines. Stephen Ambrose and John Dower, Tom Brokaw and Gary Wills, Ann Douglas and a mis-shelved Nostradamus, a flood of World War II, a spate of Vietnam. There were books I had loved, books I was curious about, and books I couldn't have given less of a damn about, but no Lifton and no one unattached to a computer to ask.

The small bookstore that, via someone's quirky taste, had once opened portals to so many worlds, was gone, and with it, a scale of existence appropriate to reading. All around me, prospective readers sat at tables or slumped on the floor, leafing through books or magazines or just gazing into space. The young exchanged glances. A kissing couple snuggled where Reference and Humor met. It wasn't so much the book that drew you here, but the palace that held it, the playland that surrounded it, the restaurant that nestled inside it. It felt opulent and unrestrained. It demanded submission or departure. So I stepped back onto the escalator and descended slowly into the atrium and then, bookless, into the Broadway night.

Just past Amsterdam, I found the aged, five-story sliver of a building. Even in the darkness of that ill-lit block, it looked battered. I climbed the steps I'd been heading toward since I first noticed the address on Marissa Kuby's envelop and, squinting in the dim hall light, read the names on the bells. 4A was M. Kuby. I pushed hesitantly. Nothing happened. I pushed again and the voice box crackled, emitting a buzz broken by flashes of static.

"Who is it?"

"Marissa?"

"Who's there?" The words arrived exhausted.

"It's Rick Koppes," I shouted. "I know it's late, but could I come up a minute?"

"Who?"

"Rick Koppes!"

The buzzer rattled like a cicada. I turned the knob and pushed, but the door refused to budge. I fingered the bell again. "Marissa, one more time!" There was another squawk. But I couldn't open it. I was peering into the stairwell in frustration when flip-flops appeared followed by the bottom edge of an old yellow bathrobe and a hand dangling a cigarette.

She stopped a few feet away and stared back at me through the glass. Had she come any closer, her weary face would have passed from sight. She let out a thin stream of smoke and considered me.

"You're not going to publish it, are you?" she said. The voice, tired and disbelieving, matched the face.

"No, I'm not."

She thought about that a moment. "Why not? James Carroll's book about his father won a National Book Award."

"I don't think yours is good enough."

"Not good enough for your publishing house or any publisher?"

"Any publisher." I didn't have words left for the finer distinctions.

"Couldn't you be wrong? You must make mistakes. I mean, who are you anyway?"

"I could be wrong, but I don't think so."

"What's so bad about it?"

I thought that over. "Something's missing, I can't tell you what."

"That's not helpful."

"I suppose not. Maybe you're just not a writer."

"I started writing in prison. Every day for sanity. This world could go up in smoke. Won't you help me? Isn't that what an editor does?"

My legs felt shaky. "Could I come up for a few minutes?"

She took another puff. "Being in jail didn't do shit for me then, did it?"

I pressed my hand against the wall, resting the weight of my body on it. I hadn't said I had her photos. She hadn't made a move to open the door.

"How could you have invited me in if you knew all along?"

I was too tired to shrug.

"Maybe you considered me a freak."

It wasn't a harsh statement, no harsher at least than the others. Perhaps I had considered her a freak. My behavior was already beyond my understanding and she was, after all, the daughter of the man who . . . "Why do you want to be a writer?"

She stared at me without reply.

"We're drowning in books, and if the world doesn't go up in smoke, it won't be a book we're thanking." This was about as philosophical as I was going to get in a dingy hallway in the middle of the night.

She took a last drag on her cigarette and crushed it with a flip-flop. Then she solved the mystery of the door by opening it in my direction and began the long climb to the fourth floor, her shoulders drooping, flip-flops slapping. I held tight to the banister, half-pulling myself upward in that gloomy stairwell.

On the fourth-floor landing, I drifted down a tiny hallway and into a modest room crammed with a life's possessions. Books ran up the back wall. A large futon, blankets thrown aside, pillows still dented, left only modest space to pass to an open-doored bathroom. Beside the bed was a small wooden desk topped by a computer surrounded by piles of magazines. Clothes and yet more books were scattered on a tiny two-seat couch. I sagged onto the futon, letting out an involuntary sigh.

She kicked off her flip-flops and lit a cigarette. "Would you like some wine?"

I nodded and without another word she passed into the next room, closing the door.

A framed mushroom-cloud poster with the words "One World or None" was on the opposite wall. Above her desk hung a group photo too small to make out. Curiosity's a powerful thing. To my surprise I found myself on my feet. Four women, two men, one a priest with collar, were arranged in a ragged line on a rocky plain that looked like the planet Mars. A woman in a flowery dress hugged a gallon milk container. Behind them I could just make out a barbed wire fence and part of a sign with the word FORBID-DEN on it. The younger Marissa Kuby was not among them and yet I never doubted I was looking at six of the Reno 7 and that she was the photographer.

I circled the futon to examine her bookshelves. It was irresistible, like a glimpse into the soul. I noted two shelves on nature: tree, butterfly, and bird guides, regional walks and rustic inns, Terry Tempest Williams and Thoreau. At floor level, where former lives tend to congregate, I found a small collection of philosophy and psychology books: Kierkegaard and Sartre, de Beauvoir and Horney, Jung and Adler. At eye level were memoirs—O'Brien, Carroll, Woolf, McCarthy, Karr, Kingston, Dillard, Hooks, Cleaver, Wurtzel, Alexie—and above them, pop psych, including a Walter Groth paperback. And then there were the nuclear books stretch-ing up one wall, complete, obsessive, by city or subject: *Hiroshima, Hiroshima Diary, The Hiroshima Murals, Hiroshima Notes, Death in Life: Survivors of Hiroshima, The Hiroshima Panels, Hiroshima No Pica, The Impact of the A-Bomb, Hiroshima and Nagasaki 1945–85, Nagasaki, A Song for Nagasaki, Living Beneath the Atomic Cloud: The Testimony of the Children of Nagasaki, The Bells of Nagasaki, Nagasaki Journey, Na-gasaki Bomb Series, Doctor at Nagasaki, The Children of the Atomic Bomb, Barefoot Gen,* and *Black Rain* among so many others. There were books on the decision to drop the bomb and the origins of the Cold War, on the Enola Gay controversy and the anti-nuclear movement. I saw Feis and Alperovitz, Boyer and Weart, Rhodes, Harwitt, and Caldicott, the transcript of *The Day After* and *The Anti-Nuclear Handbook*. I even spotted Lifton's *Hiroshima in America*.

I plucked out an oversized paperback, *Unforgettable Fire, Pictures Drawn by Atomic Bomb Survivors*. The title rang a faint bell from that late seventies moment when her movement was reaching its height. An elegant mushroom cloud enswathed in fire rose over a processional of tiny figures on an otherwise white cover.

"Everyone on earth should have a copy of that." She rested my wine and her drink on the edge of the bookshelf and pulled out another paperback. "This was the Japanese version. I picked it up at the Peace Museum in Hiroshima years ago." Her voice sparked with life. She leaned against me, looking over my shoulder as I leafed through the book. "That one, the man in the flames, you can't really see it but he's holding a rice ball, the only possession he has left. It was a central image for Jonathan Schell's *The Fate of the Earth*."

I flipped another page. "Oh," she exclaimed with a sigh. "That's so terrible . . . and beautiful. The pictures are so . . . ." She paused. "I don't know. Some of them are actually pretty. Isn't that strange? It's only when you take in the descriptions the survivors wrote that . . . here . . . " Leaning over my shoulder, she began to read a passage, her voice choking. "'This is the scene of the courtyard of the present Hiroshima Prefectural Hospital. The girl sitting in the center is me. I was gazing at my mother and younger brother who were both totally burned. My brother died around noon before my eyes.'"

She broke off suddenly. "It's strange. Even in Japan, it's Hiroshima, Hiroshima. It doesn't pay to be second. No one expects the world to end twice. My dad . . . " She paused, her voice throbbing with emotion. I thought she might burst into tears.

I reached into my pocket for her envelope. "You left this."

Slipping it into her robe pocket, she handed me my wine, picked up what might have been a gin and tonic, and walked to her desk. She undid the robe's sash, shook the garment off, and draped it over the back of the chair. She was wearing a muumuu-like white nightgown. She held out her glass. "To your visit."

She took several quick gulps and then, bunching her nightgown at the waist, pulled it over her head in a single motion. She held it wadded in one hand, while I stared at her breasts. It was unavoidable and shocking. She watched me for a moment, then dropped the muumuu, reached down, and stepped out of her panties.

I was still staring as I began peeling off my clothes. She had revealed an impressively large body, thick in the waist, pocked and scarred, reddened and darkened, ruined in the way bodies can be at a certain age. In my dreams long ago I had crept across just such a landscape, cratered and close-up, while the mushroom cloud rose, the heat seared my arm, and the city went down. Strangely, my penis began to stiffen.

We stood, looking at each other, her gaze as naked, as frontal as she was. I glanced at my penis, quivering and unsupported. I had not thought beyond this. No, I hadn't faintly thought this far.

"Would you turn out the light?" she asked.

I took a breath. This was my strangest editorial meeting. "Are you doing this because you hope I'll publish your book?"

"Probably."

"I'm serious, I'm not going to. Even if I wanted to, I doubt I'd be there long enough." That was news to me, but what wasn't that day?

I caught a flicker of emotion, evidence perhaps of fantasies, private and carefully woven, heading for the floor where our clothes now lay. She faced me, an unlit cigarette in one hand. There was something indisputably powerful about that dark patch of pubic hair, exposed and unprotected. I had an urge to be inside her and yet I yearned for words. How could you climb inside someone's skin, if it wasn't also a skin of words?

I touched the switch on the wall. The overhead light blinked out. She clicked off a tensor lamp as she settled onto the futon and we were plunged into darkness. I sank to the bed and rolled toward her, reaching out blindly. I touched flesh. My fingers moved tentatively over the roughness that was her. I tried to approach her as an editor, as if on that body I would find the manuscript she hadn't written. I could hear her steady breathing. I reached to touch her face, but whatever I touched, it wasn't a face.

Her hand, cool and firm, grasped my penis. She held it tightly, the way you might a stick. The room was laced with the musty scent of cigarettes. I peered into the darkness.

"Do you have a condom?" she asked.

"No."

"I don't either." She paused. "I guess that means you didn't plan to bed me."

I took a deep breath. "I have no idea why I'm here."

She laughed in a full-throated way and her hand shook my penis uncomfortably.

"That's how I felt in the photo you were looking at." She laughed again. "I was peeking at you. We had our wire cutters and Marsha had the pig's blood, and they were all so committed, and the only thing I thought when I took the picture, when we cut through the fence, when the MPs grabbed us, was, Marissa, whatever are you doing here?"

The tensor light flashed on. I blinked. I was eye level with her nipples, one hand on her calf, the other on her shoulder, a parody of one of those Pompeian couples who were buried in each other's arms.

"Would you like to see the second photo?"

To my relief, she released me to reach into the pocket of her robe. Then she patted the sheet beside her. I scrunched up the bed and, side by side, we considered a snapshot of a Japanese girl that might once have been destined for a school yearbook.

"She almost never let herself be photographed," Marissa Kuby said.

"Why not?"

"Shame. That was the commonest response among survivors. And look." She touched a minute dark spot above her collar. "She couldn't completely cover the keloids. They stretched all the way up her back wherever her flesh had burned."

"So she was at . . . "—I hesitated—"Hiroshima?"

"It never fails." She laughed, more harshly this time. "Akiko was four and living in Nagasaki when the second bomb went off."

"And you knew . . . Akiko?"

"The American Friends Service Committee put us in touch. I don't know how I heard of them. I was twelve. It was practically like contacting the Communist Party then. I requested a pen pal from Nagasaki."

"Did you tell your father?"

"No, but he was usually there when the postman arrived. He'd hand her letters to me when I came home from school. This was the fifties. No one got letters from Japan. I thought he'd kill me. I was so, so terrified." Her voice seemed to shiver. "But she gave me courage. And he never said anything. Sometimes when he gave them to me— this may sound strange—I'd feel like she was our special secret, like whatever I couldn't say, I said through her, and whatever he wanted to be forgiven for came back to me via her letters. What's this?" She grabbed my wrist and began spelling out Adambak.

"Someone's name."

"Do you usually write names on your arm?"

"No."

She snatched a pen off the desk and began writing K-U-B-Y just under Adambak. "Now you have two special names on your flesh." And she laughed again. "I should write Akiko's. She was so special. I visited her in Nagasaki the year I got out of prison. She had made a life for herself, even without a husband or child. They were like outcasts, the survivors. But she was such a beautiful soul. I'm dedicating my book to her."

That sobered me. Her manuscript was still with us, a small shrine to her father and a Japanese girl missing from the first six chapters, something I thought better of mentioning. "Were you ever married?" I asked.

"No, never."

I wasn't surprised. She seemed like an American survivor.

"And you?" she asked.

"Once, long ago."

"Akiko died in 1991."

"Was it from . . . ?"

"You can't prove it, but the statistics don't lie."

"How did Akiko feel about your dad's . . . "—I hesitated—"role in her life?"

When she spoke it was with discomfort. "I couldn't bring myself to tell her. Each time I found myself . . . at the edge of something and couldn't . . . go over. I felt . . . I don't know . . . responsible. But I would now." And she looked at me pleadingly. After a moment she said in a husky near-whisper, "Couldn't you please publish it?" She took a deep, sighing breath. "Couldn't you help me somehow? I'd do anything . . . "

I took a breath of my own that was, in fact, a hesitation. And that hesitation took my breath away. "No," I said, far too emphatically, "it's impossible."

Neither of us spoke.

Finally, I looked at my watch. "It's late. I'd better go."

"I guess so," she said.

Only then did I feel embarrassed. I slipped off the futon, my back to her, and didn't turn until I was pulling up my pants. She was still watching me, stretched out in a remarkably graceful S. She had the look of a ravaged odalisque. She made no attempt to cover herself and I, no attempt not to look. My penis stiffened uncomfortably in my underpants.

I said, "Don't move," which she showed no signs of doing. "I'll let myself out."

## Morning

It was almost two o'clock when I opened the door. The answering machine was blinking red. I tiptoed to the living room to turn on the small lamp, which wasn't there; neither was the table with the long legs on which it should have sat; nor, when I entered the bedroom, was Sarah, not to speak of the bed or, when I turned on the overhead light, the bureaus, the throw rugs, the chair, and the large mirror. Where the bed had been, my underwear, socks, T-shirts, shirts, sweaters, pajamas, and sweatshirts, all carefully folded, were laid out in neat rows. My belts, carefully coiled, nestled against each other like fern buds. It was a labor of unlove.

A walk through the apartment revealed that the couch, all the tables, the reclining chair, the easy chair, the lamps, the Persian rug, the paintings, any mirror except the one attached to the bathroom cabinet, and her desk were gone, as well as photos, keepsakes, pottery, plants, the CD player, and one of the two televisions. Only the bookshelves were untouched. She hadn't taken a book with her.

Touring the apartment again as if things might somehow reappear, I came to rest in that emptied living room. I opened the windows despite a chill breeze blowing in from the river and, for the second time that night, stripped down to my body. I sat on the floor. The air made me shiver. I was beyond sleep.

My stomach hung in small, reddened folds; my penis lay there, discolored and insensate; my legs were blistered, and under the skin blue veins crisscrossed uneven patches of red like so many Soviet highways to nowhere. A road map I hadn't noticed was imprinted on the body Marissa Kuby had looked at.

I don't know how much time passed before I went over to the bookshelves. Hundreds and hundreds of books rose up the walls. In the emptiness of that room, I had the sense that they might tumble down and bury me.

At least half had been saved unread. It was hopeless now. They were like an archaeological site soon to be covered by electronic sand, like Troy when Schliemann found it, the traces of so many cities, one upon another, taking you ever deeper into all that was left of past worlds, past dreams. Up there, I could see my own editing life and a truncated history of Byzantium Press, both winding toward oblivion. There were gifts sent by authors, editors, and friends; autographed books I treasured; the first book Connie ever edited; the complete works of Harry Long; and when I squatted down, *How to Read Donald Duck*, Mao's *Little Red Book*, and *The Indochina Story*, as well as the first radical reader Larry had published at Unity Press. In the highest recesses—I had to balance precariously on my desk chair—were *Red Light, Green Light*, *Thidwick the Big-Hearted Moose*, and *Pantaloon*, three books that had preceded reading into my life, while scattered elsewhere were Shirer's *The Rise and Fall of the Third Reich*, Hesse's *Steppenwolf,* Roche's *Jules and Jim*, Sawyer's *Tears of Blood*, and Chomsky's *American Power and the New Mandarins,* each from its special moment, all before the sixties ended, all stored in the only boxes I removed from the railroad apartment Connie Burian and I once shared.

I began to pull books off the shelves, restlessly fingering them. Sometimes just touching one flooded me with unexpected memories. What I couldn't do was read them.

I stood by the window, nakedly older and more run-down than I had once dreamed possible. That boy with an indiscriminant love for history and books, with an urge to help words that mattered into the world, he had been receding from me for longer than I could remember. I peered into the darkness for a sign, perhaps of a dawn still hours away. From outside came the faint, disappearing wail of a saxophone.

About 4:30, I stepped into the shower and scrubbed myself down. Then I picked new clothes from those so conveniently at hand. I felt a burst of energy. It would pass but I didn't care. I wasn't planning to go to work. I wasn't planning to go anywhere.

I approached the bookshelves once more and began to empty them. Titles whizzed by. After a while I stopped looking and just arranged the books, the most immodest of them the size of a large envelope, into neat stacks, row upon row on that previously empty floor. Soon enough I would have them ready for the cardboard boxes. It was time to empty this container.

# EARTHSHINE

On a clear night, when you sense the moon shining especially intensely, you may be experiencing earthshine: sunlight bouncing off our planet to add its faint radiance to the moon's already luminous self. Pick such a night, even in New York, and what greets you is a self-referential glow. Something of us, it seems, has always been up there.

To live through your own demise, that's a common fantasy. Sometimes it even happens. These episodes from my publishing life may already lie half-buried under transnational lava, yet here I am. As if I were Pliny the Younger *and* his uncle, as if I were on the beach *and* a tourist at world's end.

About six months after I left the Multimedia tower for the last time, Ellen Stakowicz, Larry, and I met for lunch at a tiny diner on Houston Street only a short walk from the building where my editorial life had begun. Crammed in, we had to shout above the music from an old jukebox cranked to earsplitting levels. Still, there was pleasure in such closeness, even without the frame of work that might have made us whole.

Ellen and I gossiped about publishing figures, some worse off than ourselves, and the three of us exchanged information about our freelance lives. An hour passed swiftly and yet our own departures from publishing were not mentioned. Larry and I had, in fact, never spoken of our afternoon at Le Pékin. After the waitress brought our coffees, I did wonder aloud what light we might now view ourselves in. But Larry, who generally considers metaphor an unnecessary luxury, grew cranky.

Suddenly he said, "Do you remember those old Andy Hardy films?"

"We're old," I said, "but not that old."

"I'm older than you. In Iowa we were still in the forties when all of you were deep in the fifties."

"You mean," Ellen cut in, "where Mickey Rooney would say to Judy Garland, 'Now, you'll sing and I'll play the trombone, Eddie has drums, and we can borrow old farmer Jones's barn . . . '?"

"Doesn't it occur to you that we could do just that?"

"But whose barn would we borrow?"

"Yes," I added, "where would you find the capital?"

"Ah, capital," Larry said. "Put a 'k' on it. Kap-ee-tal. You're not the first person to highlight the problem of kap-ee-tal."

"Any lout can publish a book," I replied slightly irritated. "Historically speaking, the knot's always been distribution."

"Ah, history. If you want to throw that in my face, let's start with what sets us apart from the rest of the planet, *historically* speaking."

"And what's that?"

"We're a nation of scribblers. Do you realize how highly prized literacy was among the Puritans?" He looked at both of us piercingly. "Writing your story, it's the essence of what made us a democratic nation even when two-thirds of the population couldn't vote. Every runaway slave, Quaker preacheress, shtetl immigrant, Indian warrior, Lebanese peddler, Chinese miner who made it here began to scribble, or if they couldn't read or write English, they talked it onto paper via someone who could. And they're still doing it. Believe me, it's a tradition even a lout could draw on. There's a passage in Whitman's *Specimen Days in America* . . ."

He reached into his jacket pocket and pulled out a scrap of paper on which I could see his scribblings.

"This was from his Civil War diary. 1864. He's standing by the roadside of a military camp in Virginia 'unobserved in the darkness,' as he puts it, while the Union Army marches past. They're on their way to die, of course. He writes, 'The mud was very deep. The men had their usual burdens, overcoats, knapsacks, guns and blankets—'"

"You were planning to read this to us?" I asked, amazed.

"Doesn't everyone bring obscure Whitman passages to lunch?" Ellen said sweetly.

He waited patiently, then picked up where he'd left off. "'. . . blankets,'" he said firmly. "'Along and along they filed by me, with often a laugh, a song, a cheerful word, but never once a murmur. It may have been odd, but I never before so realized the majesty and reality of the American people en masse. It fell upon me like a great awe.'"

"And what in the world does that have to do with publishing?" asked Ellen.

"The ones who didn't die wrote their memoirs," he said. "And they were all scribbling in diaries. Go find your great-grandpa's trunk in the attic and, bingo, another Civil War diary. And Whitman, what was he but an American scribbler?"

"Where are these scribblers today?" I asked.

"Just pick up the blanket and look under the covers. Believe me, after the last book biodegrades and we're reading on some unimaginable set of devices, people will still be getting us manuscripts. It's deep in the American grain. Even editors like me scribble and I'd give us a chance to publish it. How about you, Ellen?"

She looked a little sheepish. "I feel silly saying so, but I write poetry."

"And you?" Larry looked at me.

I smiled. Actually, I was considering his strange idea. "Even if we could get manuscripts—"

"Even! Ellen, do you or don't you have authors we could publish this year?"

She sat there quietly, pushing half a tomato slice around her plate with her fork while Ella sang "Isn't It Romantic." She took a deep breath. "This is crazy, but there is a young Vietnamese girl who came out on a boat, lost her parents at sea, was raised in, of all places, Nevada . . . " Her voice trailed off.

"Perfect," Larry said.

"It needs work, but, honestly, it's beautiful."

"You really think we could do this," I asked, "knowing as much as we do?"

"I think," he said, "if you want to do something, you shouldn't think about it. It's too discouraging. I did something like this in the sixties all by myself, and it was hardly less improbable then."

I found myself considering Hugh Brown's angry memoir of which I had seen only the first two chapters and, of course, Connie's stories. "I've got two possible manuscripts, but what's the point if no one knows you've published them?"

"Like the famed tree falling in the forest," said Ellen. "Maybe we should talk to other editors."

"You mean, some kind of co-op"—there was a rare hint of enthusiasm in Larry's voice—"some different way of putting it all together?"

"We are starting to sound like Andy Hardy."

"There are some wonderful editors out there." Ellen sighed. "And some agents, too, who might just be appalled enough by what's happening to lend a hand."

And so we considered well into the afternoon over Billy and Ella, Louis and the Duke, Dylan and The Band, even a cut or two of Robert Johnson doing his Delta damnedest. None of us was a fool. We had seen the giants come. We had been observers at the feast. We knew the limits. But sometimes there are worse things than dreaming. After all, a perfectly fine extinction event can occur without an asteroid crashing to earth. The Malaysian green tree frog, to take but one small example, will leave this planet sometime in the next decade without fuss or notice. A way of life can disappear buried in nothing more than silence.

A few weeks previously, Kathy Adambak—the name is a diminutive for the incised bark of a northern alder—had taken me, protesting, to a club in Chelsea. It was an hour when aging editors should have been in bed, not listening to DIY punk bands shouting their lyrics at such speed that you could scarcely catch a word. But after a while even I couldn't help moving a little. She and I have been together of late, though whether ours is earthshine or nothing at all, I don't yet know. Still, that afternoon I couldn't help wondering whether somewhere on our small, overused planet a modest number of readers might not be moved by the shouts of a tiny, aging DIY publishing house.

Larry and Ellen, I apologize for not mentioning that I was writing this book or that you were in it. I would like to thank here just a few, among the many, who made publishing an experience for me: Chris Appy, Peter Dimock, Beverley Gologorsky, John Percy III, Clark Dougan, Chad Roberts, John Lyman, Laurie Sheck, Jim Peck, Sylvie Dash, Louise Fili, Steve Fraser, Bruce Wilcox, Carol Betsch, Allan Whiteman, Jim Blatt, and Laurel Cook.

Once, looking into the New York sky on one of those rare luminous nights I had a reverie that remains with me still. I imagined another editor in a life hidden by the moon's glow: an editor born, like me, in July 1944, but with two nearly grown children for whom he feels inordinate affection, and a wife with whom barriers of time were never an issue. In that dreamy moment, I felt strangely close to him, and them. I still do, though all we could possibly share would be a birth month, an occupation, and, of course, manuscripts. But in a nation of scribblers, that's no small thing.

I won't say another word about Connie's stories here, since someday I might surprise you by publishing them. It was with her manuscript beside me that I first typed "The Last Days of Publishing" on the computer's glowing white screen. Whatever ended between us so many years ago, as long as she doesn't publish elsewhere, we still hold in common 271 pages lacking a single stutter, already luminous, to which, someday, with pen in hand, I may be able to add a faint luminosity all my own that leaves no trace. What else could one wish for?